PEOPLE YOUR MOTHER WARNED YOU ABOUT

First published in Great Britain in 2011 by Paradise Press,
B M Box 5700, London WC1N 3XX

British Library Cataloguing in Publication Data
A catalogue record for this book is available from the British Library

ISBN 978-1-904585-12-1

Cover design by David Woodward
www.designforprint.org

PEOPLE YOUR MOTHER WARNED YOU ABOUT

edited by
G. Abel-Watters

PARADISE PRESS

CONTENTS

INTRODUCTION

Mothers since the dawn of humankind must have been concerned to warn their offspring against succumbing to a dire fate. From the early cave-dwellers warning of sabre-toothed tigers, to more recent generations worried about doodlebugs or cruise missiles, maternal concern has remained unabated, with only some of the perceived risks changing with the times.

Now, in the twenty-first century, we can well envisage mothers warning their children of the perils of mixing with hoodie-clad street gangs, being groomed in internet chat rooms or flooded by the effects of global warming.

For those of us growing up with burgeoning non-heterosexuality, of course, some of the warnings our mothers were so keen to proffer had hidden meaning. How many of us have been intrigued and attracted by those dire tales of Strange Men and Unladylike Ladies, whispers of black sheep relatives or neighbours, of insalubrious venues where we might find them?

The stories in this collection, all told by lesbian or gay authors, relate these special perspectives that we have on parental admonitions; heeded, ignored or deliberately countermanded. Some relate how the queer life can be as much at risk as any other of the common human hazards; of falling victim to petty (or not-so-petty) criminals or unhappy relationships; of exploitative bosses or tourists; or of repeating the same accident as befell your sister.

Some of you may recognise your own mothers in this collection. Some of you, indeed, may recognise your children. I'm sure we all recognise the warnings, and some of the people we have been warned about.

SUEDE SHOES

Rex Batten

I was still at primary school, in the 1960s, when my father pointed out an indisputable fact. I had argued with my mother. I have forgotten what it was over; anyway that is irrelevant to the unchallengeable point he made.

'Son, if your mother says it is, it is, even if it isn't.'

And later when I was in my early teens he took me to a football match. All boys are interested in football according to my father. I have to confess it was the footballers rather than the game that attracted my attention. It was a match being played between teams of the company Dad worked for and he was carrying on matey chat with his work colleagues.

'I make all the important decisions in our household,' he claimed. That surprised me. I thought differently. Then he added to prove his statement 'I decide who the next prime minister shall be and if the Budget is fair, and important things like that. I leave the wife to make the minor decisions like dealing with the household expenses.'

I have never been sure if it was entirely a joke he was making. I, for one, did not question Mum. From my late teens she did her best to line up a girlfriend for me and with one it looked as though Dad might be right with his pun: 'Next goal for you, lad, will be the marriage bed.'

But it wasn't to be. My so-called girlfriend found herself pregnant by one of Dad's work footballers.

Mother's reaction was difficult to define. She was suitably outraged but had I been the father of the forthcoming child, I had the distinct feeling, her attitude would have been very different. She more than once hinted how wonderful it would be to be a grandmother!

That event jerked me into sorting out my sexuality. The girlfriend, before she became pregnant, had made suggestions but even kissing her I found off-putting. There was certainly no arousal. In fact I was more than a little relieved when the group that I'd been going around with broke up leaving me and a couple of other guys to go for a drink on our own. That suited me. I was still a virgin but being close to those two guys did stir things up a bit, stirring that was best relieved by masturbation in the shower where all traces of misbehaviour were washed clean away. I was more than a little aware that Mum did look at the sheets.

Being without a girlfriend after the pregnancy episode was, initially, accepted by her as a natural reaction to the disappointment of being two-timed, but as time went on she would ask questions as to whom I'd been with. It was all very casual, of course; the last thing she wanted to appear was domineering. This was in the 1970s. Gay sex between two males in private was legal but it was to take another decade or more for it to be an acceptable subject in TV soaps.

She was sure my two mates were OK. She had met them, but she had obviously been doing some research. She had discovered the name of a bar in our part of the world used by 'those sort of men'. When she said they were men who did not fulfil their function as men I knew what she meant. I did look into the bar. It was early in the evening and as I was the only customer I didn't stay. What she didn't know was that I had created a fantasy sex world of my own with no experience but which has since proved to be remarkably accurate.

I knew nothing of the cottaging scene. I had warnings from Mother, but the only two public conveniences in our neighbourhood had attendants who kept an eye on whatever might or might not be going on. Then one night when we were alone in the house she produced a list of ways to recognise 'those men'. Mine was a very suburban way of life and the more outrageous camp descriptions did not fit anyone I had ever met. The one that did stand out a mile was the simple fact that 'those men' wore suede shoes.

Suede shoes! In spite of a couple of incidents at school I believed I was the only young man in my part of the world who thought the same way about other men but here was the information, the guiding light, I had been looking for. I was not alone. I wouldn't have gone so far as to say there were hundreds of others like me but there were certainly quite a few.

I assured my mother I would bear in mind everything she had told me. I did not question her findings. Why should I? She was Mother. She could not be wrong. I would not have questioned anything she said.

What was to be my next move? I spent the next few days with my eyes glued to the ground. Bumping into people was an occupational hazard.

More than once I heard 'Look where you're going!' Sometimes the 'f' word was included.

A week passed before I knew my world had opened up. I was chatting in a bar to a very good-looking guy who was wearing suede shoes and, what was more to the point, was very friendly. There could be no doubt about it. Mother was right. This had to be the man for me.

Just after ten he said it was time to leave.

I agreed.

We both went outside.

He didn't seem in a hurry to get away.

We were standing in deep shadow.

I extended a hand of friendship and got a black eye.

My assailant/lover spat out 'You...' as I lost my balance and fell to the ground unable to hear his description of me. Then he disappeared into the night.

I felt my face. There was no blood but it was very sore. There was no choice but to go home and get to my room without having to give any explanation. It was not going to be my day.

'Have you been in a fight?' greeted me as I tried to make for the stairs.

'No, Mother, I tripped. I fell. I didn't see where I was going.' That lie contained more than a grain of truth.

'My poor boy.'

'Don't fuss.'

'I am your mother.'

I was led into the living-room and made to sit under a light and undergo a thorough examination whilst all the time thinking 'Had I not listened to you this wouldn't have happened.' Then very gently she rubbed cream over the bruise, soothing the pain. That was the sort of thing Mother always did. Ever since I was a child she could soothe away pain. How could I be angry with her? And all the while she talked as she always did. After what had happened I did not feel like listening to anything she said but some words did seep into my consciousness.

'I am beginning to wonder if all you read is true,' she said, and I thought 'I have a black eye to prove it.' After taking a breath she went on 'You really do look as though you've been in the wars. I expect you will have a headache in the morning. I will put some pain killers by your bed.'

Whilst she was finding the pills and getting me ready for bed she continued 'I went across to see Maud tonight. Well, as you know, I always do on a Friday.' Maud Barker was a close friend of Mother's. They spent hours together gossiping. 'Well, her son Richard, you know him, of course. He's in the Navy. You know that, of course. He's home on leave. Maud couldn't have expected him or she would have told me. It must be nearly two years since I saw him. I must say, he's a very good looking ... I was going to say boy. He's not a boy any longer, he's a man. He must be a good four years older than you. My, how the time does fly. Why he won't wear his uniform I do not know. He should be proud of it. But there you are. He said it was orders and do you know what? He was wearing suede shoes! It does make you think. It really does.' She paused as she handed me the pills. She held my hand as she looked into my face. Then she said with a smile 'And another thing I read is that those men... you know what I mean, I have explained it to you... those men are usually very good to their mothers, but you are always very good to me. Now it's time for you to go off to bed.'

And I agreed.

A couple of days later I met Maud's son Richard. He made a joke about my black eye and I just as jokingly told him Mother's suede shoes theory.

In spite of the first test failure of Mother's information, her readings proved to be correct on both counts.

Bless her.

QUIET ENDING

Elsa Wallace

'It'll be a quiet funeral, just immediate family and a few friends,' said Evelyn.

A quiet *funeral*? thought Maisie. Weren't they all *supposed* to be quiet, a bit hushed? Unless one went for a rousing wake, which was unlikely in this case. One heard of people planning a quiet *wedding* but Evelyn's stipulation of a quiet funeral seemed superfluous.

'I'll just send a donation to her favourite charity,' said Maisie, 'if you let me know what that is. I assume she didn't want flowers.'

'Oh, I like flowers,' said Evelyn.

Maisie looked sideways at her. It's not what *you'd* like should be the criterion. Surely Aunt Amy's wishes come into it somewhere, if anyone knows what they were. Amy was the original retiring spinster-aunt, such a gentle soul. Maisie had seen more of her in her childhood; occasional teas at Amy's: her father would drive them there when he wanted something of Amy or, more rarely, she needed something of him. Maisie recalled how at the end of the old-fashioned teas Amy would produce a plate of thinly-sliced bread and butter and say 'Would anyone like a quiet ending?' And now, according to Evelyn, it was necessary to state that *this* ending should be quiet.

'What should we wear? Full black or not?'

'Decide for yourself, I think.'

'What are *you* wearing?' Maisie persisted.

'I've got a white and navy thing will do. It's more white than navy actually. Depends on the weather really. I don't want to be sweltering. Summer funerals can be ghastly. Her church is really small and stuffy, and then we'll be going to Jonathan's afterwards and his windows can't be opened since the burglary. Though there is his garden; the overflow could go out there.'

'What's the parking like?'

'Dreadful. Don't think of driving. It's no distance from the station to the church. But it is a bit of a hike from the bus stop to Jonathan's.'

'*Bus stop?*' Maisie could not help her exclamation.

'I expect it won't come to that. We'll find space in what cars there are. There won't be that many of us, and they may not all want to come back anyway.'

I'll wear my walking shoes, thought Maisie, even if they don't quite go with my outfit. She was relieved that Evelyn, her ex-sister-in-law, seemed happy to take on the brunt of the arrangements with Cousin Jonathan and someone from Amy's Centre.

In the event she didn't have to walk, squashed instead into the back seat of a Renault between the Romsey twins who insisted on fastening all three safety belts, no matter what collision of elbows with ribs this entailed. They irritated her further with what some described as their nervous habits, Anselm playing the air-piano and Theodore humming or whistling a melody. The really maddening or eerie aspect was that when the 'pianist' appeared to stumble, the other simultaneously reproduced the stumble faithfully in vocal form. On this occasion it was *Farewell to Stromness*, and, by the time she had identified it, Maisie decided she had had more than enough music for one day.

All of me, why not take all of me had wailingly introduced the service, if service it could be called. Whose idea was *that*? And then to be nearly blasted out of your pew by the Firework Music, which seemed to go on forever, prayers and addresses being necessarily short.

She had noticed some people giggling during the interminable Handel – and what people! Evelyn had hinted in a last-minute phone call that there would be a 'representation' (as she termed it) from Amy's Centre. Naturally, Maisie had expected a couple of staff members and a few token old dears in a minibus, not this heterogeneous mob of – mainly – men.

Few had made even a pretence at wearing mourning. Three women in stately West African traditional dress at least brought some decorum to the proceedings. There were people in jeans and even flip-flops. It was a hot day, but even so...

And then there was the matter of the officiating parson – a woman in a grey suit and rainbow scarf who spoke briefly on the subject of being oneself and extending that self into the lives of others. 'Ronny made her mark on the world, and if we all do as competently and selflessly as she has we could be well satisfied.'

'Ronny' it seemed was her nickname at the Centre and widely used, as testified by cards on the many wreaths and sheaves. 'Our Ronny, always ours, missed and remembered.' Some cheeks were wet. Maisie couldn't even feel near to tears. What was there to feel sad about? Amy was old, she had had the life that seemed to suit her. Maisie couldn't recall her ever appearing dissatisfied. She hadn't been complacent or smug, just contented perhaps. And evidently she had had plenty of friends the family were unaware of, if this lot were a sample.

A large rosy man with silver sideburns took over the pulpit to announce 'There's a party for Ronny, a bit of a celebration, at the Centre and you're all very welcome.'

Maisie had expected Jonathan to be miffed at this encroachment upon his prerogative, this upstaging of his modest get-together, but he appeared impassive and only nodded.

They trooped out into the over-warm afternoon, Maisie glancing about for Evelyn. She had much with which to tax her and noted how Evelyn had seemed to be deliberately avoiding her eye in the church. In particular there was the glaring feature of this funeral – that there had been no coffin! The grey suit had alluded to this, indicating the hecatomb of blooms. 'Here we have only flowers, as Ronny perhaps wished – though I am not so certain of that; she was famous for avoiding waste as anyone who tried to throw away a paperclip soon found out. You all know she willed her body to Science, and we recognise her character in that.'

Do we? Maisie felt she recognised nothing about this peculiar occasion which seemed to be focused upon someone she had never known. No coffin – Amy's trim little body stored somewhere for medical students to hack about. She suddenly thought of the callous raffish physicians in *The Pickwick Papers*, Sawyer and Allen, trying to shock with their insensitive remarks about bidding for the arm or leg of a corpse.

What had possessed Amy to do this? What interest had she in science or medicine? Maisie vaguely associated her with homeopathy and herbs. When she was tiny and fell down Amy's steps and became hysterical she had been given arnica.

It was being brought home to her that she didn't really know Amy. There'd been lunch or tea a couple of times a year when she was a child, never Christmas as far as she could recall. Amy always left London for that. Perhaps what she knew of her was largely what she had assumed about a woman of her generation – Amy was much older than her brother, Maisie's father, and in fact behaved more like an aunt to him too. She wracked her brain trying to grasp at some facts about her aunt. Amy had been a book-keeper; she attended St George's; when she'd retired she'd gone to this Day Centre or whatever it was, a sort of church thing, Maisie had assumed. But perhaps it wasn't? There seemed to be no real clergyman about today, unless the grey-suited woman was one of these new priests. And that was another thing: that woman had done most of the talking and had not once mentioned God. Very strange. Irreligious herself, Maisie had been prepared to hear a lot about God today and this omission was disconcerting. What else was there to say about Amy? Maisie had a vague idea there had been a romance but no one ever talked about it. Some clergyman, no doubt; perhaps a Catholic priest.

She had the impression that the Centre had become Amy's life. Once when, guiltily, she had forced herself to phone and invite herself over, Amy had said placidly and not regretfully, 'Oh sorry, love, not tomorrow, I'm at the Centre then. Perhaps next week?' Maisie had felt put out that Amy wouldn't make a change in her routine to accommodate her.

And now, she thought, Amy couldn't even be bothered to be at her own funeral; after all Maisie's own effort getting here (there had been train trouble and she had been late, missed the start of the service and didn't get her proper place in the front pew) and now in this awful heat compressed between the eccentric twins. Her black skirt was hopelessly crushed when she extricated herself from them and the car.

'Hello, darling, you must need a drink.' Evelyn hoiked her inside and gave her a tall glass tinkling with ice.

Maisie said 'I really want a word with you. I'm not happy about any of this...' and would have continued but Evelyn pushed the large pink man towards her, saying 'You'll be getting a lift back with Bill so you may as well get to know each other,' before scrambling away through the french doors into the garden.

Bill grinned at her toothily and said what a generous and thoughtful person Ronny was.

Maisie said stiffly 'We always called her Amy.'

He chuckled. 'Yes, awful. She hated it.'

'Did she?' Maisie felt her hackles rise. 'She never said so.'

'No, I suppose not. She was like that.'

'Why *Ronny*?'

He looked surprised. 'Her middle name: Veronica. But she said that was too long, and she liked being Ronny.'

Maisie frowned, wondering if she had ever known Amy's middle name.

Bill was going on about how Ronny knew how to give a gift. 'She had a real talent for that, hadn't she?' He lowered his voice. 'She's left me all her Pyms.'

'Pimms!' exclaimed Maisie. Was it likely that Amy had bequeathed crates of Pimms to this man? Whatever next?

'Her *Barbara* Pyms,' he confided. 'First editions. I could hug her. I only became a Pymite through Ronny. She will always be with me in that.'

Maisie found there was nothing with which she could reciprocate. She hadn't exactly shunned Amy but she had not sought her out very often. She supposed she had rather aped her mother in disregarding Amy. She recalled her mother saying once, critically, 'Amy's a great reader. She even takes a book on a picnic. Now that's rude. There are times when you have to be sociable.'

When they did meet it was true Amy's chief conversation was of books one had never heard of or had no intention of reading. And every year she went away on a retreat; that was off-putting. Maisie had always been afraid Amy would embarrass both of them by wanting to discuss religion, but she never did. When she was a child she had once been intrigued enough by the idea of the retreats to ask what Amy did there.

'I read, mostly,' said Amy.

'Now there's a novelty,' said Maisie's mother.

Of course Maisie hadn't given her much opportunity to discuss anything. In later years they had rarely met. Amy would phone Maisie for her birthday and Maisie would say they must meet, after her own holiday, after she'd got this tranche of work done, always after, and always never. If she were honest she thought of Amy as someone with whom she had little in common, if not someone actually boring.

And now this bewildering funeral, and this Bill eulogising away, and all these people at the church to whom she clearly meant so much, certainly more than she had meant to Maisie or the rest of the family.

She knew she was being illogical in feeling resentment that these people had, it appeared, taken over Amy and almost claimed her for their own. She felt shut out. Cutting short another of Bill's reminiscences (not only was 'Ronny' the perfect confidante, but also apparently a whizz at fundraising) Maisie went in search of Evelyn.

The air was unmoving in the garden but it was a relief to be outside.

'Oh, you've just missed her,' said Jonathan, now looking more relaxed. 'She's gone off with Mrs Chuku to the Centre. Aren't you joining her there? With Bill?'

'No, I'm not.' Maisie looked at her watch. 'I've got to get my train, if it's running. This has been a very peculiar day, don't you think? Trying, to say the least.'

'Oh well.' Jonathan shrugged. 'We've all learned something new, that's all.' He turned away to dead-head a hebe.

She returned indoors and explained to Bill she would be on her way soon; she felt sure it was getting cooler.

He insisted he would drive her; no trouble, he had promised Evelyn, besides he had someone to meet and he'd go on to the Centre later, once the party got going.

One would have thought Bill would have had a car commensurate with his size, but, on the contrary, a black and silver Mini was his choice.

'Not a day for putting a quart into a pint pot,' he joked as he inserted himself into the minute vehicle.

The traffic was dense and as they poodled along Maisie made use of the time by probing him on Amy, or rather

Ronny; he opened up, like an unfolding rose, she thought, once she had got him started.

'Oh yes, those retreats. I used to twit her about them. I said "Funny thing, isn't it, Ronny, wherever it is you go, France, Italy, Bavaria, it's always one of the prettiest spots and with a rather good local wine." She blushed. And why shouldn't she treat herself; she worked hard enough the rest of the year. I always knew, when I couldn't staff the helpline or reception, I could rely on Ronny.

'Of course I didn't know her in the early days. She was there right from the start. No one much knew what she was doing then. The bigotry and prejudice. It's still here, of course, but not as it was then. And she stepped right in, did her counselling course, and she was there, in the right place, at the right time, as she used to say. And that was a grim time, wasn't it, the eighties; all those deaths. There weren't the drugs then, or enough support. I said to her once "I can't go to any more of these funerals." *She* never said that to me. That was the difference between us. I know her own loss made her strong; she never forgot it. She used to recite that Emily Dickinson poem to me:

They say that "Time assuages"–
Time never did assuage.

She *knew*, you see. I needed that when I lost David.'

He laughed suddenly. 'I remember once somebody tried to fit her up with this librarian, Françoise; thought she would be the ideal woman for her. Ronny was just amused. She said to me "But Bill, I've *had* the ideal woman. There is no other. I am what I am, a lesbian widow." I remember that – it was the first time I'd ever heard the term.'

'It's a first time for me too,' said Maisie.

REVERSES IN TIME

John Dixon

I was born on the 29th of February, Leap Year's Day, in the tenth year of my parents' otherwise childless marriage. My father was old enough to have been my grandfather. My mother was half his age, and joyless and dutiful. I doubt that my birth brought them any rejuvenation. I myself had no childhood and was born middle-aged.

I was barely twelve (in solar years, that is; three in birthdays) when my father died. Everyone expected my mother to blossom and make the most of her loss. Within a year, however, she'd been diagnosed as having a disease that would prematurely age her. It was almost poetically just. My parents had taken my childhood from me; and now one of them was dead and the other was going to age fifteen physical years for every solar one. I wouldn't, after all, have to wait before I could make up for lost time. Everything had changed, and in some cases gone into reverse.

Take, for example, table manners. As a child I'd been bombarded with all the usual orders: 'Stop sucking your thumb. Sit up straight. Keep your mouth shut when you eat. Don't talk with your mouth full. Hold your knife and fork properly. Put them down neatly between mouthfuls. Put them together when you've finished. Don't gollop your food. Don't make a noise when you're eating. Don't turn your fork over to spear peas. A knife is always necessary. You may eat cake with a fork. And be careful of your new clothes.'

I didn't resent these instructions or later try to laugh them off; indeed I found they earned me considerable praise. How exemplary! How polite! Foreign women in particular were to think of me as a true English gentleman.

But now there is Mother, accelerated in the slowing-down process, doing all the things she told me not to do. She spills her food as her shaking hands don't quite coincide with her uncontrollably nodding head. Her false teeth clack on solid food; her lips suck and slurp at liquids. She drops peas on the floor and crushes them into the carpet under her slippers.

Not only this. There has been a verbal regression. She's begun again to use those babyish simplifications of words that she once invented for my benefit. 'Creamy molk-molk. Be-beff. Din-dins. Beautiful, isn't it? Boo-flins. Boo-flins din-dins.'

I can still visualise her bulk hovering round my rickety baby form, thrusting a spoon into my mouth and making chicken-calling noises, suffixing every remark with a question tag, at which she smiled and nodded – and expected me to do the same. 'Good. Isn't it? You like that. Don't you? Nice? Cluck! Cluck! Isn't it? More? Pop it in. You wanted that. Didn't you? Chew it first. Won't you? Don't swallow it straightaway. Will you?'

It all reminds me now of those necessarily one-sided dialogues in the fellatio scenes of pornographic videos. 'You like a big mouthful. Don't you? You do? Yeah? You wanna take it all in, eh? Suck that dick?'

Poor Mother! Her early discipline didn't have the long-term effects on me she desired.

Perhaps she sensed the reversal in her own fortunes and realised that she'd ceased to be any sort of role model. She never failed – in her progressively rare lucid moments – to advise me on whom I should emulate: the school captain of games and the head prefect, emphatically not those dreadful rough boys. And though her own life was now totally hand-to-mouth and her memory spasmodic she had a disconcerting way of remembering my school timetable. She would even point to my PE kit on the days we had games. I played along, took the kit, but rarely attended the sessions. I never felt any enthusiasm for following rules or fitting in with the wishes of others; and absolutely no desire that my team should win. Whenever possible I skived off and made excuses about my mother's deteriorating health and having no father and being the only child and so on. If I did attend I'd spend the time on the playing field or in the gym spectating the other players. More often I simply arrived late – in time for the showers, which I was happy to join in.

How keenly I observed the growing boys! Their hair dampened from exercise, partly straightened by sweat on their foreheads and now totally flattened by the spray; the entangled forms enveloped in the steam; the emergent delineation of the musculature; the blossoming of the inverted triangles of pubic hair; the buttocks opening as the bar of soap was retrieved from the floor; the vigorous towelling down that caused a swaying of the willie. Is it roundhead or cavalier?

In time I grew out of these delights and hardly went into school at all. I spent more time at home. Mother was pleased to have my company but in an unexpectedly lucid moment might blurt out advice on punctuality and regular attendance. She'd hold me close and say 'You know what happens to boys who play truant!'

I'm not sure that I did; and I didn't for a moment suppose she did either. I reassured her that we had long free periods to study independently. I'd come home early and say that I'd been studying at the local public library. I never told her that the window seat at the library gave a fine vista of the entrance to an adjacent public lavatory, a location which was more pleasing than any playing field and peopled with more interesting men – and devoted to what I now realised was my true sport!

'What did you do at school today?' Mother would ask with a supreme effort of mental concentration and breath control.

'Maths. Approximation. Estimation. Conversion.'

'What's that involve?'

'You have to estimate the size of things and then convert the measurements.'

'I see,' and her head nodded uncontrollably. Of course, she didn't see; her mind had wandered even before she'd finished the sentence. But it was a great comfort to her that I should be continuing the conversation even after she'd lost it.

'For instance,' I went on, 'if it's a good nine inches long then you multiply by 2.5 to get it in centimetres.'

I also absented myself from that other communal school event – school meals. There were times, however, when I dropped in simply to pass on food to the younger pupils. Mother insisted each morning I make sandwiches. She also forced on me items left over from her own special diet – rusky, anaemic, diced. She would point to the food, and nod uncontrollably as if to say 'Take this. You need this food to stop you getting what I've got.' I played along; I ate my sandwiches and waited just outside the school dining hall, furtively opening the food container. In no time at all I was surrounded by a group of younger boys. Some of them, even though they had just eaten, would say 'Let's have a bit' or 'What's she given you today?' I kept them in tow, never fully satisfied but never going without. One lad often said 'I wish I had a mother like yours.'

'Yes, I expect you do,' I said, greatly doubting it. I bribed him to do little jobs for me – including masturbation.

But I wasn't really interested in my own age group. I liked the older men I saw from the window of the local public library. They went wild over me. I used to return home from school wearing the casual clothes that had become de rigeur for our year and then go to the public lavatory having changed into the school uniform – which was now far too small. But what advantage a collar undone, a tie askew, a rakish cap and a shirt tail hanging out! How they loved my growing up and my unchanged cherubic looks! On the days we had games at school I'd spend the whole day wearing the kit. That drove them mad. They gave me little tips – which I spent in the local sex shop on nude magazines, pornographic videos and, above all, bottles of poppers.

I was soon openly asking for tips. 'Can you help me?' I'd say in my most helpless voice. 'You couldn't make it a bit more, could you?' if necessary adding truthfully 'I have an incapacitated mother at home.' If they questioned this I'd reel off a convincing list of surgical appliances, medical routines and medicaments. Whether they believed me or not, they always thought me deserving of some recompense. Well, not pence. No coins, please. Notes in double figures. And many of them.

I felt no qualms about using Mother as an excuse, any more than I did in writing excuses to school and forging them in her increasingly quavery signature. The more I used her as a way of giving myself free time and easy money the less I saw her as a liability. Not only this; I used the money to buy her little presents, items of interesting food not on her diet, wickedly indulgent snacks that would have horrified her doctor. I realised I had a deep yearning to give pleasure by redistributing, to use any means to take from one to give to another.

Inevitably, the truancy extended to all subjects and despite my ingenious excuses I feared the school might write to Mother or send round some nosey-parker of an inspector. It wasn't, however, my absences that caught up with me. The school couldn't really complain about my academic progress. I did all the homework at the local library. I read extensively, far beyond the limited school syllabus. I have always believed self-education is preferable to tuition. I overtook the clever pupils; the ones who, like the pacesetters in athletics, burn out halfway through. When the exam results came out the masters could not understand my success. It made their work seem superfluous.

I was summoned by my form master. 'You've been away a lot. I didn't realise quite how much.'

'It's my mother, sir. She's ninety-five.'

'Don't be silly. How can she be ninety-five when you're only fourteen?'

'It's the ageing process, sir. It's accelerated in her. For every one year we get older she ages fifteen. Next birthday, she's a hundred-and-ten.'

'I see.'

'It's not funny, sir.'

'I wasn't laughing.'

'A lot of people do, sir. And that only makes it worse for me, and it's a problem enough as it is.'

'I – I'm sorry,' he said contritely. 'I can imagine – I think – what you have to bear. Anyway, does the problem impede your ageing – I mean – your learning process?'

'I do my best, sir,' I said, sweetly. 'I spend a lot of time in the local lava – I mean library.'

'That's good. Well-stocked, is it?'

'It's good enough for me, sir. I always hand the set-work in on time.'

'That's true – and very commendable.'

'Are any of the masters cross with me, sir?' I asked in a plaintive voice.

'Not that I – well, not exactly but – let's put it this way. I don't think all the masters would be as understanding about these things as perhaps... er... I...'

'Oh, dear.'

'If there's any problem – if you want anything – you will come to me first, won't you? You know I wouldn't want you obliged to talk about your problems to everyone.'

'That's very kind of you, sir.'

'Here's my home telephone number. We must keep in touch,' he said, putting his hand on my shoulder. 'I hope circumstances improve. We all want to see a lot more of you.'

The master had been very good to me. I felt I had to repay him in some way. That night in the public lavatory, as I sat idly and still fully-buckled in a cubicle, I wrote in indelible ink below the existing graffiti 'For a really good time telephone...' and added the number he'd given me.

My school attendance didn't improve; I could see that school had little to offer me. I spent more and more time studying in the library. I was also able to save some of the money from my 'tips' to help Mother, for we weren't a particularly well-off family. It gave me satisfaction to think my way of life was benefiting her. When she saw my exam certificates she seemed quite happy for me to spend time at home with her. We seemed to be moving to an unspoken truce.

The circumstances and the nature of that truce arose in this way. I was at home quite legitimately for the fortnightly visit of Mother's doctor. I have to admit his visits were among the few times I would have actually preferred being in class. He never failed to treat me as a child (more so even than Mother had done before the onset of her illness). He warned me one day as I was showing him to the front door 'I'm sorry to have to tell you but your Mummy's got a Dicky Ticker.' He patted himself on the chest to emphasise the point. 'I'm going to give her some quick-dissolving pills. She must pop them under her tongue. They work almost instantly. Under no circumstances must she get over-excited.'

'She's not likely to, is she? Housebound, in a wheelchair – and virtually confined to bed?'

'You'd be surprised the passions that can exist the less their outlet.'

I'll second that, I thought, and looked upon the doctor with new respect.

'She must also,' added the doctor, 'have a home help.'

There have been a whole succession of them. Few survive Mother's tantrums. She gets worked up if a speck of dust is missed, little realising the amount of dirt she creates herself. Anyway she hates another woman in the house. (PROMISE Mummy – I'll never bring one home.) Indeed the very presence of a woman near her, even on television, seems to rejuvenate her and slow down the ageing process. Above all she hates anyone going into her bedroom.

The bedroom is her inner sanctum, preserved unchanged since Father's time, including the double bed I was born in and he died in. Almost every surface is decked out in beauty creams, scent bottles, pomanders and other vanities. Her favourite piece is an atomiser with a long lead ending in a small rubber oval, like a rugby ball. She positions the atomiser in the direction she wants it to spurt – usually behind her ear – and squeezes the ball with her elbow. She keeps it even nearer to the edge of the bed than the box containing the pills for her Dicky Ticker.

I like that expression – Dicky Ticker. At night when I'm in my own bedroom flicking through magazines and sniffing poppers and performing a clockwork (and to a lesser extent pendulum) action with my member I think of the phrase and say it's Dicky Ticker Time. Under the sudden onrush of the poppers to the head I feel I'm about to have a heart attack and listen aghast at the insistent pounding, which reverberates through the whole house – and which on one occasion turned out to be Mother calling for help, banging the rubber end of her walking stick into the pea-encrusted carpet.

And there she is – on the edge of the bed, the pill-box spilled over the floor – leaning as far as she dares, her gnarled fingers gathering at the nearest pill. I pop it under her tongue and prop her up on the pillows. The bright redness of her face soon drains away, growing paler than her normal colour till it becomes the ghostly grey of cremated bone ash. The pill is having no effect. Her breathing is becoming slower and more laboured. I cannot find her pulse.

I panic, rush to my room and grab the bottle of poppers and thrust it under her nose, flattening each nostril in turn. She flushes bright red, bugs out her eyes and begins breathing heavily. I tuck her up and pick up the bedside phone to call the doctor. She cuts me off, shakes her head and stretches out for the bottle. I put it down among her scent bottles. She smiles her gratitude.

She has little time for the doctor now, refuses to have a home help, and has come to look on me as her special saviour in times of need. She rarely gives advice and has forgotten my school timetable. And she no longer objects to my going into her bedroom. Why should she? This was the room in which I was conceived and in which I was born.

And which I now keep clean. I'm careful not to dust round the framed photo of Father supporting me in my early steps. I do not move – or use – the scents or jars of cream. My main task is to check out the bottle of poppers, now given pride of place, next to the atomiser. I must say she gets through it at a remarkable pace. In my role as redistributor – unacknowledged righter of the world's wrongs – I buy her bottles from the tips I get from my clients.

I feel less furtive now in my ever more frequent visits to the sex shop. Buying things there for one's own mother undoubtedly cuts down any residual guilt feelings!

BREAD AND MEAT

Jeffrey Doorn

'Never match bread with bread. Or meat with meat, for that matter.' Len was telling me about his latest 'disastrous affair', though it didn't sound that disastrous, and could hardly be called an affair. Len does tend to over-dramatise.

It seems he fancied the pants off this number, courted him madly for weeks, and when he finally got him home, found he was a classic case of butch in the streets, bitch in the sheets. Bread and bread – not very appetising. Nor was that the first time Len got his anus all aflutter in anticipation of a good rogering, only to have 'Roger' hit the bed and promptly turn over. Poor old Len, always a bridesmaid...

If I were a drama queen, I'd say both my affairs really were disastrous. The first was what Len would call meat with meat. 'Ham' walked into my life the day I landed my first job. The letter had arrived that Friday morning confirming my appointment as a graduate trainee in the PR department, starting the following Monday. I went out to a well-known gay pub that evening to celebrate, and there he was.

We talked, we drank, we laughed, we got horny, we went back to his, we – no, we didn't fuck (this was in the early days of AIDS), but we did practically everything else. We started meeting every Friday night, and then more often.

I suppose it started getting serious when he introduced me to his friends. The gay ones immediately called me Ham's boyfriend; they said his nickname referred to his fondness for the back of the thigh. His straight mates said it stemmed from his being ham-fisted. And here I'd thought it was simply that his surname was Bacon.

Ham worked in a B&Q and fancied himself a DIY expert. He'd done some repair work in that awful little room he rented, and set about redecorating it, which brightened it up a bit. He thought my flat poncey; but I'd only to say something wasn't working or needed attention, and he'd be there with his tool-kit. Whatever the job, he insisted he could do it, though I often had to call in a real plumber, electrician or builder afterwards.

Then the room adjacent to his fell vacant, and he pressed me to move in. He persuaded the landlord to re-open a previously blocked adjoining door; and with sole use of the kitchen on the same floor, we had a more or less private flat.

That's when the trouble began. He'd never let me do anything. I wore suits and worked in an office, so I couldn't possibly get my hands dirty. Domestic chores were all right, food shopping, the bulk of the cooking and so on. I think he wanted a male wife, circa 1950s, while I saw myself as a young executive of the yuppie Eighties.

This conflict was also, naturally, played out in the bedroom. I'd always hated it when I was first having sex and people, usually older men, would ask 'Are you active or passive?' At the time, I was experimenting, trying this and that variation to see what I liked. I didn't want to be labelled or pigeon-holed. While I let guys fuck me occasionally in my late teens, I came to realise I preferred to do the fucking, given half a chance. If I did take it, I liked to straddle him; that way I was in control.

Ham didn't mind my straddling him, which I didn't do that often; but he kept trying to get me to lie on my tummy, which I didn't like. And as for returning the favour, heaven forbid!

'There are other ways to have sex,' I reminded him.

'I know, but they're all foreplay; they don't completely satisfy.' We'd often end up sleeping back to back; eventually our sex life more or less dried up.

Things weren't going that well at work, either. After a great start, doing my training and slotting into an admin post, then rapid promotion to executive officer, it all started to go pear-shaped. We were privatised and the whole ethos changed. Instead of working to serve the consumer, we were there to sell to customers. Former partners who all co-operated for the good of the industry were now rivals in competition for business. Any employee tainted with the old mentality faced redundancy or the sack.

I'd become friends with Len, a personnel assistant a few years younger than me. He told me horror stories of staff in their forties and fifties, who'd devoted themselves to the industry, being treated like shit as one by one they were pushed into early retirement, 'voluntary severance' or worse. I thought it couldn't happen to me; after all, I'd only just turned thirty. Len, however, saw the axe coming and did what he could to soften the blow.

First my department head went, then the branch head. Next, my section was merged with another. Finally, I was told one Friday afternoon my services would no longer be required. I cleared my desk and went home, hoping for a sympathetic cuddle at least. What I got was indifference, a callous coldness which brought out all my anger and resentment. It touched off a row which didn't resolve itself in bed, as previous rows often had, but simmered for a week, sparking and flaring up again and again.

In the middle of the final screaming match, I suddenly stopped. 'What the hell am I doing? I don't need this.'

'You need me, that's what you need. You're in a state 'cause you lost that poncey job. Get a real job, not prissy public relations shit. In the meantime, I'll take care of you.'

'You'll take care of me? Go fuck yourself.'

I moved out that night, slept on Len's settee for a couple of weeks, then found a new place and, before long, a new career. It was in my new office that, several months later, I found a new boyfriend.

Clovis seemed more my type: friendly, outgoing, affable and sweet-natured – as long as he got his own way. By a strange coincidence, he knew Len. They used to go to the same clubs, and sometimes double-dated; that is, the pair of them would go trolling for men. Once they'd ended up back at Len's, having failed to pick anyone up. 'We didn't do anything,' Len hastened to explain. 'Bread and bread. We spent the whole night chatting and giggling, catching sleep between jokes and dissing everybody we knew.'

With our proximity at work, and Len's approval, Clovis and I were soon a couple. After a few months he moved into my flat. No sooner was he ensconced, however, than the demands started. First he took over the menus – my diet was all wrong, it seemed. I went along with it to please him. Then my 'rubbish' music collection was banished and replaced by his CDs. That hurt; I really resented having my favourite sounds consigned to a cupboard, but bit my tongue. Next, he started changing all the furniture, moving or ditching whatever he didn't like, often without bothering to consult me. The loss of one cherished item led to our first row, in which I wounded him to the core by comparing him to a cat spraying his new territory. From that point it just got worse.

I wish I could say that the sex compensated, but sadly, our bed became a battleground as well. He used sex to get what he wanted, to placate me when he'd gone too far or reward me for going along with his schemes. The worst example was when he used his charm, and arse, to get me to abandon holiday plans to a destination I'd long fancied, and instead go to a gay resort I'd always avoided. Once there, I hardly saw him; he'd return from the dunes for dinner, then hit the clubs, where I'd join him for the first couple of hours before staggering back to our room. He didn't stumble in until after four, and one night didn't get back at all.

After that the gap between us widened, though there were still occasions when the hissing, clawing cat became a sex kitten, romping and wheedling and purring.

Soon all our colleagues knew the exact state of our relationship on any given day: we brought our home life into the office and the office home. There was no respite. I started applying for jobs in other departments, eventually getting a transfer to an outstation. This did not go down well with Clovis, who accused me of abandoning him, though I suspect he was secretly pleased.

While I felt a somewhat guilty relief being free of Clovis during the day, I came to dread the evenings. He would persist in chatting about the office, but appeared restless and distant if I mentioned anything about my new place. Finally, I banned all discussion of work matters or people. However, any subject I raised was dismissed as boring. After hearing that word once too often, I snapped. 'If you're so bored, why don't you leave?'

'You'd like nothing better. You could go back to your crappy old furniture, your rubbish music and your dull, dull life.'

'At least it would be *my* life.'

That was it. Within a month he'd moved out, and I began erasing all trace of him from the flat, except for a few photos and mementos. After all, it wasn't all bad. It was harder to erase my brooding thoughts about our relationship. I kept replaying scenes and conversations, analysing what went right and what went wrong and what I could have done to make it better. Needing to get away, I booked a holiday, to the destination I'd been prevented from visiting before; it helped clear my mind a bit. Afterwards, with the coming of an English summer that stretched out and burned everything in its path, the healing process began to take effect.

I made two decisions: one, I did not want another boyfriend; two, I was better off living on my own. Len offered consolation. He felt terrible, having encouraged my affair with Clovis; but I told him not to be so silly. 'These things happen. Anyway, I think I prefer friendship to love.'

Really, if it weren't for Len, I probably wouldn't get out much. Oh, I've renewed a couple of other old friendships as well, but with Len I always feel I can just relax and be myself. Plus, he talks so much about his exploits, it takes my mind off my own situation.

Last night we were out on the town and fell back into his for a nightcap. That's when he told me his bread and bread tale.

'What a cock-up,' I laughed.

'That's just the problem, it wasn't a cock-up, but a bum-up. And I haven't been shagged in months.'

'Tell me about it.'

'Well,' he giggled, 'if you don't think it would spoil things, we always have each other.'

'Are you serious?'

'What are friends for?'

THE HAIR OF ISABEL

Hilary Stanhope

Elizabeth's eyes, heavy with the seeds of sleep, yet bereft of slumber, cast their gaze along the knots and whorls of the ceiling of the Great Chamber. For at least an hour she had traced their forms and flourishes, thinly flattered as they were by a coat of lime wash, applied, she did not doubt, just days before her arrival.

As her mind span plots and resolutions, she saw there, in that moulding, Henri III of France, there King Philip of Spain, and over in the far left frieze her cousin Mary, locked away at Fotheringhay, but hatching schemes with one or other. The mind of a Queen was never truly at rest. Time there had been when these long hours of the night were ones that she cherished, when, freed from the hubbub, the presences and the audiences of the court, she could be alone with her thoughts, with her dreams. But now the hours were at once agitated and wearisome.

At length, she rang the bell beside her bed. Seconds later, her chief lady-in-waiting, the Marchioness of Macclesfield, appeared. Not much older than the Queen herself, but clad in black, set off by the starched unyielding whiteness of her ruff, Lady Macclesfield had been the Queen's chief servant for more than half the twenty years of her reign. Her spry discreet austere intelligence, coupled with her talent to predict her sovereign's whim, had made her what the Queen herself was wont to call 'my fourth arm' – the third being the ever-present and prescient Lord Burghley.

'Lady Castlebar, Ma'am?' the servant enquired. Even the gloom, lit by Lady Macclesfield's solitary candle, Elizabeth discerned a half-raised eyebrow that in others she would have condemned as insolence.

'My lady, I would say that you know my mind better than I do myself. What would philosophers have made of that?'

The black figure departed, and minutes later a very different form appeared in the doorway. The Countess of Castlebar, despite being herself a widow, was enswathed in purple velvet, an indulgence that her sovereign had herself permitted her. She glided silently into the chamber, even the floorboards knowing better than to creak under her tactful feet, and settled on the chair at the foot of the Queen's bed. In her hand she clasped two small leather-bound volumes.

'Homer or Ovid, Ma'am?'

'I think we shall try the Greek this night, Isabel.'

Haltingly, and awkwardly, Isabel began to read. The hesitation came from the fact that while her eyes saw Greek, her lips spoke to the Queen in Latin. The Queen then re-rendered the words in Greek, whereupon Isabel would compare them with the original. Perhaps fortunately, she seldom had cause to make many corrections.

Looking at Isabel's auburn tresses, illuminated by the candle's guttering light, Elizabeth thought, not for the first time, that she saw her younger self. Who else in the court could have played games of translation between the two great ancient languages? Who else would dare to match her own sharp wit? In some ways she saw that Isabel excelled her. Elizabeth had never really believed herself a beauty, whatever a thousand glittering portraits or a million gilded words of flattery might say to the contrary. She saw them for what they were. Her features had always been too angular, her gaze too sharp and knowing, for her to be an Aphrodite. The many princes who had wooed her in vain had done so first for her Kingdom, perchance for her mind, but last of all for her feminine form.

Isabel was different. The intelligence that shone from her eyes was ample and yet soft, seeming to reflect the sumptuousness of her bosom. And then there was the poetry of her fate. She had been married at nineteen to the Earl of Castlebar, one of the most dashing men in all Ireland, but sadly with a tongue and a heart as sharp as his rapier. He was said to have treated her cruelly, banished in her lonely castle on the Atlantic shore, while he dived into the taverns of Dublin.

When he was ambushed and murdered, while most saw it as the work of Popish rebels, there were some tongues that wagged about the work of the Countess's young lover. But Elizabeth had been sufficiently charmed by her arrival at court to have none of it. And now, months later, she stood second only to Lady Macclesfield in her esteem.

At length, and after several verses, Elizabeth's mind began to yearn for rest.

'That is sufficient, Isabel. Thank you, you may go now.'

She held out her hand, allowing Isabel to kneel and kiss it. The yielding moistness of the lips on the Queen's veiny hand caused her to stir awkwardly. Such a point of contact was rare. She half wished that she could ask her to stay. But some limits were not to be crossed, even by a sovereign Queen.

The morrow was taken up with hawking in the park that surrounded Scraggsfield Hall. The house was as old, as venerable and crumbling, as her host and hostess the Duke and Duchess of Banbury. Married for over forty years, almost as long as Elizabeth had been alive, their obvious love and devotion was at once a charm and a taunt to her. She also appreciated the fact that, whilst other subjects would build whole wings, dig new lakes and set up fountains flowing with wine to mark her visits, her Lord and Lady Banbury would simply tidy up their tottering pile to make room for her.

Even the old state bed with its great posts had lately been found to be riddled with woodworm. Elizabeth, who would not hear of usurping her hosts from their own bed, now had an unfamiliar but welcome sense of openness when she retired to her chamber.

It reminded her sometimes of her girlhood days in the rambling old palace of Hatfield, when she was at once more fearful and more carefree. Hence she would return to Scraggsfield again and again, forsaking grander palaces. But Lady Banbury held a faster and more penetrating place in her affections. She had not only served as a young lady-in-waiting to her mother Anne Boleyn, but had, in an errand that could, had she been caught, have spelt painful death, smuggled a letter from the condemned Queen in the Tower, just days before a French swordsman sliced away her life. The letter had been addressed to a daughter whom she never dared think might one day reign.

For years Elizabeth had carried the letter with her, but now each word was chiselled so deeply into her heart that she scarcely needed the used and yellowed parchment. She silently recited its opening at least once a day, though she had never shared it with a soul.

To mine own dear daughter that I shall never now see grow to womanhood, I would that thou shouldst ever know that, while thy father the King hath much wronged me and traduced me, I have ever loved him, and still would be his humble servant even unto death. My Elizabeth, mayest thou know greater happiness than hath been the lot of thy poor mother.

But to this end, two things. First, fear always the love of princes as much as their wrath. Yet fear but one thing more, and that is the regard of the women who would be thy sisters. They may wield neither sword nor axe but yet they can send daggers into thy heart.

So grow fair and strong, Elizabeth. If there be place that I may watch over thee when my light is out, then so shall I always.

Thine own loving mother, Anne.

Elizabeth had certainly marked her mother's words through every year of her reign to date. They had borne weight in her numerous rejections of marriage. Most saw in this simply the balanced wisdom of her politics. A Queen with a Consort was in truth a Queen only in name. Her poor cousin Mary was the embodiment of that, her beauty and learning crushed under the weight of three marriages.

The lack of male flesh was something that she had borne with equanimity. About even the handsomest of her courtiers there hung something of the absurd, even about her Lord Leicester with whom she had been most closely tempted to wed. With their struttings, their peacockry, their ludicrous ruffs and codpieces, there was nothing that she yearned or hankered for when she lay cold and alone in the midst of her large bed.

The maternal warning against women seemed equally well marked. There were the two Marys who had been the twin burdens of her life. Her sister, though not perhaps as bloody as her enemies had painted her, had held her in fear at Hatfield, even if she had finally spared her to assume her place in a Protestant sun, eclipsing Rome from England's shores. And Mary Stuart, once her lawful heir, who would have usurped her, still plotting, even from her rocky midland prison.

And now Elizabeth could wryly reflect that, her loins past the point at which they could bear fruit, she was no longer to be nagged into marriage with a man, and marriage with a woman was something that even her beloved Greeks could scarce imagine. And yet now, there were nights when she awoke and sensed that she longed for something more than company, more than the crossing of intellectual swords.

With the court's sojourn at Scraggsfield approaching its close, the whole household was in unusual animation, as the Queen prepared for her monthly bath. Elizabeth had always cared as little for her ablutions as most of her subjects, and with the passing of her flush of youth, she cared even less. Time had perhaps worked less cruelly on the contours of her body than those of her ladies-in-waiting, many sagging like sows under the weight of so many children born into sorrow, and often as not to immediate death.

Her skin may have greyed and yellowed through age and the application of rouge and paint, but the flesh below was still taut. It was flesh that only an honoured few could see, presided over, as ever, by Lady Macclesfield, but now with Isabel also in attendance. Screened off from the lesser servants by muslin cloths, the Queen lowered herself into the tin bath. Lady Macclesfield began to rub the fragrant oils into her back, while Isabel read a passage from the Iliad.

'My Lady Macclesfield, it is my wish that the Countess of Castlebar have the honour today.'

'So long as you do not expect me to read Latin, Ma'am,' Macclesfield replied with a scowl.

'It's Greek, my lady!' retorted the Queen, provoking a further darkening of the black widow's countenance.

Isabel set to applying the oils, smoothing them into the Queen's shoulders. Elizabeth was soon lost in reverie and, forgetting herself, almost smiled.

'Proceed further, Isabel,' she continued, inviting the latter's hands to scoop round to apply oil to the royal breasts which had never felt the lips of man or child. They were firm and supple rather than ample. 'Pigs' bladders,' Elizabeth herself had joked in one of her bawdier moments. But now those smooth fair hands were lifting them and easing in the soap and oils, with a tact and a wisdom unknown to the hands of Lady Macclesfield. Elizabeth's instinct was to lie back further, but then, perhaps recalling her mother's words, caught herself falling much, much further.

Suddenly she sat bolt upright.

'Enough, Lady Castlebar. Enough!' she hissed. 'The Queen is now clean, and has no more need of your attentions.'

Lady Macclesfield dismissively nodded at Isabel, who retired to the corner of the room as though her fingers had been burned. The ablutions continued to their customary conclusion and the Queen and the court set about another day of business and forced revelry.

And yet, even as she parried noblemen and ambassadors, Elizabeth could not help returning to those moments of aquatic transcendence. That night, after just two reels with their Lordships Braintree and Portishead respectively, she claimed a headache, and retired to her bed. She took the great bolster and clasped her arms around its linen firmness, which comforted her. Yet sleep was as fitful as ever.

At length, rather than ring, she stood up and walked over to the casement. Pushing back the curtain, she saw what she took to be an owl flapping across to a great oak tree. If owls really did have wisdom, then this was a sign that tonight she must learn something not written of, even in the classics. She crossed to the door and pulled it open, to startle a snoring servant.

'Send Lady Castlebar orders to attend to me at once!' she barked.

Minutes later, the familiar figure stood in the doorway, bearing the two volumes.

'Latin or Greek, Ma'am?'

'Tonight it will be neither, Isabel. Come, sit with me.'

'On the bed, Ma'am?'

'No, on King Philip of Spain's haunches! Sooth, woman, I have thought you many things, but never dim!'

The younger woman perched shyly on the counterpane.

'Why do you serve me, Isabel?'

'You are my sovereign. Your word is my pleasure.'

'And if I were just an ordinary Joan, borne down by the cares of running a house?'

'But you are not, Ma'am.'

'But if I were?'

'Then I am sure that I would love you still.'

'Love me for what? My mind, soul, my body?'

'For all those, Ma'am. You are more than a Queen. You are a good woman.'

'Lie beside me!'

Isabel laid her length along the counterpane, staring at the ceiling as if in her final repose.

'What do you see on the ceiling?'

'I see ships and worlds, and dreams of men and women, and countries perhaps.'

'Why, Isabel, if you had said "I see paint and cracks, and lumps of plaster" I should have banished you this moment. But now I see that you are a woman after my own heart. Oh Isabel.'

'Ma'am?'

'Oh, call me Elizabeth, a name I never hear.'

'But, Ma'am, that is not seemly.'

'Wouldst thou defy thy sovereign's order?'

'Very well. But only for you, Elizabeth, my Queen.'

And Elizabeth reached out and ran her fingers through Isabel's tresses, brushing them away from her ears, then passed her fingers over her lady-in-waiting's lips. She felt their soft pressure in return. Her hand continued its royal procession down to her corsage. Loosening the neck ruff, Elizabeth disrobed the breasts. Not firm and rounded like her own, but more ample in their flowing whiteness, each one crowned by a ceremonial rose, a rose whose scent

Elizabeth now longed to smell and kiss, and this she did, eliciting soft murmurings from Isabel.

And then the latter turned and pressed her lips against Elizabeth's own. Elizabeth was conscious of the blackness of her own teeth, but this did not repel Isabel's tongue. And then Isabel's hands were invading areas of the royal clothing where even the most audacious of courtiers never ventured. Elizabeth felt fury, but then another feeling stronger still. The hands continued their invasion into territory where even her personal physicians would not have dared to trespass.

Elizabeth now scarcely knew what she felt, only that she felt. And then it seemed as though the many castles of her kingdom were shaking at their foundations. And great waves rose up upon the lake at Kenilworth, crashing down and sweeping away the Earl of Leicester and his Palace, and then the walls of the chamber where she lay began to cave in.

'Oh, Isabel! Mercy!' It was as a low heart-stopping growl. And with that, Elizabeth's convulsions ceased. Moments later, Lady Macclesfield burst through the door, accompanied by two guardsmen.

Isabel wrenched herself away, as if she had plunged her hand into the flames, which in one sense she had.

'Her Majesty was in a disturbed sleep. I rushed in to steady and comfort her.' Her own flushed face seemed to tell another story.

Yet the seconds taken in this utterance saw Elizabeth's ecstasy transformed into real rage, unadulterated now by more curious feelings.

'My Lady Macclesfield, how durst thou storm in upon thy sovereign as if she were some drunken sailor in a tavern! I summoned Lady Castlebar to attend to me. That is enough!'

Lady Macclesfield knew better than to linger, much less argue.

The visit to Scraggsfield ended in the same vein as many before it, and Elizabeth left with genuine regret, and not just because she had seen, and felt, what had previously been beyond her imaginings.

She continued to keep Isabel close to her. Even when word got back to her of mutterings about her new friendship, she thought little of them, until one day Lord Burghley himself took her aside.

'Part of your great strength, Ma'am, and the esteem in which you are held by all of your people, lies in the fact that you are seen to favour no particular man or woman. Why, there are some familiarities, some liberties, which even I, as your oldest and, I hope, most loyal of servants, would never dream of taking.'

'It is not your manner to prevaricate and preamble, my Lord Burghley. Spit it out like a man, and not like the snivelling servant you pretend to be!'

'It has been noticed that your servant Lady Castlebar, loyal as she is, has come to feel need of you in ways unseemly for a subject. She is young, and no doubt she knows not what she enters into, but I would not be doing my duty if I did not warn you.'

'You dare, old man, to warn me. But be thankful that you are indeed old, and be thankful likewise for your doddering gait and long grey beard, for it is by virtue of that and that alone that I do not have you whipped for your insolence.'

Burghley was familiar with these outbursts, though he was seldom the direct object of them. But inwardly Elizabeth herself quaked.

And that night, for the first time, in the darkness of her chamber, Elizabeth Regina knelt, knelt not before her God, not before man, but knelt to sup of the cup of woman, a communion that was at once more bitter and more sweet than any that had touched her lips, the cup of truth and life, and she felt the strange transubstantiation pass through her.

After this epiphany, Elizabeth knew to her bones that a boundary had been crossed, though she hardly knew what form the changes would take.

When, days later, Isabel took suddenly to her bed, Elizabeth was distraught but hardly surprised. Putting decorum to the winds, she hurried to her servant's chamber, and looked knowingly yet all the while unknowingly upon her pallid visage. The white smooth skin had turned a greenish hue, a green that could spell only one thing.

Later that day the terrified cook lay prone at Elizabeth's feet, begging mercy. And Elizabeth knew, in truth, that it was not this poor wretch who had poisoned Isabel; her Isabel. That would have to bide its time for later. With pity mixed with contempt, she dismissed him from her presence.

Isabel's agony, though short, was intense. As she groaned and perspired, Elizabeth's mind was wrenched back painfully to earlier very different writhings and groanings, and thought how similar sounds and gestures might mean direct opposites. Soon she was barely conscious, but still Elizabeth refused to leave her side.

When at last it was over, Isabel seemed peaceful, even to the point where some of her usual colour returned to the cheeks and lips which Elizabeth now kissed for the last time. And then Elizabeth took a pair of scissors and cut away a lock of Isabel's auburn hair, and then walked away.

In the weeks that followed, Elizabeth tried to uncover the truth. Nothing could be pinned on Lady Macclesfield's breast, but in her heart Elizabeth knew that if not actually guilty in deed, she was in heart, and had her banished to her estates in Cheshire, never to set foot at court again. It was said that the next time that Elizabeth truly smiled was when she heard that the woman had fallen from her horse, fractured a collarbone, and then died of the resulting complications.

Lord Burghley, who would normally have been relied upon to send his ferrets in to root out any poisoners within a hundred leagues of the Queen, mysteriously drew a blank, indeed insisted that the Royal Physicians had concluded that the unfortunate Lady Castlebar was a victim of the dropsy. And Elizabeth knew that Lord Burghley, who had so often and so piously lied on her behalf, was lying now to her face.

A man and a woman had betrayed her. She could punish one, to a point, but the other one she could not live and rule without. It angered her that her father would have sent a faithful servant to the scaffold for half such a crime. But part of her had died with Isabel. She would live on, she must reign on. From thenceforth she would be the Queen, and Queen alone.

It was late March, and the first buds were beginning to form on the trees in the park at Richmond, but young Margaret felt little of the spring about her. Her great lady and sovereign had passed away the previous day in the seventieth year of her age and the forty-fifth year of her reign. As she looked upon the cadaver she was more than ever aware of the degree to which artifice had disguised the approach of death, layering it beneath creams and paints and velvets and satin and jewellery. It was hard now to believe that this assemblage of bones and skin and plumage had ever been alive, let alone that it had once been young.

And yet Margaret had known her in her later years and loved her. She had stolen in to the chamber to bestow one last favour. Reaching timidly into the Queen's cold corsage she felt the locket, and pulled it out, breaking the fine silver chain. Inside, as she had been told, was a lock of auburn hair, slightly faded. Whose it was, she knew not, indeed it scarcely mattered. She took it away, and, the following day, sewed it into the lining of the shroud in which the Queen was to be buried.

And so Elizabeth descended beneath the cold stones of the chapel that her grandfather had built in Westminster Abbey as the temple to the Tudor dynasty, of which she was the last. And the hair of Isabel descended with her into the earth, and into the discreet forgetfulness of time.

TWO PAINTINGS STORY

Jimmy Driver

Arnold and Steve sat on their sofa in the living room, coffee cups conveniently poised on small tables. The television programme they were watching showed a man and a woman standing in front of an oil painting, surrounded by a lot of other people who were looking at them intently. The woman, wearing a smart business suit, was talking about the painting, the artist, the style and so on. The man listened attentively. Eventually, she asked 'Have you any idea of the value?'

'No, not really,' he replied.

The look on the man's face turned from interest to astonishment as she named a huge figure.

'And I bought it for a fiver in a junk shop!' he said.

Arnold turned to Steve and smiled. 'Why does that never happen to us?' he said. 'Why can't we find something worth a fortune? Come to think of it, why haven't we won the lottery yet, either?'

Steve replied without turning round. 'Well, maybe one of my paintings will sell for a fortune. Or maybe we will win the lottery this Saturday.' He continued watching the programme. 'Or maybe we'll just find a pot of gold at the end of the rainbow.'

Arnold turned to look at the painting on their living room wall.

'That view of the coast is lovely,' he said. 'You've captured the visual impact so beautifully!'

'Oh, don't praise me like that. It sounds so, so, so...'

'So what?'

'Well. Yes. So what!'

Arnold looked at Steve again. He knew this was Steve's way of ending a conversation. He expected Steve was embarrassed by too much praise. He considered Steve a very talented artist. But Steve had never generated serious income from his art. The painting had never brought in enough money to live on.

Arnold stood up and took a step towards the kitchen, knocking over one of the small tables. The coffee cup dropped and broke on the floor. A small patch of coffee extended over the carpet.

Steve glared at him. 'You pillock!' he snarled. 'You had to break one of the best china cups, didn't you? You couldn't break one of our cheap mugs, could you?'

In the ensuing row, the insults traded got steadily louder and more hurtful. Eventually a truce was called.

Arnold remembered that their friend Georgia was expected that evening. As he reminded Steve, she needed cheering up; her boyfriend had just left her.

'In that case, I'll leave her to you. I'm going to the pub,' Steve said, and went into the bedroom to change.

The doorbell rang some time after Steve had left. Arnold welcomed Georgia into the living room and they sat on the sofa.

Arnold felt pleased to see his friend. It was such a relief after what had happened earlier.

'How have you been?'

'Well, gradually adjusting. Yes, recovering gradually,' she said. She told him how her life was changing; how she still felt lonely and unhappy now such a big part of her life had gone; how she was finding some solace with her friends.

Arnold thought the worst of her pain was over.

'You're managing really well!' he said. 'You deserve a medal.'

She talked some more about the difficult time she was going through.

'Well, remember I'm your friend and you can always talk to me!' Arnold said with just a hint of self-congratulation.

Georgia and Arnold talked on well into the night. Eventually, she phoned a minicab to go home. Realising it was well after chucking-out time, Arnold wondered why Steve hadn't come back yet.

'Oh, I expect he's waiting for a cab, too,' Georgia said reassuringly.

They talked on for a few minutes, then the doorbell rang announcing Georgia's cab.

'Goodbye! And don't forget, just get in touch if you need someone to talk to.'

'Will do! Bye!'

Around midnight, Arnold was pacing up and down. Steve hadn't appeared. Arnold phoned Steve's mobile; it was turned off so he left a message, hoping Steve would pick up his voice mail and phone back that night. After waiting for some time longer, he eventually turned in.

The next morning, a Saturday, Steve had still not returned. Arnold phoned again and left another message, but still no reply. Had something happened to Steve? Was Steve coming back later? Or at all? Arnold paced around the room. A lot of thoughts were going through his mind. Had Steve had an accident? Had Steve fallen ill? Was he in hospital? Could someone have called an ambulance for Steve? If they had, wouldn't they have phoned Arnold to let him know?

Steve couldn't have just abandoned Arnold, could he? He thought of phoning their friends. Maybe it was better not to. At the back of Arnold's mind, he was afraid of hearing the worst. Eventually, he decided he had to know and he did phone round. Nobody had seen or heard from Steve, or so they said. He sent one more text.

After that, he phoned Georgia and told her Steve hadn't come home. Georgia reassured him. There was probably nothing to worry about. She said nothing too bad could have happened or he would have heard by now. The hospital would have been in contact if Steve had been badly injured. Maybe he had gone to a friend's place to let Georgia and Arnold talk in peace.

Arnold took solace in a glass of whisky with only a little soda to dilute it, and went to bed.

That night he had a strange dream. He was trying to use his land line to phone Steve. He picked up the receiver but he couldn't get a dialling tone. He kept trying and trying, but still no dialling tone.

Then he dreamt he was at a train station, on a platform with a crowd of people. Steve was on the platform opposite. He called out to Steve to come over to him, but Steve didn't reply. Then a train pulled into the station and blocked his view of the other platform. When the train departed, Steve was gone.

The phone rang on Sunday morning. Steve's voice was even. 'Hello, Arnold. Sorry I didn't answer your messages before. I'm on my way over to you. I'll explain.'

Arnold's voice seemed to rise an octave or two. 'Where the hell have you been and what's happened?'

'I'll explain. Don't worry. Bye.'

Steve terminated the call. But Arnold did worry.

Within an hour, Steve was opening the door of the flat.

Arnold couldn't contain his rage. 'Well? What the hell happened?' he shouted.

'You can guess what happened,' Steve answered coolly.

'What? You've met someone else?'

'Yeah, I've met someone else!'

The row that followed was more violent than the one about the broken cup. It seemed to go on for hours.

Eventually Steve said 'Arnold, you know I haven't got the gift of the gab.'

'What do you mean?'

'Well, I never was very good with words.'

Arnold could sense trouble coming.

'So what?' he said. 'It doesn't matter. You express yourself through painting. You're a talented artist.'

'Well, this isn't about painting. I'm moving out.'

'WHAT?!'

'Yeah. I don't want to live with you any more. I've realised I don't love you. I don't know if I ever did.'

'You can't leave me for this one night stand. Or this two night stand.'

'Oh no, I'm not leaving you for him. I want to live alone for a while. I'm going back to my parents. Then after that, I'm going to find my own place. Sorry.'

Arnold was gobsmacked. 'What've I done to deserve this?'

'You haven't done anything. Neither have I. Sorry! Now I'm going to pack.'

Steve went to pack his things, leaving Arnold fuming in the sitting room. Then he went into the kitchen. He appeared at the doorway leading to the bedroom, holding the best china coffee cups. Steve was leaning over a large sports bag and an open suitcase on the bed.

'Here,' Arnold screamed. 'Don't forget these! You're so fond of them!'

He threw the china cups at Steve's head, missing badly. The resultant shower of broken china was nothing like as spectacular as Arnold wanted. Two of the cups landed on the bed and didn't even smash.

Steve remained calm. 'I think you'd better stop doing that, Arnold,' he said in a quiet, even voice.

Arnold looked at Steve, enraged. Steve was some years younger than Arnold and in a lot better shape. He was a regular at the gym. Arnold, despite the pitch of rage he was in, assessed that it would be unwise to provoke further the man he had once loved, and still did love in a way.

Arnold carried on looking at Steve, only silently now. Suddenly, he was overcome by a wave of unbearable grief. He burst into tears and sobbed uncontrollably.

At first, Steve said nothing. He just continued packing. Then he turned to look at Arnold.

'Look, I'm sorry, but that's the way it goes.'

Arnold was still dumbstruck with grief. He found it too painful even to look at Steve. He went back into the sitting room and sat on the sofa, in silence.

It would, he realised, be pointless pleading with Steve to stay. He looked around the room and couldn't help noticing the painting. He thought he must try something, say something to Steve. He walked back towards the bedroom and almost bumped into Steve, who was coming the other way, encumbered with the sports bag and suitcase.

He said 'Look, Steve, please, just wait a bit and think it over.'

Steve still resolutely refused to shout. He just said 'No' in a quiet voice and brushed past Arnold.

The next sound Arnold heard was the door banging shut. Steve had left his keys on the inside.

Arnold was devastated. First he paced helplessly round the flat, then he spent some time sitting, staring into space. Then he burst into tears again. He put his coat on and went for a walk in the park, but he just found himself wandering aimlessly around the paths, staring at the ground. He returned to the flat still feeling shattered. Then he knew what to do: he would phone his best friend.

'Georgia, it's Arnold. I feel devastated. The most awful thing has happened.'

Georgia's voice was deeply concerned. 'What? Is it Steve?'

'Yes. He's left me. Just walked out. Just like that.'

There was silence on the line for a few seconds. Arnold continued 'I couldn't believe it. Just like that. Just walked out on me with no warning. And I had no idea.'

'Oh, Arnold, I'm terribly sorry to hear it! I'll come round. I'll come round straight away.'

Arnold was struck by the look on her face as she walked through the door. He thought she seemed more devastated than he was. He was now at the numb, rather than the grieving, stage. She held out her arms and gave him a hug.

After that, they talked. Georgia asked Arnold how he was feeling.

Arnold's state of mind was anaesthetised. He managed to say a few sentences about how unkind of Steve to leave him, and over such a little thing. He had had no idea, no premonition this was going to happen. Then they just chatted about other things: accommodation, transport, shopping, the usual Londoners' concerns.

Then it was time for Georgia to go. She kissed him goodbye and they went to the door and opened it. Suddenly, Arnold didn't want Georgia to leave. He had to say something. 'Wait, Georgia, er...'

She turned and looked at him. He realised he hadn't acknowledged her kindness to him.

'Thanks for coming round. I feel better now.'

They spoke on the phone again a number of times over the next few days and weeks. They saw each other often. One day they were sitting on a park bench together. Arnold turned to Georgia.

'You know why we get on, don't you? Because we're both in the same boat.'

Georgia looked surprised. There was a pause. Then she said 'Well, I think we've always got on.'

They looked at each other in silence for a moment. They felt a shared tenderness.

'Arnold,' Georgia continued. 'I've been thinking. Living with someone doesn't have to mean going to bed with them, does it?'

Arnold laughed. 'Or doing it on the kitchen floor? Or anywhere else?'

'Or anywhere else,' Georgia agreed. She looked into his eyes again and was confirmed in her opinion that the moment had come. 'Arnold,' she went on, 'I've got something to say to you. Since we get on so well, why don't we live together? We can keep each other company. We'll have separate rooms, of course, so we can keep apart when we want to.'

'Georgia!' he answered. 'I was waiting to say the same thing to you!'

She guessed he was lying, but she didn't mind.

They walked back to Arnold's flat, talking all the way. They sat on the sofa in the sitting room; then Arnold went into the kitchen to make coffee.

When he came back, Georgia was standing looking at Steve's painting.

He said 'You've got to hand it to him. He's a good artist.'

'Maybe so,' Georgia replied, 'but I don't like having it here.'

Arnold was surprised. 'What?' he asked. 'Don't you like it?'

'Not because it's a bad picture. I don't like it because it'll always remind us of Steve. That's all over now. It's all in the past.'

Arnold was looking at the picture, still holding the tray of coffee. His mood turned to one of annoyance. He said 'But I do like it. I think it's a beautiful scene.'

Then he looked at Georgia. He realised he was part of a new couple now and he had to make allowances. He put the tray down on a small table, and looked at Georgia again.

'Oh well,' he said. 'I'll take it to the charity shop first thing tomorrow morning.'

He poured the coffee and offered one cup to Georgia. 'Here,' he said. 'Let's drink to the future.'

THREE, THREE, THE RIVALS

Zanna C. Mayhew

There were three of them. They didn't look alike. But there they were, three mares, all racing on the same afternoon at Maiden Moor point-to-point meeting. Sisters.

They had different owners, which meant I was wearing different racing colours for each; they had different trainers, different breeders, even, and were sired by different stallions. I would never have known they were linked if I hadn't been sitting in the ladies' changing tent reading the race day programme with studied detachment, trying to calm down between races.

The first was called Cat Bells, a youngster in steeplechasing terms at five years old; tall, leggy, a dark bay-brown with a white star no bigger than a ten pence piece on her forehead. I saw her for the first time in the parade ring before her race, walking round eyeing up the crowds nervously, ears and nostrils flickering. She looked fit and well, her coat groomed to glossy perfection. She had raced twice before, showing promise without getting very close to the winners, and now was running in the maiden race. That's a race for horses who have not yet won.

We set off, bowling along comfortably in the winter sunshine, keeping to the outside of the other horses so she had a clear view of where she was going and the fences she had to jump. She took hold of her bit at the 'off' with enthusiasm, jumped the first two obstacles cautiously while she assessed the course, then the third one, the first open ditch, fluently and confidently, clearly enjoying herself.

Her owner reckoned she'd be better next season after another year to mature, but already she was pretty good.

She jumped the fourth a shade too enthusiastically, too big, stumbled slightly on landing, recovered herself and went on, hardly needing any reassurance. The fifth and sixth she jumped like an old stager, still galloping along easily. We swung round the bottom bend and faced up to the second open ditch.

I thought she was approaching it just right, would fly it easily. Then a few strides out she faltered.

Novices do that sometimes: suddenly think they can't fly over a fence from their steady gallop, even though they have before. So you pick up their reins, steady them, put them on a shorter, bouncier stride and get them to pop neatly over the fence rather than take a flying leap at it. I did that, and we'd have been in just the right place to be able to take one more shorter stride and pop over carefully.

But Cat Bells didn't like something. I urged her on, but she faltered and faltered again. I felt her flounder, then almost at the point of no return remember her training, decide to oblige me, to go for it... and a fraction of a second later realise she'd gone for it on the wrong stride, would have to stretch to reach the fence at all, wouldn't make it... decide to try, to dive at the fence, even though she couldn't make it, would crash through the top and land on her head...

I grabbed the reins, jamming the brakes full on, pulling on a left-hand-down full turn to get out of the way of the approaching fence. There were choruses of swear words, from the riders behind us as they tried to get their horses out of our way, and from the ground staff as Cat Bells's hind quarters crashed through the wings of the fence in a shower of white plastic tubing. Never mind, wings are meant to be knocked down easily. Cat Bells came to a halt and stood trembling. Two horses had been carried out and missed the fence altogether; their riders told me exactly what they thought of me and, too far behind to be able to rejoin the race, headed back towards the beer tent muttering to each other about 'women drivers'. The ground staff collected up the white tubes, and everyone else continued, now two fences ahead. I slid off Cat Bells's back, trembling myself, and stroked her sweaty neck.

They say horses can be telepathic and I've often had experiences that could bear this out, but never anything like this. Nor have I ever ridden a horse who has dived at a fence and landed on her head, and I hope I never do. I've known it to happen, of course; one moment leaping mbitiously and the next a broken neck and that's that. I don't know if any of them have known what was going to happen, but just for that instant I swear that Cat Bells did. And was going to dive obligingly at that open ditch regardless.

It didn't happen. We stood there shaking, appalled at the thought of how close we'd come to what might have been. Another rider, whose horse had refused at an earlier fence, came jogging along on the way back to base and halted his mount to ask if we were OK.

I pulled myself together. I was supposed to be responsible for Cat Bells, looking after her not winding her up to greater heights of horror. She had turned round to face the fence and was standing with her head and tail held high and ears pricked, staring not down into the ditch on the take-off side, as some novices do when they've suddenly realised it's there, but over the fence at something on the far side.

'I think so... ' I said to the other rider, and tried to explain what had happened.

'Oh, crikey!' he said. 'How rotten. Glad you're both on your feet, anyway.'

He and his horse set off again. The ground staff were putting the white tubes back together. No-one offered me a leg up back into Cat Bells's saddle, so I walked and led her. As soon as we got round to the landing side of the fence she stopped, turned back to face it and stood there staring again. I coaxed her to come on, chivvied her, even tried shouting at her before she relented and walked on, and even then she kept looking behind her at something until we'd passed two more fences.

Her owner came scurrying down the track to meet us, a middle-aged ruddy-faced farmer who kept a couple of horses stabled in a corner of the farmyard and trained them himself. I wondered what to say to him, but he was too concerned to be cross. He tore apart the Velcro holding the protective boots round Cat Bells's shins, felt all four legs with practised hands, watching critically while I got her to trot, then stood absent-mindedly smoothing bits of wind-blown mane back into position and feeding her peppermints while I tried to explain. Cat Bells by now was much recovered, tossing her head about in high spirits and trying to get her nose into the pocket with the mint packet.

'Thank goodness!' he said. 'So many of these boys would have kicked her on regardless. You're both safe, that's the main thing. Much the main thing. You can ride her again.' He dug out the last mint. 'I'd hate anything to happen to her. I got her from a very dear friend... That's the lot, darling; there's no more. Time to get you sponged down.'

I'll draw a hasty veil over the unpleasant interview with the Stewards running the race meeting, and move on. The second of the trio was the oldest and most experienced, and was running in the Open race. Countess Natasha was her name. I'd seen her before, in that I'd twice found myself vainly pursuing her tail and flashing hooves as they vanished into the distance. She was generally thought to be in with a chance, though there were one or two whose tails I reckoned we might find ourselves vainly chasing. I'd been rung up the previous night and asked to ride her, as her usual pilot had failed to get doctor's clearance for the ribs he'd cracked the previous Sunday playing rugby.

She walked round the parade ring like an old stager who knew all the ropes and saved her energy for where it mattered. Not very tall, long back, a muddy sort of bay colour which might have been rich and bright before her winter coat was clipped. She went to the start like an old and, set off like an old hand, bowling steadily along just behind the leaders in fourth place. She popped neatly over all the fences, swung round the bottom bend, faced up to the second open ditch.

She didn't falter like Cat Bells had, didn't hesitate or flounder. She just stopped. One stride from the fence she threw her head up and dug her heels in. There was another chorus of swear words as the riders behind us tried to prevent their horses cannoning into her backside. She came to a standstill with one front foot just in front of, and the other on top of, the thick orange pole that marked the take-off side of the ditch. I felt myself sliding gracelessly over her right shoulder, bouncing off the fence of springy black brushwood on the far side, landing on my bum in the ditch. Someone else's hind legs crashed through the brushwood not a yard from my left ear.

The stragglers all piled over the fence somehow, someone whose horse had seen us stop and followed suit came round for a second try and refused again, to the accompaniment of more bad language, gave up and set off back towards the tents and parked 4x4s. I scrambled to my feet, decided to ignore his shouts about 'back to the kitchen sink', climbed out over the orange guard rail brushing earth off the seat of my jodhpurs, and caught hold of the reins. Countess Natasha was standing immobile, still with one front foot on the guard rail, staring at something on the far side of the fence with head high, ears pricked and eyes wide. I urged her to come along, tugged on the reins, pushed with one hand on her chest to get her to step backwards, clucked my tongue to her, all to no avail. The other horses would be coming round again soon on their second circuit...

It was several long moments before she suddenly unfroze, shook herself slightly and consented to step back, turn round away from the fence and walk off the track itself. She appeared to be perfectly sound. Still no-one offered to give me a leg up. I sighed to myself: another long walk. Better get on with it.

I led her round to the far side of the fence to start the journey. She stopped again, swung round to face the spot where the horses land, staring into space again, let out a high-pitched nervous whinny. I stroked her shoulder, murmuring soft reassurances and urging her to come on. She consented after a fashion, walking most of the next two hundred yards sideways looking back all the time. Then suddenly she turned round as if she'd forgotten what had been bothering her, and walked on like the old-timer who'd plodded round the parade ring saving her energy.

Countess Natasha was owned by two ladies in their fifties, with very County accents and greying hair in nets. They would, I knew, be blaming me for losing them the race. They kept her, and their other horses, in one of the big livery yards that turned out many point-to-point winners every season. The proprietor was no fool and, so long as he didn't think you one, a reasonable man. I did my best to forget I was all muddy and had foolishly fallen off one of his horses; to keep my chin up, my gaze level and my voice steady.

'Is that,' I asked, 'what she usually tries to do? I wish you'd warned me!'

He gave me a very strange, considering look.

'No,' he said. 'I've never known her do anything like that before.'

The third of the trio was a stocky, sturdy dapple-grey officially named Spacewoman One and known as Vicky. She belonged to a family who kept her, another hunter and some ponies in the mews behind their paper shop and galloped her on the beach. They were always advertising for another 'Person Friday' willing to do both the horses and the baby-sitting. I couldn't blame anyone for not wanting to stick the job as being around the family felt like living in the middle of an over-acted soap opera. Vicky's mane and tail always looked as if they'd been plaited by earnest children practising for a Pony Club test, and her winter coat had been clipped from her belly two inches further up one side than the other. But one could forgive all that as she was a lovely, friendly, obliging horse to ride, and was developing into a good racehorse too. I'd ridden her twice before and last time won a novices' race at Badbury Rings.

This time she was running in a long-distance race, over three and a half miles rather than the usual three. Her owner was thinking of running her in a hunter chase on a big racecourse, had heard that hunter chases required more stamina than point-to-points and wanted to try out her stamina in one of the rare longer races. I didn't bother to think he was crazy. I wanted to ride Vicky in a hunter chase.

The longer distance meant going to a different starting point; not turning left out of the parade ring past the horseboxes and the Portaloos to the usual place, along the side of the course heading towards the top bend. This time, we turned right past the crowd clustered round the winning post, past the dusty Land Rovers with people perching on the roof racks to get a grandstand view, and round the bottom bend to a point near the end of the back straight.

Vicky and I lobbed along at a steady canter in a bunch of runners heading to the start. We passed what would be the last fence, the second-last fence, were about to pass the open ditch and round the bend...

Vicky was not about to pass any open ditch. Fifty yards from it she flung her head up, squealed, whipped round and set off at full gallop. I hung on grimly somewhere over her left shoulder, struggled to get one leg back on each side and my mud-stained seat back in the saddle, while the grass close below sped past in a blur... Damn it, I wasn't going to fall off twice in one afternoon!

Vicky was heading straight for the hedge dividing the racecourse from the road. I tugged urgently on the reins, trying to stop her, turn her away before she joined the long list of road accident casualties. She had her ears flat back to her skull, her neck at full stretch, and was paying me no attention at all.

An expensive camper-van drove along the road, sun glinting on its metalwork and flashing off its windows through a thin patch of hedge. Vicky spun round away from it in another ninety-degree turn, again nearly dislodging me, galloped past the end of the car park, across the course before the last fence and set off across the triangle of open ground in the centre of the track.

In between race meetings this was sheep grazing country, grassy but never guaranteed safe underfoot for galloping horses. Despite all my soothing words and rein-tugging Vicky continued at full bolt, leapt a rocky outcrop, skidded down a hollow, picked herself up and carried on.

The sheep had been rounded up and put in pens near the top bend. Their bleating calmed Vicky where mine hadn't. She slowed to a jerky trot and then a shambling walk as we arrived back on the track and turned towards where the other horses were circling at the start. I didn't bother to think of what they'd be saying about us. Vicky snorted. I stroked her neck. She was sweating, panting and trembling with fright. For that matter, so was I. I didn't think she'd have much chance of lasting three and a half miles in a race and I was sure I wouldn't.

The starter was striding about impatiently. I found my stirrups again and we mustered a trot. Two vets were at the start and ready to inspect Vicky who instantly disliked them. The starter didn't wait for their verdict before telling me curtly he'd withdrawn her. The vets pronounced Vicky to be sound but spent and to have lost a shoe somewhere. One of them actually legged me back up and the starter got the race under way. I pointed Vicky in the other direction to walk back the long way, round the top bend and down the side of the course past the three mile start and the Portaloos. I was in no particular hurry for another unpleasant interview with the Stewards and I wasn't going anywhere near that open ditch again.

A few days later, at the stud office where I had my day job, I answered a phone call from Jean Bennett, a breeder I knew slightly. She was enquiring about sending some of her mares to one of our stallions. I remembered seeing her name listed as breeder of Cat Bells, so I asked if she still had the dam.

'No,' she said. 'She died. Why do you ask?'

I pictured Jean, brown smiling eyes, round friendly face framed in bits of wispy hair escaping from her grey suede baseball cap; saw her striding round her yard in multi-coloured leggings and those jodhpur boots with the buckle-up ankle straps, calling all her horses 'darling'. I explained.

'Oh, goodness! Well, you have met the family now. I'm so glad they're all right.' She sighed. 'It was very sad. I came round at afternoon stables – must have been four years ago last Saturday, now I think of it, and Cat Bells a year old almost to the day – and found her lying groaning in her box. Couldn't tell how long she'd been there, but she'd been fine at lunch time. Turned out she had a twisted gut. I sat down beside her and called the vet on the mobile, but her heart gave out before he arrived.'

‘Oh, the poor girl!’

‘Yes, very sad.’ I thought I heard a couple of sniffs. ‘We were all very fond of her. “The Ginger Mountain” we called her. Or “The Ginger Monster” if she was being a nuisance... not that she was vicious, she wouldn’t hurt a fly, but she was insatiably nosy, had to see everything you were doing and would never stand still... Chestnut, she was, and eighteen hands if she was an inch, off the scale on the girthline measuring tape, with great big ears, and a white blaze with ginger freckles on it.’

I must have sounded surprised. None of the three I’d ridden were a bit like that.

‘No,’ said Jean, ‘none of her offspring were at all like her. She only ever had the four; she was never a great one for letting the stallions near her. We didn’t manage to get her in foal again after Cat Bells was born, and we weren’t having much luck the following year, either. Just wouldn’t have it, she wouldn’t. And at eighteen hands, what she wasn’t going to do, we weren’t going to make her. I reckon that was why she’d changed hands so often, the owners got frustrated. You can understand it. I’d never have sold her, though. I suppose I can sympathise, but anyway, I wouldn’t have parted with her.’

I’d known a few mares like that, too.

‘She was more interested,’ Jean went on, ‘in Cat Bells... and, do you know, there’s the strangest thing. We later heard that her first foal was killed that same afternoon. Coincidence or what?’

‘Not,’ I asked, feeling the back of my neck start to prickle, ‘the second open ditch at Maiden Moor point-to-point, by any chance, was it?’

‘I don’t know. At the races, certainly, but I don’t know which course.’

I’d look it up, I thought, but I already knew what I’d find.

'That was a mare too, reddish-bay, quite small. She started favourite, or so I heard. Stood too far off one of the fences, dived at it, hit the top, landed vertically on her head. Broke her neck. Killed instantly.'

So near, I thought. So close we'd been to having that happen twice.

'There couldn't really be any connection,' Jean said. 'Rationally, it's impossible. But our Ginger Mountain was always so protective of her youngsters. They warned me when she first came here that she'd never let us near the foal, she'd be so determined to keep her safe. And she always did keep a very close guard on Cat Bells, inspect everything to see if it was safe for her, warn her away if not... ' She paused. 'I haven't thought about it for years, but now I can almost hear that special whinny she had that warned Cat Bells to come away, leave that alone... So motherly. You can just imagine her poor heart breaking if anything happened to one of her daughters, something she hadn't been able to warn her against.' Her voice had a cracked edge. I heard another sniff and a big gulp. 'Sorry, I'm being silly. It couldn't possibly be.'

Couldn't it? I thought. Something had warned those three away from that open ditch.

Jean went on: 'I didn't have her for long – The Ginger Mountain, I mean. She was already in foal with Cat Bells when she came here. I wish I'd kept Cat Bells now, but you know how it is, on a stud, selling the youngsters is how you make your living. She was called Cat Bells because she was a Little Mountain... '

I nodded. 'In the Lake District. It was the first fell I ever climbed. I must have been five... '

'You too? Same here... And I'd already promised her to a very good friend... Look after her, won't you?'

'Cat Bells,' I assured her earnestly, 'is just fine. She had a bit of a shock, but she's OK now, and she's going to be very good indeed. I promise, I'll take the most exquisite care of her.'

Jean laughed. 'I bet you will! And listen: Cat Bells is quite like her mother in some ways. I'm sure she'll take good care of you, too.'

There is a theory that 'three, three, the rivals' in the song Green Grow the Rushes-Oh *refers to a triple-peaked mountain range called Yr Eifl, north of Pwllheli at grid reference SH 237345. The Welsh name, meaning 'fork', has often been rendered in English as 'The Rivals'.*

PANDORA AND THE PROFESSIONALS

Simon Dessloch

'We're both professionals,' I said to Pandora, tracing a finger from the tip of Pandora's nose to the end of Pandora's dick. Smelling my own shit. Downstairs on the first floor the mental guy was singing the same incomprehensible sentence over and over and I said to Pandora 'How does an intelligent boy like you end up in a dump like this?'

'Through being intelligent and a boy. I'm OK really. And thanks for the fifty quid. Things could be a lot worse. I could have been even smarter or I could have been a girl. You wouldn't come here any more if I was, would you?'

'No.'

Pandora rolled a joint. It was part of our deal. Pandora lit up, gave me the spliff. I took a hit, another and – the idea of Pandora dickless lingered on my mind like the insane looping sing-song on the first floor. I wished Pandora hadn't said that, that thing, that girl thing.

I clasped the boy's penis, held on tight until the horror image went away. Panda was still hard. The Viagra had done that.

Serenity took hold.

Where would I go if I couldn't come here? To this beautiful dump of crazy people and car crime and cannabis? Of Pandora. Of Taste and Judgment.

What wouldn't I do to keep things exactly as they were!

I was content. With little margin for error. Life had to be near perfect for me to be merely OK.

I was on the borderline. I could do being a man. It wasn't enough. But it was just possible for me to earn high, respectable job, normal, and have this other life, have Pandora. Pandora made it enough.

I put the joint down for the last time. Pandora rolled on his belly. I mounted him. Gave him the dick a little more suddenly than he would have liked. 'Keep going.' Pandora was a tight strong springy thing and the mattress was firm.

Passion drove me now. It was exquisite. The way the dope intensified emotion and delayed orgasm. Forcing me to reach for higher levels of pleasure to gain release.

Normal life was intolerable.

I was on the borderline. Pandora was beyond. Outside. Incapable of normal life. Dysfunctional. Untogether. Unrepressed. Allseeing. Making connections between unconnected things. What a great cop he would have made. But it was impossible. To get to the top you had to travel the road of mediocrity. Discipline. Hard work. Ego. Competitiveness.

Professionalism.

Sweat made our bodies slippery. Pandora was smiling that desperate smile, breathing hard and keening softly. I was so proud I had the power to make this boy happy.

'I love you so, Pandora. You make my life possible.'

Pandora wedged the fifty pound note between the bedside table and lamp. 'Fifty quid is the difference between surviving and living,' Pandora said. He had no reason to give up his low-life. No way to, either. 'Supposing I could land a job. It would leave me with no gain. To get a well-paid job, I would have to be someone else. Someone I'm not. It's too high a price to pay. But I'll save up the fifty. I've seen a pair of Hugo Boss jeans. They are so cool. A hundred quid.'

'Why don't I just give you the other fifty?'

'No need. They're only a pair of drop-dead gorgeous jeans. I don't *need* them. Not really.'

A call came in for me. Pandora left to brew coffee. The guy downstairs was ranting again. Ten minutes later my business partner arrived.

'How you doing, Panda?'

'Very well, thank you, Greg.'

I showered, dressed, only got a smidgen of Panda's coffee. Gregorio drank the coffee, smoked the pot, allowed his eyes to wander, but then he went home to fuck his wife.

He was a good partner, respecting my life-style, joining in at the narcotic level, just like I accepted invitations to dinner at Gregorio's with his wife Gloria and the children.

Those were strange experiences. The level of repression I had to exercise in that setting made me come across as reserved and mysterious, especially to the children – Clara, eleven, and Sidney, nine.

'They think you're James Bond,' said the wife.

Sometimes I wondered what it would be like if Pandora were – sort of – my wife. If we shared a house in the suburbs with garden and pets. Panda loved cats. In a big house he could keep as many of them as he liked.

I sprayed cologne on myself. Checked my reflection in the mirror. I looked respectable and powerful.

Pandora waved bye-bye, cradling the Siamese in his arms.

Electric Six on the London motorway tailback. We both loved them, Greg and me. Their songs of deviant sex, het anal, two men singing sex to each other, het love in a gay setting, a future in which you were *all that you could be.* And then Greg asked 'What's it like?'

I'd been dreading this moment. 'Uhm, Greg, you might ask Gloria if she might – '

'Done that.'

'She said no?'

'She said yes.'

'Oh.' I focused hard on the road, the cars, overtook on the fast lane, trailed back into the middle. Was Greg propositioning me? 'I could ask Panda?'

'Oh, just tell me, Cody. I know you don't owe me. I just want to know.'

'Well, it's – ' Ahead of us common sense gave way to road rage: a silver Merc rammed a red VW.

'Cody!'

I braked hard and avoided colliding with the two cars involved in the accident. And then we got hit from behind. Not terribly but enough to ruffle our feathers. I saw a smear of blood on Greg. 'OK?'

'Yeah.' But some part of him had definitely connected with the car. I rubbed my neck. Felt the burn of the seat belt on my chest and my hips. I saw the two guys in the accident cars moving slowly and carefully in their vehicles. The crash had knocked their rage out of them.

'Well, Greg,' I said, 'It's kinda like that. But it can be done safely. No. That's a lie. We should help these poor fuckers, and when it's over, we'll have a drink, and I'll tell you all about it.'

We ended up bruised and battered with minor whiplash and safety belt injuries. Greg's car was trashed. Greg told Gloria not to worry and he'd be home soon. And then I took Greg to The Out Side. It pleased me to take a man like that to a place like this, even though it wasn't true that Greg was mine. Just to see the looks we got. Appraisal. Approval. Desire. Envy. The wandering eyes weren't bothering Greg, or didn't seem to be.

Pandora never came to The Out Side. 'They give me funny looks,' he once told me. It was a strange thing. We'd known each other for five years, so many nights I spent in Panda's bed, yet we never went out together. Not once. I made a mental note to rectify that situation.

Why were things the way they were? So much queer politics, and yet a straight man could walk into a gay bar and be accepted just coming over respectable, as long as he left his wife at home, while the queerest of us, perhaps the bravest of us, got shunned.

I bought us double vodkas with coke and ice and thought about how beautiful Greg looked with those slight injuries he was carrying. The cut and the bruise made him look rough, ripped away the pristineness.

We sat by the window, safe behind the glass.

'This feels good.' I drank for thirst. The drink was finished before I felt the booze. Greg paid for the next round.

I thought about how adversity can bring two people closer and how I felt it now for Greg, how that minor car crash had somehow put an intimacy there that had not existed before.

'So tell me, Cody.'

'Well – with Panda and me – I don't just give, I take too. That's what the money's for. Shit, that sounds horrible.'

'Why? Straight guys pay for it, see whores. For the stuff their wives won't do, or *can't* do.'

'I don't have a wife.'

'No, but you have Panda, to be spouse and whore both. Sometimes I envy you.'

'Sometimes I envy you. Not for the woman, but – the security.'

'Well, there's gay marriage now. You two could get hitched. You wouldn't have to pay him any longer. But to keep him, that'll cost more, and not just money. *Nerves.* Will you go for it?'

'Don't know.' I thought again about having Panda live with me and the danger that existed right now between Greg and me. I wouldn't make the first move.

'How about a coffee?'

'Cappuccino for me, please.' I smiled. Hard man Greg and his creamy chocolatey coffees. I preferred mine black – straight. Panda did too. 'So between you and Panda, is it fifty-fifty give and take?'

'Roughly.' It was more like forty-sixty. Panda gave more. That's what the money was for. And Panda needed the money more. And that was why he had to give more. If we got hitched –

'What are the rules?'

'No rules. Well yes. You know what the rules are. You've got children. You – it's not so different with us.'

'So what's it like – taking?'

'Ask Gloria.'

'I'm asking you.'

Shit. Shit. Shit.

'I'm a man. You're a man. No point asking Gloria. I'm asking you.'

We got a cab. The driver asked where to take us. Greg said nothing and I looked at him and he looked at me and the driver was grinning in the rear view mirror. Greg was playing it so cool. I hated him.

'Battersea.' My place. Once inside the little virgin was all over me before I could say *how about a Mochaccino?*

'I know I have no right to and I know you don't owe me,' he said but he didn't stop. 'If you can't tell me, show me,' but he kissed me before I had a chance to say no. I could have in the car. I could have in the bar. I shouldn't have let it get to this point. I could have still pulled it back, if I'd wanted to. I just didn't want to.

There were awkward moments. Hesitations. Jump cuts. But the pauses never lasted more than seconds. Afterwards he rolled on his back and laughed and laughed. Laughed until I joined in and then some. Like a great weight had just been lifted from both of us. Like, why didn't we do this a long time ago?

I checked my phone and there was a message. Left half an hour ago. Gloria, I thought, and felt a twinge of regret. It was way past midnight. But the call was from Pandora. 'Trouble. I'm in Wandsworth Road.' Panda sounded panicky and the call stopped there or was interrupted. We fished for our trousers, shirts, boots. Greg drove my car while I tried to call Panda with no success. Left a message. Called the landline.

Greg knew my car better than I did myself. Wandsworth Road wasn't that far.

No response from the landline. Pandora's flat was just off there.

'Shall we check out his place first?'

'Let's drive up Wandsworth Road looking for Panda. If we don't find him – '

'We don't know if there is anything to find.'

We found nothing between the south end and where I usually turn right to Pandora's. I saw Greg smiling and wondered whether it was because he loved danger or because he didn't take Panda's message seriously, because of what we'd been doing an hour before or all of the above. A call came in. I prayed it was Panda.

'This is Gloria. Are you two still alive?'

'Shit, Gloria, it's been one of those days. One emergency after the other. I'll get Greg to call you back as soon as possible.' And I wondered if Greg had even checked his messages. I hung up on Gloria.

Greg turned left into the car park outside Sainsbury's, which itself was closed. I saw Panda sprawled on the ground. The grotesque position of his body. Nothing living could be this way. His upper body was on its back with arms in surrender mode. From the waist down he was turned and twisted unnaturally and obscenely. Like in that horror movie *Society*, Panda's ass was his front.

I approached cautiously, saw blood on Panda's hands, his face. And then Panda looked at me. I drew back instinctively, made myself step forward, bend down to his level and make contact. His eyes were clear. The rest chaos. He was messed. I forced myself to caress his fractured face.

He was wearing those fancy designer jeans he'd been talking about. Tucked in at the knee they were, with bright yellow decorative stitching, zips down the calves, bottom seams upturned once like shirt cuffs.

'What kind of guys did this? How many? Did you recognise any of them?'

With virtually nil volume, Panda said 'Not guys. *Girls.* Maybe eight or ten. Teenagers. Don't know them.'

Somewhere to the right Greg was calling 999. Then he kneeled down on the other side of Pandora. 'Shit, Panda.'

Pandora looked at Greg, at me, with a smile about as unkind as I'd ever seen, or maybe it was the effect of his bashed-in face, but I knew that he knew. I held his hand. It slackened. He closed his eyes and in my mind I said: *Die, Panda, die. You don't want to live, not like this.*

But Panda didn't die. His back was broken, his spinal cord severed. He's in a wheelchair permanently – paraplegic. And of course that means he can't feel anything down there now.

Greg dumped Gloria and the kids. She would have kept him, even knowing what Greg and I did, but Greg just didn't want her any more. Greg moved in with me and it's great sex. There are just some things Greg can do that a lightweight thing like Panda never could, even when he could. Greg and me are truly fifty-fifty.

Panda's in a nursing home. Greg and me inherited the Siamese. Every other Saturday we collect Pandora for the weekend. We give him kisses. We roll him joints. What else can we do? Part of me feels that I should have had Panda at my place permanently but it would mean giving up everything and I just can't. Panda made it easy for me by saying 'Don't ask me to stay. You think I want to sit in the chair listening to you two fucking?'

I haven't spoken to Gloria since that night. Greg visits her and the kids but not very often. Gloria doesn't even know Panda exists.

The other day I got close. I ran into Clara and Sid at the DVD counter in Sainsbury's. I said 'Hi' and Sid just froze and stared at me. Clara's eyes glazed over. She gave me a very grown-up nod like she was an old woman, then pulled Sid away with her. All along Sid's eyes stayed glued to me as though I was the weirdest, most unfathomable thing he'd ever seen, like he had just discovered a universe of terror and wonder and she had just realised that she didn't matter and she never would.

HOME

Tom Wright

In his waking dream, Anthony recalled the men of The Rainbow; the gods in white T-shirts, burly and bold. He watched as they laughed and flirted, touched or pressed in a single assembly, like a game of swans – and he felt mesmerised.

The scene only altered with the thud of an electric beat. And the gods began dancing, dry ice consuming their awesome physiques. And, for a moment, Anthony found within him the audacity to join them, to introduce himself and to try to belong. But reality soon triumphed; the beats of the bar became the rings of his alarm and in an instant Anthony was awake.

'Ah shit!' He reached over and turned off the tyrannical clock.

'Anthony, are you up yet?'

'Yeah!' he groaned.

'It's quarter past!'

'Right!'

'That bloody alarm!' added his dad.

'Mmmm.'

'Do yer wanna cup of tea?'

He opened his eyes. A gritty darkness still penetrated his room; familiar objects seemed to be mere shadows of themselves.

'Please!' he responded and turned to the bedside lamp.

His room, lit up now. The same room he'd woken up in for nineteen years. He crashed his head back on the pillow and let out a long, exhausted sigh. Closing his eyes he returned to his visions, making his tired-out face begin to smile; he would go again to The Rainbow tonight – yes! The mere thought of it made him quiver...

'Anthony, yer tea's ready!'

He longed for his magazines... 'Right!'... but he settled his thoughts on the night ahead.

'Again?'

'Yeah, Mam, again.'

'What do yer think, Ian?' Mary turned to her husband for support.

'Let 'im go out,' he replied.

'It is Thursday, Mam.'

'I know but you've... you've been out every single night this week.' There was no disguising his mother's concern but Anthony now was unbeatable.

'I'm not asking for permission, Mam.'

'Oh, that's nice,' she sighed.

'I'm just going out with people from work, that's all.'

'What do yer get up to?'

He took a gulp of his tea. 'What do you mean by that?'

'I mean...' said Mary, biting into her honeyed toast, 'how can you afford to go out every single night?'

'I'm earning now.'

'Where's me lunch?' Ian interjected.

'It's in the fridge.'

'Right, well I'll be off then.'

'Am I the only one concerned 'ere?'

'Turn that thing down!'

Anthony lowered the volume on the radio as instructed (*Tainted Love* had just begun playing.)

'Just let 'im 'ave 'is fun.' Ian took the Tupperware box from the fridge and pecked his wife in a perfunctory way. Anthony watched, envious of his ease, reassured by their solid familiarity.

'Bye, Dad,' he added.

His father dismissively mumbled an 'Aye' and left.

'Right,' the young man said, 'I'll get myself ready then.'
'OK.'
His mother turned to the taps and began to fill the sink. Anthony returned to his room and began to undress.

I wonder if I could trade myself in? For a new upgraded model?
'I'll have the one without the acne, please, and with the newly-improved, well-toned physique. That's it, the one with the muscles.'
'Certainly, Sir, can do.'
Anthony smirked at his reflection: if it weren't so tragic, it would almost be comic, how he despised his physique.
He took one last look at himself in his wardrobe mirror before removing his new white T-shirt and placing it in its carrier bag. Then, re-opening the wardrobe, he took out an ironed shirt. He would only watch the men at The Rainbow, he decided, buttoning up his shirt; he wouldn't approach them yet. *I'm not ready.* No, he would work; he would enrol in a gym, build up his biceps, train, push, endure, transform his physique (he knotted a tie) and he would wait; wait for as long it took to look like them.
There. He looked better in a suit, he decided; shrouded and compatible – 'Anthony, you'll miss yer bus!' – although he did still have the look of a schoolboy on the first day of term.
'Anthony!'
'One day,' he began, but then was at a loss what to say next. He looked at himself uneasily in the wardrobe mirror, hesitated as if something was missing, then grabbed for his bags and rushed out to work.

'Anthony, right, I'm Max. How are you?' Max offered a hand to Anthony.
'Good... thanks.' Max's handshake was solid and tight.
'I've seen you in here before, you know?'

'Really?'

'Yeah, but I've always thought you must be with someone. Are you waiting for anyone tonight?'

'No, no.'

'Good. Well then, Anthony, tell me all about yourself.'

'Well...'

It didn't take long for Anthony to explain (a few muddled sentences loaded with 'only' and 'just') but Max seemed satisfied with the brief response and effortlessly moved on to himself.

'... so, you see, you've got to keep following your dreams, I think,' he concluded, 'no matter what challenges lie ahead. That's why I love this place, Anthony, it's my place to escape from all the crap, from my tedious job whilst I wait for the right agency.'

'Right.'

'And I love a bit of glamour too, you know? The Rainbow has some very good-looking men.'

'I know.'

'Like the one I'm standing talking to.'

Awkwardly, Anthony responded 'So... you... come here a lot, then?'

'Yeah, I do. I even work here occasionally, you know?'

'Really?'

'Oh yeah! I have a lot of friends here, Anthony. It's like a home. I'll never forget this place, no matter how successful I become in the future. It's important to remember your roots, I think. I'm quite a shy guy, really, underneath, you know, really, and this place, it's given me such confidence. It's made me realise who I am. I can truly be myself here.' He paused. 'Here and Beacon Hill.'

'Right.'

'Do you know Beacon Hill at all?'

'Yeah, I used to go up there with me family.'

'It's great there; it's so peaceful. It's where I go to think, you know? Whenever I'm really stressed out. You need your own special place, don't you think, Anthony?'

'Yeah.'

'Have you ever been up there at night?'

'Erm, no.'

'Oh, that's when it's at its best, you see the whole city all lit up. It's beautiful. Why don't we go there tonight?'

'What?'

'Let's go. I haven't had too much to drink, and I've still got my car. Believe me, it is amazing.'

'All right then,' Anthony conceded; for this beautiful man was asking him out and he needed to grasp at such an opportunity.

'Great!'

And with an all too sudden abruptness Max stubbed out his cigarette and began to put on his coat.

The November night was black and still; a biting cold gripped the city. On first entering Max's car Anthony had felt relief; the car's heating quickly defied the early winter chill. But then, as familiar suburbs began to fade away, the striking pits passed, a sense of discomfort, a wave of anxiety, rose within him; a startling awareness of the situation he was now in. By the time the roads became winding country lanes, Anthony was tense and still. It was then that Max put his hand on his knee.

'Are you all right?' he asked.

'Yeah,' Anthony responded, and it was partly true. Of course the whole escapade was dangerous and stupid, but still, he was in a car with this awesome guy, a guy who had just put a hand on his knee.

'You're really quiet, you know, Anthony.'

'I'm fine.'

'Do you want some music on?'

'Yeah, all right.'

'I've just got the Frankie Goes To Hollywood album, you know?'

'Yeah.'

'It's fantastic! Listen to this song...'

And so on they went, the rest of the ride being led by the tracks: *Relax, Two Tribes, The Power of Love* – the melodies gliding over their heads and seeping out away from the car allowing the lyrics to enchant and disturb the dreams of the sleeping world through which they passed, so that when they awoke the birds would be queer and the bulls would fall in love.

On and on they drove, climbing determinedly up Beacon Hill, until, at last, Max stopped.

'Right. We'll need these.' Max took from under his seat a pair of binoculars and stepped out into the icy night. Heart pounding, Anthony followed.

'This way!' and with that Max vanished through a wall of green.

Through the prickly darkness there came a view that made Anthony gasp. It was clearly his city but seen in a startling new way; lit up like a toy model, it gave one the impression that it could all be picked up and simply thrown away.

'It's good, isn't it?'

'Yeah,' Anthony sighed.

'Look over there!' Max added, passing across his binoculars. 'Can you see? Just by the Council House, follow that road through to the right and that's where The Rainbow is. On a clear day you can actually see the flag flying.'

'Really?'

'Yeah.'

'Wow.'

And then Anthony quietly turned his attention elsewhere: to home. It was difficult at first to find his bearings but soon he followed through the familiar landmarks until finally he could see the roads that he used to play in as a boy. He tried desperately to find his actual home, but it was lost amongst a clutter of other similarly shadowed fronts. As his search continued he felt Max's arm surround him. Lowering the binoculars, Anthony looked directly into the eyes of his protector.

'Are you warm enough?'

'Yeah.'

'Come here,' and he squeezed Anthony tightly. 'I really like you, you know?' he whispered.

'Really?'

'Yes, of course. You're beautiful.'

Then Max kissed Anthony deeply. For the first time in his life Anthony was kissed by a man. He could feel the stubble and the teeth and the tongue and the saliva and the bliss.

'Thank you,' he responded, knowing at once that it was a stupid and inappropriate thing to say, and yet it was the only thing that seemed right.

'You're so innocent, aren't you?'

Anthony shrugged. Max paused.

'I want to see you again, you know.'

'Me too.'

'Then take a look at yourself in the mirror.'

'What?'

'Nothing...'

'Oh, I see...'

'Meet me again tomorrow, yeah, in The Rainbow? I'll have a surprise for you.'

'OK.' And Anthony desperately wanted to add 'And I love you too,' but he managed to hold it back, gripping instead to Max's hand and returning his sight to the streets of home, which again seemed strangely different.

'What time did you get in last night?'

'Dunno.'

Mary forcefully opened the bedroom curtains. It was a bright but frosty morning; the windowsill was sodden.

'It was gone one.'

'Ah! Then why did you ask me?'

'I'm not gonna have this, Anthony.' She turned to leave him alone with his tea.

'Mam! Have what?'

'What are yer up to?'

For a moment there was an opportunity; Mary looked at her son in a plea to understand.

'Nowt.'

'Right, well, you'll be late to work for nowt then, won't yer?' and decisively she left his room.

Propped against the bar, Anthony waited once more. Max hadn't said what time he'd arrive but twenty-four hours ago, in this same spot, he'd been here, telling the boy how wonderful he was.

To pass away the time Anthony had been playing a silly game. It involved guessing the names of the various people in the bar. The gorgeous guy behind the counter, well, he was called Brad (of course) and the old man in the corner who kept winking and grinning, he was Colin or Walter perhaps. Indeed it now seemed that the whole of the bar was divided between Walters and Brads. And Anthony watched them all, still waiting.

'Ladies and gentlemen, well, gentlemen of sorts...' The bar had swiftly become crowded and the cabaret had now begun. 'Let me welcome you to The Rainbow for our weekly extravaganza!' Groans. 'Yes, it's that time again for the Sodom and Gomorrah Cabaret Night!' Cheers!

The lights in The Rainbow went down and on a small stage, by the loos, a silhouette appeared from behind a screen. It was of a man dancing, and as he danced he began to unrobe, until finally, stepping away from the screen, his shadow became a reality; he was naked and hard. Making his way into the crowd, the stripper began to encourage the men to rub oil onto his strong, toned frame. The men wallowed in delight. And that's when Anthony caught his face. It was Max, approaching him, now, directly – beaming and raw.

'I told you I would surprise you!' he whispered, pouring the lotion into Anthony's hand. 'Put it here.'

Max directed Anthony to his balls. Anthony held them and began to rub the lotion onto one; it felt like he held the earth in his palm.

'That's nice,' Max responded.

And for a moment it was just the two of them, alone and intimate, and then, abruptly, it became a crowd of people watching a spectacle and laughing and delighting at the stripper with the boy. Anthony blushed.

'Suck him off!' a voice called.

And with that Anthony stood and rushed to the door.

'Watch out!'

'Calm down!'

A chorus of tired whooping came back from the bar. He left it behind yet paused in the entry. The whooping, he heard, had now become cheering and chanting and calls for more.

'Are you all right, mate?'

The voice made Anthony jump.

'Yeah.'

The barman, whom he'd earlier named Brad, had appeared from the bar. He lit a cigarette.

'Do you want one?'

'No thanks.'

'You just ignore them, you know. They don't mean any harm. They get that way, excited. It's just fun.'

'I know.'

'Are you going to come back in?'

'No, I'm going to go home now.'

'Are you sure?'

'Yeah.'

'All right. Well, come back again, won't you?'

'Yeah.'

Anthony looked across the entrance foyer to the sign which he'd always noticed on his way out, and which had never made any sense to him.

'Actually I have got one question.'

'Sure.'

'That sign, what does it mean?'

'What? Oh! I'd forgotten about that! Huh! "I guess we're in Kansas now." Well, I guess it means ... it's from The Wizard of Oz, you know?'

'Oh, right.'

'You did know that, didn't you?'

'No.'

'Wow.'

'What?'

'Nothing. It means that when you leave here, the bar, you return back to the real world, I guess. Maybe you might prefer to be there, the way you feel tonight.'

'No.'

'Good. So I'll see you here again, yeah?'

'Yeah.'

'I better get back.'

'Right.'

'Take care then, erm...?'

'Anthony.'

'Anthony. Right. Well, take care, mate. I hope to see you again. I'm in here all the time. My name's Brad, by the way.'

'Brad?'

'Yeah, see you again.'

'Absolutely,' replied Anthony, with a startling new certainty.

HOLDING OUT FOR A HERO

V. G. Lee

I noticed her hair first because it was glossy and mostly the other women's hair was dull and stiff with lacquer. It snaked in dark blonde coils to her shoulders. She should have had bigger hair, say like *Charlie's Angels*. Big hair of that quality would have looked stupendous. Instead, at the front it hung limply around her face and as the evening wore on it got flatter and more untidy.

She was in her late twenties; squashed into hipster, black leather trousers and a skin-tight, see-through shirt. She wore her clothes with the confidence of a woman who'd once known her figure was desirably voluptuous. That must have been at least a kilo ago. Her name was Karen.

'Karen, what you having?' someone asked.

'Vodka tonic.'

Later the bar ran out of tonic.

Better say now: while all this observation was going on, I was standing in the ballroom at the end of Hastings pier. It's a flea pit of a pier although the council refers to it as 'Covent Garden on Sea' since it was refurbished a few years back. I hadn't been able to bag one of the chairs arranged around the circular tables at the edge of the dance floor so I had to stand, my shoulders against a barred and padlocked fire door. Each time I moved, my feet came off the carpet with a nasty sucking sensation. Outside it was December and freezing cold, inside stifling. The ballroom was packed, at least a thousand people, ages ranging from twenty to sixty; women dressed up, men dressed down. Because it was near Christmas some of the women wore sparkling deeley-bobbers in their hair while their men wore Santa Claus hats and thought that was enough to incite roars of laughter.

I was there because I didn't want to be at home alone on a Saturday night. I knew no one. I'd dressed all wrong. What I should have worn was Lurex or leather but I'm a jeans and pullover kind of woman. To combat the cold, I'd come out in woolly trousers, a man's cardigan over a polo neck jumper and my anorak. I kept the lot on because I didn't trust the cloakroom staff. They were tossing the coats just anywhere and getting the ticket slips muddled up with the raffle tickets they were selling.

I watched the dancers, I watched the band. I tapped my plastic beaker of warm white wine with my index finger in time to the beat but as the evening wore on more and more I found myself concentrating, without appearing to, on Karen. My gaze was like a small bird settling for a moment before fluttering away.

After noticing her hair and clothes I'd seen her face. She was lightly tanned. Not a fake, tanning salon tan; more as if she had some Mediterranean blood. I want to say she was cat-like but that's too easy – her nose was thin, a good shape, her mouth was thin but again a good shape. Her eyes were a brilliant green, slanting, and they held me. Setting aside their colour, her eyes appeared shuttered as if nobody was going to read what was going on behind them. This impression was so very definite that it surprised me to see how relaxed the other people at her table were with her, as if they hadn't noticed.

The other tables were all full, most of them reserved by the local retail outlets for a staff Christmas outing. Karen's was for a south coast chain of wine bars. A piece of white card sellotaped to the table top said *George's Wine Bars – the place to eat and drink in Sussex.* Everyone seemed to know and like each other. There was a young guy, probably the spoilt baby of the team – he had badly dyed hair, his fringe curling up in the sauna-like heat; then there were eight men and women around Karen's age, generally worn out, downtrodden and tired-looking, plus two older guys who looked like Maintenance and an older woman in her fifties, who might have been a manageress. I put her down as possibly a lesbian like myself. She wore quite a bit of eye make-up, a mustard-coloured, slippery blouse that kept falling off her shoulders, black trousers, sandals, chunky jewellery – would have passed as straight; still, you get to sense these things. A couple of times during the evening she looked over at me and I looked back. Old dyke spots young dyke and assesses. We both broke eye contact at the same time.

Twelve people, thirteen chairs. Everyone trying to be happy and animated except Karen. Everyone in the early stages of getting plastered. The support band shambled off. They'd been useless; a bunch of middle-aged geezers. You get hordes of these in Hastings, incomers who grow what's left of their hair and wear it in a pig's tail of a pigtail. If it sounds as if I despise them, it's not meant to. I see them on the sea front in their too-tight jeans and checked shirts, battered suede waistcoats hanging open to hide their paunches. Sometimes they stare out at the sea with desperation as if Hastings is their last chance saloon. Makes me quite emotional behind my dark glasses. Way to go for me yet.

The band was replaced by sounds of the seventies and eighties: Abba, Blondie, early Madonna. Ricky Martin and Natalie Imbruglia thrown in as a sop to anyone under forty. Then back to the seventies: Hot Chocolate, *You Sexy Thing.* I groaned silently. Chair occupiers scrambled to their feet. At a table on my left a middle-aged bloke with a huge beer gut straining his skin-tight tee-shirt simulated sex with one of the deely-bobber women.

I was about to see if the crush at the bar had diminished when a short man in a smart blazer pushed through the heaving crowd. He came round the back of Karen's chair, poked her shoulder, she looked up and he jerked his thumb towards the dance floor. She shook her head. He jerked his thumb again, more insistently. Without looking at anyone she stood up and followed him. They didn't dance. He held onto her hips and sang the words at her:

'Yesterday I was one of the lonely people –'

I went to the bar.

I was away some time. The ballroom bar was packed six deep with punters waving tens and twenties. I gave up there and went outside onto the pier, past the bouncers, big blokes in big boots and mega-big overcoats.

'You had your hand stamped?'

I held up the back of my hand.

Going outside doesn't mean you are outside on Hastings pier. It's not that easy. Poky shops have been built facing each other, under cover, sort of a tunnel of shops. Without the lighting the tunnel's dark, even with lighting it's not a cheerful place to be. Hippy shops selling candles, ethnic artefacts and crushed velvet, a nail bar, a musical instrument kiosk, empty carcasses – dark inside with broken boxes and scraps of paper on the floor left by the last occupier. It's all poverty trying to look colourful and bohemian. At home I've got stacks of candles because I feel just so sorry for the woman in the candle shop, sitting in her big jumper and fingerless gloves trying not to shiver.

I found the Pub on the Pier. Shabby's good in a pub. I waited ten minutes to be served. I didn't mind – at least the temperature was near normal; my feet warmed up, my body cooled down.

I forgot about Karen. It was still the start of the evening, only ten o'clock. My interest at that point could have disappeared if I'd seen better. I bought a half pint of white wine for later and a whisky to warm me up and took my drinks to an empty table. Plenty of overspill from the dance. There were groups of women with faces like carefully prepared masks; dyed hair sprayed into shape – not even a gale would have shifted their fringes. Nearly all of them had the ferocious fake tans that made their skin look pockmarked under the harsh pub lighting. I picked out the ones that went to the gym. They were thin with good muscle tone in their upper arms. The ones that didn't go to any gym were the flabby ones wearing distracting chiffon scarves and flashing gob-stopping ear-rings. And the ones that didn't need a gym – the younger girls, the shiny, straight-haired girls with skin like rose petals. The men I took no notice of. I registered them, that was all; loud voices, *fahking* this, *fahking* that, *stupid cahnt!*

Whisky finished, I thought of Karen and how her face had been while The Blazer was grinding and singing. Resigned. Removed. Carrying my beaker of wine I left the pub and returned to my station in front of the fire door. The dance floor was emptying. Nobody was ready to slow the tempo down for *California Dreaming*. It was too early. Karen and The Blazer were returning to their table. He walked ahead of her. He went to the chair next to the one she'd been sitting on. Karen peeled off and took an empty chair further round the table. He gave her a hard stare. She kept her head down. While they'd been away someone had refilled the glasses and she grabbed her glass and knocked the contents back as if she was dying of thirst and vodka was no stronger than water. She turned her attention to the older dykey woman.

I'll tell you a bit about The Blazer. He must have been fifty, short, and stockily built. His head was bullet-shaped, emphasised by the close cut of his vigorous, iron-grey hair. He wore polished, slip-on shoes and grey trousers, a blinding white shirt under the blazer, and a club tie. Old-fashioned in that way rich blokes can get away with. The others at the table were polite but not really at ease with him, which made me think he must be their boss.

Karen was getting drunker quicker than anyone. I noted a protective tenderness amongst the rest of them. The drunker she got the more vulnerable she seemed. The Blazer couldn't keep his eyes off her. No tenderness there, more like hunger.

Time passed. People went walkabout. The closely-held boundaries of each party began to merge. The bloke with the beer gut asked Karen to dance. When she stood up she was a head taller than he was; her breasts came just below his chin. She laughed. He buried his face in her breasts, grabbing hold and wobbling them against his cheeks while she stared over his bent head with a vacant expression on her face as if this was just routine, and let him get on with it. The older woman (I'll call her The Manageress) stood up. With great good humour she inserted her arm in between Karen's breasts and the bloke's face so he had to step back. As he did so, The Manageress latched onto his shoulders and smoothly drew him out to the dance floor. The Blazer was on his feet; he took hold of Karen's arm and shook it. 'What the fuck do you think you're up to? Well?'

'Well what?'

She brushed his hand off her arm like she was brushing away a speck of dirt and sat down. Before he could reach the next chair The Manageress was back and sitting in it.

About that time I started to take more notice of The Manageress. I put her down as Karen's protectress and began rooting for her as if she and The Blazer were in a contest, with Karen for the prize. She had short hair and a smoker's face: angular and lined. She didn't look as if she'd ever been happy, because the lines on her face had all settled, going in one direction – downwards. She'd positioned herself sideways so Karen could lean back against her. After a while she casually draped an arm around Karen's shoulders. With her free hand she lit a fag, pulling on it before gently putting it between Karen's lips. They were like two people who'd just enjoyed good sex together.

The night should have been interminable. It wasn't; it shot past. Each time I glanced at my watch another big segment of time had ticked away: ten, eleven, midnight. The main band was due on. The deeley-bobber women came over to the *George's Wine Bar* table and asked if someone would keep an eye on their handbags while they went out for chips. The Blazer said 'Bring us back some chips and we might think about it.'

'Of course we'll keep an eye on your bags,' The Manageress said.

'I'm serious about those chips,' said The Blazer.

'Anyone else for chips?' the deeley-bobbers asked.

No one else for chips.

I queued for the toilets. The women in front of me went quiet. They wanted to say 'The Gents are next door,' but they weren't quite sure. I stared down any curious looks – you need nerve to be a butch dyke in a small town.

Got back. The Manageress was out on the dance floor on her own, giving all she'd got to Bonnie Tyler's *Holding out for a Hero*. Her eyes were shut and she looked as if she needed no one.

Back at the table The Blazer was eating chips from a Styrofoam carton. At one point he leant across the table and offered Karen his fingers to lick. She knocked his hand away. He came back at her, pushing his middle finger at her mouth.

Each way her face turned, his fat, greasy middle finger followed.

Almost, then, I saw myself grabbing him by the collar and slamming his chip-greasy face against the metal table top. Karen unsteadily scraped her chair round to face the dancers. With a laugh he sat back, took out a white handkerchief and wiped his hands.

What next? The raffle followed by the main band. Snow White from the pantomime at the theatre across the road had been booked to announce the winners but she got waylaid by fans at the bar so the organisers hauled someone's granny on stage who was celebrating her fiftieth wedding anniversary even though hubby had been dead for fourteen years. Everyone cheered. Women shouted 'Aahh!' and looked at each other as if that must be the sublime outcome to a perfect life.

As raffles went it was a good raffle. The ticket holders got really excited. I saw a foot spa, a giant Body Shop basket, and a six-pack of Asti Spumante being carried past me to the deeley-bobber table. The *George's Wine Bars* hadn't bothered to buy raffle tickets so they all looked bored. The Manageress went off with one of the older guys to get more drinks. Snow White was found. There was a general cheer until she tried to talk about the pantomime running for another ten days and how the tickets were ten pounds, twelve pounds for the circle, with special rates for children. She had a high piping voice which was fine for being Snow White but useless getting heard over a drunken crowd.

Someone yelled 'Piss off now, darling,' and lobbed a plastic cup.

Twelve-thirty. The ballroom lights dimmed, the stage lights switched off. There was a drum roll while smoke from dry ice seeped across the stage. Red spots drilled the smoke. Eight blokes ran on stage, two of them wearing pork-pie hats and sunglasses to look like The Blues Brothers. That was the only resemblance.

'Do you want to rock?' they shouted.

'Yes,' we shouted back.

'DO YOU WANT TO ROCK?'

'YEAH!'

'THEN LET'S ROCK,' and they creaked into *Jumping Jack Flash*.

Everybody was up on their feet, all the tables emptying. I watched faces. The crowd was transformed, imagining themselves young Mick Jaggers or young Mick Jagger's girlies. Karen climbed unsteadily onto a chair. She pulled up her shirt and tucked the ends into her bra, then began an inept belly dancing routine. From the crowd she picked out a bloke who looked a bit like the actor Alfred Molina. He'd won a four foot high teddy bear in the raffle and seemed happy to dance with it for the rest of the evening. Alfred had a nice face. I put him down as middle management in a caring, sharing building society. He held Teddy in front of him and worked Teddy's arms so they waved at Karen and in return she undulated her whole body and made sexy passes in the air for Teddy's benefit. Everyone was laughing. It looked innocent and funny. Then she fell off the chair. Not gracefully; the chair tipped up and her leather-clad legs shot up in the air as her bum hit the ground. Alfred and his teddy bear rushed over to help her up. She was OK, laughing and rubbing her backside.

He got her to her feet and she fell forward into Teddy's arms, resting her head on the bear's shoulder while slipping her hands under Alfred's jacket. Alfred looked pleasantly bewildered but too drunk to engage properly with what she was doing. At this point The Blazer, who was the only one left at their table, got to his feet and marched over. He didn't seem annoyed or jealous. He looked as if he was quite unemotionally retrieving his personal property. He peeled her away from man and bear, led her back to the table and sat her down. He sat next to her.

She wouldn't look at him. He stared at her averted profile. He put one hand on his knee and the other on

Karen's knee. His head was as close to her face as he could get it. Her expression was blank as if she'd cut him and everything else out. Suddenly she noticed that the buttons of her shirt were undone to below her bra – you could see nearly all of her breasts. With difficulty she did up two buttons. It took her ages to get button through buttonhole. All this time he continued talking steadily to her although I don't know how she could hear because the music was so loud. I counted *Rockin' All Over the World, Love is the Drug* and *Nutbush City Limits* and still he kept on talking. At one point she held out her hands, palms up against him like she was pushing his words away. I noticed her nails; they were false, long, squared off and painted silver with a tiny diamond above each cuticle.

By then I'd moved nearer, stood at the edge of their table, rocking slightly to maintain my balance. I was very drunk. My circle of awareness had reduced to Karen and *mister blazer, mister bullet head, mister in your face intrusive.*

Karen jerked her chin up as if she was trying to keep her head above water, her eyes everywhere searching for... blue sky, a hero? All I needed was one look, a plea to step in. I rehearsed the words 'Is he bothering you? Are you OK? Nobody owns you.'

I looked into her eyes. No, I can't exactly say I looked into her eyes because her eyes wouldn't be looked into – nowhere in her face did I read a plea for help. Her head tipped higher and higher to get it out of his range while he kept on rabbitting.

I searched the crowd for The Manageress. There she was, part of a circle dancing to the band's lousy rendition of *Brown Girl in the Ring*. They were all singing along. Even The Manageress was singing though she seemed too world-weary to relish a sing-song. She didn't look happy. None of them in the circle looked that happy. Nothing like the deeley-bobber crowd who were so happy they might start fighting soon.

The Blazer took hold of Karen's wrist and yanked her to her feet. He pulled her towards his all-dancing, all-singing, unhappy staff. They broke the circle and let the two of them in. The Manageress was on one side of Karen, The Blazer on the other. The Manageress took her hand while he kept his grip on her wrist. Between them they stopped her from falling or from just slipping down onto the floor. Karen didn't really dance, she jerked about like a badly-controlled puppet. Her shirt had ridden up and there were glimpses of white fleshy stomach. I sat at their empty table, in the seat Karen had just vacated. I drank what remained of the vodka in her plastic glass. Now there was no sign of Karen or The Blazer or The Manageress, they'd gone deep onto the dance floor. I saw Alfred Molina with his teddy bear. He looked well pleased with the bear as if he'd found a true friend. He saw me watching him and he grinned, lifted the bear's paw and waved it at me. I waved back.

On my way home. Three a.m. In my head, Bonnie Tyler still begged for a hero. Early mornings are one of the best times, when the town's almost deserted but not quite. The odd taxi purring by. A few clubbers on foot, shouting, swearing or just heads down and dogged for their warm beds.

I was about to turn into St Mary's Terrace when I saw the two of them, The Manageress and Karen. They were heading away from me, both very straight and tall but holding their bodies carefully as if they'd had a skinful – arm in arm, their shoulders touching or stopping the other from falling over. Karen wore a leather coat with a fur collar and The Manageress was in loose tweed.

I had an appointment on the hill with another insomniac but I decided that could wait. I thought I'd only be a few minutes; they didn't look capable of walking far or fast. I paused to tie my boot lace, I paused to clean my tinted glasses. We were in St Georges Street. At last they stopped, The Manageress rummaging in her shoulder bag for something, I presumed a key. Yes.

Not a bad house: blinds at all the windows, the original Victorian tiling on the steps leading up to the front door, red and black checkerboard pattern. The Manageress was coping better than Karen. She was up the steps and putting the key in the lock while Karen clung to the wrought iron gate.

The Manageress half-whispered 'Karen, for God's sake...'

'I'm sorry, Frankie. I can't manage the steps, I'll have to crawl.'

They were at an impasse. It didn't look as if The Manageress wanted to navigate back down the steps to get to Karen. She said despairingly 'What am I going to do with you?'

'Can I help?' was out of my mouth and floating in the ice-cold air.

Karen didn't look round. The Manageress did her best to focus on the voice. She said 'Could you give her a hand up the steps – she's not very well.'

I lifted Karen's hand from the top of the gate and slipped it under my arm. 'Come on. Lean on me.'

She started singing 'Lean on me, I'll be your strength, I'll help you carry on... how does it go?'

I hauled her up the steps and through the front door. The Manageress switched on a light in the hall. 'Could you bring her through to the kitchen?'

She didn't wait for an answer, but strode off. I did notice as she strode she touched the walls to keep her balance. In the kitchen the phone began to ring. Gently I deposited Karen in a wicker chair. The Manageress picked up the receiver. 'Yes, we're home. No, Karen's fine. Talk to her on

Monday.' She put down the receiver. 'Just bugger off,' she muttered, reaching for the kettle.

Karen was smiling: at me, at The Manageress. It changed her whole face.

'And you are?' she said.

'Your hero.'

'Who says I need a hero?'

'I do.'

'And you are?' she said.

'Your hero,' I repeated.

THE CATHEDRAL OF THE SPHERES

Henrik Harrysson

As Anthony stepped into the cathedral, he couldn't help but look up; look up again in awe, the same awe he had felt when he was last there, fifteen years before; more than a lifetime ago as it now seemed. The building did not so much tower as swoop upwards on all sides, while the thrusting metal rods seemed delicate as lace, and quite incapable of supporting the great glass ball that crowned it all.

'Glass,' the Founding Father Jahomus had called for, and glass in abundance he had certainly got. Glass to reveal the urgent wonder of the heavens, an exercise of depth and passion that no Michelangelo, no Leonardo could approach. On even the dullest of days the glass contrived to sparkle, refracting the light into a thousand coloured shafts that played on the congregation far below. And at night the constellations seemed to canter across, leaping over the bars, while the moon, when it appeared, seemed magnified into a great disc of pale purity.

That was part of the revelation of the Founder Jahomus, the melding of the awe of the ancients with the need for the divine. Anthony still thought it the most beautiful building he had ever seen, whether empty or, as today, brimming with expectant worshippers. So sad, he thought, that all of this would soon be dust and shards, and the people blown away with it; but sometimes the destruction of extreme beauty must serve the needs of extreme truth.

His mother had warned him often enough against places like this, against the people who had built them. He had listened to her, then not listened, then again listened with a vengeance that she could not imagine. He had had every benefit that an irreligious upbringing could bring. His father had once told him that, to believe in God, you have to be either a fool or a genius. Anthony knew that he was neither.

With both parents encouraging him to think for himself and make his own mistakes, he had done well at school, excelling most in science, but a good all-rounder. When, aged sixteen, he first fell in love with another boy in his class, no parents could have been more supportive, or more sympathetic when months later the boy turned his affections to girls.

Having been made a fool by love once, Anthony was damned if it was to happen to him again. He soon discovered that his own body was a wonderful resource for pleasure; pleasure with other boys, pleasure with men, pleasure even occasionally with girls and women, who were as much seduced by his bashful charm as by his slightly fey physical beauty. He would test his mother by feeding her selected revelations, but while he would occasionally be gratified to see her flinch, he could somehow never goad her into condemning him.

Eventually even the fascination that he felt for sex began to fade, there being only a finite number of positions and partners, and each conquest seemed to show diminishing returns. His parents had encouraged him to drink, in small doses, from an early age, hoping that alcohol would lose the lustre of 'forbidden fruit'. His father was equally more than happy to share the odd joint. The tactic worked so well that Anthony, seeing that this was tame, boring, puerile stuff, fairly quickly graduated onto cocktails of harder drugs. Even finding him in bed in the early afternoon, his face smeared in his own vomit, his mother had merely sighed and stroked his hair.

One morning Anthony woke up and realised that things had gone rather far, even for him. He was lying on his back in the park. His mouth and throat tasted like the inside of a drain, his eyes felt as though their orbs had been rubbed with sandpaper and his head seemed about three sizes too big for his skull. His shirt and his trousers were both half hanging off him. Had he had sex? Could he have been raped, for that matter? He simply hadn't a clue.

He looked up and saw the branches of a weeping willow, the willow in the park that he remembered from his childhood. The lower tendrils were gently stroking his face. And as if in sympathy with the name and the motions of the tree, Anthony did something that he had not done since he was a child: he began to cry, a cry as much of a boy, filled with frustration, fear and rage, as of the grown man that he liked to think he was.

He opened his eyes again, and was startled to see what appeared to be an angel – could his parents, his whole world, really have been so wrong all the time? The longish blond hair, framing a pale face with kindly green eyes, and a worried, worrying smile.

'Fuck!' was Anthony's next thought. 'The first decent bloke I've seen in ages and here am I, looking like a tramp that's been thrown out with the rubbish.' But then he looked again, and became more perplexed. The man or boy (who could tell?) was certainly beautiful, but he wasn't exactly sexy. There was something too clean, too regular about him.

He pulled Anthony to his feet.

'I'm Kalparan,' he said, still holding firmly on to Anthony's hand. 'I want to be your friend, but you need someone stronger than both of us.' While Kalparan was wise enough not to tell him immediately that he belonged to the Church of the Holy Spheres, Anthony ought to have suspected as much from the name. Converts adopted a new name, keeping only the first and last letters of their birth-name as proof that, while the outer self or 'frame' remained, they were innerly transformed.

Instead Kalparan (who had been born Kevin) announced that he was taking him to meet some friends, who had helped to set him right. And thus it was that Anthony came within the sphere of Father Dacossian. The latter, who had started life under the more prosaic label of Dean, seemed, within minutes of meeting Anthony, to know more about him than he did himself. One of the great precepts of the Founder was that, for the church to win over the millions, they had to convert the individual man and woman, and that entailed finding the unique path to their hearts.

Dacossian saw that Anthony, walking heap of a young man as he was, was nobody's fool. He also saw, beneath the layers of dirt and degradation, something of fire (what the ungodly might call 'charisma') that could make him a leader as much as a follower. He not only argued with Anthony about everything from Kant and Descartes to Quantum Mechanics and the Problem of Evil, he let Anthony fight and lose, and then eventually win the arguments himself.

The Church also encouraged converts to keep in touch with their families, the love of family being part of the love of God, be it of a minor kind. Besides, those whose faith could not withstand this test were scarcely true believers. Anthony's mother, fearing the worst after he had simply seemed to disappear, accepted his apparent death to reason as at least something a step or two above actual death.

Anthony learned so quickly that within weeks he was ready to be introduced into the faith, jointly sponsored by Kalparan and Dacossian. And so he saw the Cathedral of the Spheres for the first time: the approach, past the lake, past the Founder's monument on the hill, the hill on which Jahomus had first seen his vision of the wholeness of Creation, and then the cathedral itself. Swept along inside, he waited impatiently, until his moment came to be introduced to the congregation as Agradray.

Standing in his robes, under the dome, he felt more than just a sense of pride and belonging; he could feel, seeping through his veins into the marrow of his soul, the sentiment balanced between peace and ecstasy that defied words.

While most converts were released back into the world to 'seek out the word of love in every street and every gutter', Agradray was thrilled to be asked to remain as one of the select few men and women to be prepared for the priesthood. If he found it curious that most were unusually beautiful, this did not much bother him. Perhaps the greatest joy of his conversion had been the renunciation of the flesh and all the angst and distraction that went with it. He felt free, free to admire the beauty of man or woman, much as he might gaze upon a sunset or a dolphin, with wonder untainted by lust. He sometimes thought he would expire through happiness, through the sheer intellectual inevitability of it all.

Having successfully passed tests in the practical and the philosophical, Agradray was granted one of the most humbling honours of all, the task of painting the Monument to the Founder. His statue, the height of several houses, knelt in all humility gazing at the sky, supported only by a stone column some hundred metres high. Jahomus had never sought such a monument, and there were those who thought it almost idolatrous, but, on its hill overlooking the lake, it was the first sight that most pilgrims had of the place, almost its defining emblem.

Since scaffolding would be an affront (to the faith as much as the eye), the monument was painted, almost in perpetuity, by just two initiates, suspended from the summit by ropes. Agradray found that he had been promoted to join Garremat, a sandy-haired young man with grey eyes and, if anything, a rather plain and forgettable face; certainly someone whom Anthony would not have looked twice at. Garremat was also quiet, almost distant, but had a way of conveying in a few words, or in a gesture, thoughts that might, for another, take a book to tell.

Each morning, at sunrise, they would approach the monument from their separate quarters, unlock the door and then climb the long, narrow spiral stairs to the statue, before lowering themselves over the side. As he gazed down on the fields, the lake, the cathedral and the ant-like creatures below, Agradray felt outside of the world, with only Garremat there, working away, occasionally throwing a glance, or exchanging the odd word.

One day, their painting for the day complete, Garremat suggested a swim in the lake, a race out to the island. Agradray had never been much of a swimmer, and also felt, for no particular reason, that this ought to be out of bounds. But something spurred him to agree. In fact, once in the cold water, he found his fins, and as they approached the island was edging ahead. It was then that Garremat grabbed his legs, pulling him back. Agradray struggled free and made the last few metres onto the island. Garremat followed, leaping like a flying fish from the water, racing after him, and seizing him, pushing him over and then holding him prone on the thistly ground.

As the warm, taut flesh pressed down on him, Agradray felt that the past few months, which had seemed like a rising flood of truth, were now ebbing away, receding like the tide to reveal something more complex, more ineffable than was to be found in any catechism of the faith. Lying prone, with the wonderful warmth of the other man working its way through his skin, his bones and into his soul, he felt the world go strangely vague.

And then something stranger still; the face, the ordinary face, the lips were touching his, and seemed by their breath to suck out all the certainties he had gained over the last months. And with that simple, ordinary sense of human warmth, the castles and palaces he had built in his mind, his very idea of heaven, began to dissolve, to crumble to dust.

Agradray and Garremat had lain there for some time, moving their minds to meet the new certainties of their bodies and their souls.

For a few weeks afterwards, life had continued as before. Each day Agradray would unlock the door at the bottom of the monument, and they would climb up and spend the day painting in silence.

Agradray was still torn. He wanted to possess Garremat fully, to be one with him. And yet he did not want them to skulk around, or steal away like escaped convicts. So one day he asked Garremat to marry him.

'I shall be your husband, and you mine; and we shall show a faith that will shake the cathedral to its foundations.' And Garremat had simply kissed him in consent.

Marriage meant instant disqualification from the priesthood – Father Dacossian banished them, with the words 'Agradray, you are my first failure. May God forgive you.'

'I am Anthony again now,' he replied with pity in his voice, pity for an old magician who had lost his wand. They left without looking back, though Anthony kept in his pocket the key to the monument.

And so Anthony married Grant, as he once again was, and his mother and father looked on, happy at a son lost and then found again. As he looked across to his husband, Anthony saw that beauty can transcend the physical. The first five years of the marriage were perhaps the happiest of Anthony's life. For once the passions of the heart, the body and the intellect seemed to have come together, and every act from shopping in the supermarket to writhing naked on the kitchen floor was imbued with mystery.

In the next five years their love morphed into something more settled, more silent, more mature. If Anthony's heart no longer skipped several beats on the mere sound of Grant's voice, and if he was now happier curling up beside him than clawing every fibre of clothing from him, that seemed only for the good. Anthony's career, now Professor of Physics at the local university – the youngest in decades – brought him a passion that he no longer sought or needed at home.

The first signs that a crack was appearing came as Anthony passed the age of thirty, and then the perhaps more critical age of 33.3. A third of a century; a long playing record (as his grandfather had once told him). And where exactly had this brought him? A husband, but not children. (Anthony had poured icy water on Grant's suggestion that they adopt.)

He began to see his husband, still happy in a humdrum job, as a growing hindrance. The chance for a Chair at the University of Vienna was thwarted, because Grant would not leave his brother and his parents behind. He saw Grant start to grow fat and careless of his appearance, complacent. Anthony began to look at other men with more interest. Thirteen years of faithfulness; why, that was almost unnatural, almost immoral.

And so, when a particularly young and winsome missionary from the Church of the Holy Spheres knocked on their door one day, Anthony did not do what he had done several times before. He did not set out to give the boy rope before tying him up in intellectual knots and then finally sending him off confused and defeated. He decided that, instead, seducing him would be a pleasure that was also a duty – there was also that tell-tale spark in the young man's eye that told him that he would, in the end, be willing prey.

In fact it took all of Anthony's charm, all of his verbal skill, before he had his quarry where he wanted him, prone and whimpering, simpering with delight, in the back of the family car. Yes, he felt guilty, a traitor, a cad, but somehow this increased the frisson. The thought of Grant sitting, still trusting, waiting for him at home, was horrid but exciting. And even the knowledge that he was now more loved than he was loving made him feel a benediction.

But when the would-be missionary left the Church, and changed from the rather charming Lahoxe back into plain old Lee, Anthony felt the control, and with it the pleasure, draining through his fingers. Lee now insisted that he was in love with him. Anthony knew that he could not leave Grant, at least not yet, and began to sense that to have two lovers was to halve rather than to double one's love.

He began to drink as he had not done since that night in the park. At first Grant was annoyingly considerate, almost cloyingly so, reminding Anthony of his mother, chiding him only gently when he came in slurring his words. Then he wrote off the car that he had lately defiled and was banned from driving – with a most unflattering picture of him printed in the local press, for Anthony still cared greatly about his looks. He was given a written warning for turning up drunk to a lecture.

At last, even the love of the all-forgiving Grant seemed stretched as thin as a spider's web.

'You're not the man I married!' (Trust him to use a threadbare cliché.)

'And you're not the man I've been fucking! At least not these past six months!' And then added, for good measure, 'Yes, even you can work out that it's that sweet little blond thing from the church, except of course I've shown him where he belongs.'

Grant didn't reply, didn't even react much. For a week or two things carried on much as before. They even had sex, after a fashion, for the first time in months. Then, one day, Grant was gone, a note in his neat hand stuck to the hook where Anthony always hung his coat.

Gone away. Have to think. Will call when I'm ready.
Love G.

'How unoriginal,' he thought – Anthony would have come up with something much more incisive. And then the 'love' at the end, like a let-out, a reassurance that Grant would eventually be back.

So Anthony didn't worry overmuch. He carried on with his work, even managing to turn up to most of his lectures both sober and on time. If the days were nearly bearable, it was at night in the early hours, when he would awaken and reach by instinct for the reassuring smooth warmth of Grant's body, and feel only a cold void, that his heart began to deaden with dread.

After a month, he could feel the legions of panic beginning to assemble and creep up his limbs before invading his spine. He no longer had any desire to see Lee, and turned limp and flaccid on the one occasion when they did meet.

Even so, he was surprised to awaken one morning on the bathroom floor, his head marinated in his own urine. He knew then that if there were lower depths, they were ones he must not see.

His desperation to see Grant thudded against the cold marble-like reality that he knew nothing of his whereabouts. And then, even as Anthony washed the filth from his body, he saw land, on the doormat, a letter that could only be from the man who, despite all logic, still seemed to be the love of his life. His shaking fingers, still wet from the shower, tore it open, the water causing the ink to run.

I have been thinking about you. Am at the cathedral. We should meet. Love? G.

Love with a question mark this time, but it extended to Anthony a straw just strong enough to pull himself away from the edge. That Grant should be anywhere near the cathedral was a blow, but perhaps that was just his way of getting back at him. And quite an elegant one, he thought.

Two days later another letter followed.

I'll meet you by the lake under the monument on Saturday.

The lake, where they had first felt that strange link of heat. Anthony could hardly wait. He felt like a teenager again. He went out and bought himself a new suit, in the black that set him in his best light. He counted the hours. He hardly slept.

And then, in the early morning, before he set off for the cathedral, a ring on the door. A policeman and woman stood there. Somehow, before they began to open their mouths, he knew, knew that this new hope, this new chance was dashed. Dashed as the body of Grant, which, the policewoman told him, had fallen from the monument. The rope which had been holding him as he painted had snapped, somehow. They assured him that death must have been instant.

Anthony, not responding, then seemed to know, briefly, that strange, almost sweet nothingness, the welcome void that is the extinction of all hope. The inquest returned an accidental death; the rope had been distressed by time, apparently. The body was returned to Anthony, as next of kin, for disposal. And Antony could not help but kiss the cold and yellowing face and hands that he would never hold again in warmth, before consigning it to be burned.

But something else was burning, burning in his mind and heart, a searing sense that something had to be done. And slowly a cold clear plan was born, born of necessity and rage. Anthony could not bring his Grant back to his arms, the Grant he had himself so casually thrown away. From his side he saw justice in this, but there was a much greater justice to be hatched.

And so, two months later, all was in place. He returned to the cathedral, hardly bearing to look up at the monument as he passed it. In one pocket, a photograph of Grant, taken on their wedding day; in the other the key to the tower.

He half-wondered that they made no attempt to challenge him. The elders of the church had spoken of the need for security, of the threats from fanatics of other, failed religions. But Father Dacossian had rebuked them. The church should be open to all. Better one murderer let in than that a thousand souls should cringe in selfish fear.

On one of the High Mass Days of the year the cathedral was packed. As Anthony advanced along the aisle through the ocean of the faithful he felt as Moses must have felt in the Red Sea. His eye was caught by the kindly glint of an old man and woman.

'Soon you will be dust. And it is right.' For he knew that had they known him fully they would curse him into hell.

His eye then fell on young children, full of the provisional joys that come with being three or four. They too would die, but surely, according to their own creed, he would be sending them to a better place, far from the evils that would curse their time here.

And so at last he approached the altar, the optimum place to detonate the bomb. And there he saw the familiar, handsome form of Father Dacossian, the hair still magnificently thick and black. A miracle, the faithful said. A bottle of dye, or perhaps a wig, replied the infidels. Yet it was not Dacossian's eye or gaze that Anthony's met. Instead he crossed glances with a young man – brown hair, grey eyes, about twenty-five, otherwise unremarkable – which made him start and almost stumble. The young man smiled bashfully, and Anthony felt that he was staring into the face, the soul, of Grant.

He knew it was a nonsense, but at the same time he knew that he could not kill the boy, or splatter and dash his blood across the shattered myriad panes of glass of the exploding cathedral. And if he could not do that, neither could he destroy the others. And the people, young and old, whom he had passed and cursed regained their humanity. And he stood there, not as the avenger but as a cheap, cold-blooded murderer, who had already killed his Grant as much as they had.

With a cry of 'No!' he turned and ran back down the aisle, no-one attempting to stop him. Bursting through the great doors, he carried on running, down to the lake. He sat down under a tree, swaying and moaning quietly. At length he decided. He could no longer commit mass-murder but he could, he must, do something.

Waiting until night fell, and the place was empty to the light of the moon and the sound of the owls, he walked back up towards the monument. Taking the key from his pocket, he discovered that, even after fifteen years, it still turned in the lock. Again, no alarm or security, but why should there be?

Climbing to the top, he looked out, for one last time, at the spherical dome of the cathedral, sparkling with the stars and moon, and down at the lake. He took Grant's portrait from his other pocket, and kissed it. Fitting that they should die in the same place. But then, as he prepared to detonate, another thought. He had lived through thirty-five years of heaven, and hell. To what purpose should it end now? He still had many amends to make. Death would be too sweet, too unearned. Grant had earned his, but he, Anthony, felt that he had work to do.

He unstrapped the explosives from his waist, and placed them, reverentially, halfway up the spiral stairs. Fortunately he had a timing device, one that he had fitted lest his nerve fail him. In fact he felt much more nervous walking down the stairs, and then away from the tower. He was almost down at the lake again when he heard a dull roar.

He had known that the monument, built 'to last a thousand generations' would do no such thing. He had seen the flaws in the engineering, built as it was by Dacossian's younger brother in thanks for his recovery from opiates and other drugs. In reality he had used cheaper labour and materials to continue funding his habit.

And so the bomb's work was made much easier than it should have been. The tower telescoped down, the statue swayed, and then, most splendidly, the great head toppled off and fell to the ground with a thud, before rolling down the hill and coming to rest in the reedy mud.

Anthony felt tempted to kick it, but knew now that he had other, better, nobler things to do. He might be caught; his past would most likely catch up with him in some form, indeed he almost hoped it would. But he was ready. And as he caught his own reflection in one last look at the moonlit lake, he seemed to see his own face, and for the first time in many moons looked himself in the eye, and smiled.

BIG RINGS

Elsa Wallace

In fact it was not my mother who warned me about us; I suspect she knew little on the subject, perhaps not even enough to disapprove. Or was I wrong? Did she know enough *not* to disapprove? My aunt once told me 'When your mother was a girl she used to bring home the strangest women and take them to her room and talk for hours. We never knew what they talked about.'

What my mother did warn me about was the white slave trade; I should beware of people who tried to lure me into upstairs rooms from where I would never be seen again. This impressed itself so powerfully on me that when, aged eight, I was invited by her good friend Iris to join her on the first floor balcony of the ice-cream parlour I instantly identified her as an agent of the nefarious trade and refused the treat of an ice. It did not seem at all unreasonable that the slaving business might flourish in an obscure Karoo town and with the librarian as one of its employees.

The warning about us and what sort of people we might be came in my teens from an acquaintance of my mother's who had been to Jo'burg – city of sin – and whose daughter had been accosted by 'one of them'. She had stroked Nolene's cheek and told her 'You have lovely skin, my dear.' Mrs Murphy said 'Now at the time Nolene's skin was very poor, not like it is now. The woman wore one of those big rings. They *all* wear big rings.'

She passed on this information dispassionately, so perhaps it was not so much a warning as part of a field guide to lesbians.

Then came the Sixties when it was fashionable to wear large Perspex fun rings, but I supposed those did not count. We had now moved to the Copperbelt and my mother as usual quickly assembled round her a group of women who came to tea on Sunday. Most of them were Catholics but Mrs Irwin and Mrs Temple were not, and some were between husbands. The dashing Mrs van der Spuy was looking forward to her third husband. Mrs Irwin said 'I don't know why she bothers. I think once you've got the kids it would be nice if the men buzzed off.'

I was not often required to be present at the tea parties but when my mother had her wrist broken by being knocked down by a large dog, I was useful in making tea, fetching hot water and helping to make the cakes: Victoria sponges, fairy cakes, shortbread and peanut biscuits.

The conversation never struck me as particularly engrossing; tips on cooking or sewing mainly. Most made their own clothes, as the shops had a scant and dull collection. Mrs Irwin had natty linen suits run up by Mr Chauhan in the Second Class Trading and Mrs Branch had to go with her when she ventured off the beaten track in that way, it being 'not done' for white women to go there alone. They discussed exasperations at work and with gardens and 'garden boys' – 'I told him to cut the grass and found him with the secateurs trying to cut the glass in the front windows.'

Pets featured quite strongly. Mrs James went on about her budgie Fifi's vocabulary and Mrs Atkins about her boisterous Schipperkes. The male got hysterical when the female was on heat. 'So when I'm not breeding I just sedate him. I wake him every six hours for food and what have you, otherwise he just sleeps through it.' Mrs Branch said 'I wish I was able to do that to you-know-who,' and there was shocked amusement.

The third most interesting afternoon was when Father Luke popped in to see how the sewing was progressing for the church fête. He was duly presented with a box of oven gloves and aprons. He was a plump little Italian who seemed to find much of life diverting. This time he told us of a parishioner who had come to complain of poltergeists and wanted his kia exorcised. Father Luke was not inclined to oblige. 'He said these people are dancing and singing on his roof at night. I told him, good, you've got your entertainment free, you don't need to pay to go to the bioscope.'

The second most interesting occurrence at these afternoons was when Mrs Webb told us of witnessing an arrest in her street; a black man handcuffed to a lamp post and a black constable beating him. 'Now I'm British, I can't put up with that and I ran out right away in my shortie nightie, my little shortie nightie,' she tittered. The nightie had no effect on the constable but eventually a superior officer turned up to take charge.

I wasn't supposed to hear the most interesting item of news. My mother had had wind of it and despatched me to the kitchen to put cheese spread on cream crackers, but the excited buzz reached me there.

Mrs Irwin had been found in bed with Mrs Branch by Mr Branch who had come off shift unexpectedly. Who would have thought it? And they have both got grown-up girls.

Mrs van der Spuy was critical. 'What surprises me,' she said, 'is that they let him jump to the right conclusion. Why didn't they just say they'd heard a noise in the night – a poltergeist – and were scared?'

'Being scared doesn't make you take off your clothes,' said Mrs Webb.

'Well, drunk, then. They should have said they were drunk.'

'Who would have thought it?' said my mother again. 'Joanie Irwin had only just got that Hollerith job.'

'Penny plays a lot of golf,' said Mrs Temple.

'*I* play golf. Sometimes,' said Mrs Webb indignantly.

'But *you* don't play to win,' said Mrs Temple. 'Penny had shelves of cups.'

There was silence while this intelligence was absorbed.

I gleaned later that the two promptly eloped to Cape Town and that Mrs James (with her husband's permission) tried to cheer up Mr Branch with casseroles and salads, as he was too despondent to eat at the Mine Mess and all his own cook could run to was bacon and eggs.

'He just sits there at the kitchen table,' she reported, 'his head in his hands. He can't fathom it out. Who can? There was no sign. There he sits with her rings in front of him on the table. I'll say this for Penny Branch: she left him her rings and she needn't have. My God, the *size* of that diamond!'

AS THE CROW FLIES

Jimmy Driver

Daniel said goodbye to his boyfriend, Brian, on the bus, went into the tube station and through the booking hall to the ticket barrier. He took out his pass and went through the machine without getting stabbed in the ribs.

'Over the first hurdle!' he thought. He went through the station and onto the down escalator. As soon as he could no longer see daylight, he felt he was being hidden underground.

'I feel like some dark secret the earth is hiding from the sun,' he mused to himself, as the escalator carried him deeper and deeper underground. At the foot of the escalator, he stepped off into a cavernous chamber full of people. He thought Hades must be a bit like this modern underworld.

As Daniel expected, the platform was packed with commuters. He felt he was just being added to a great mass of anonymous humanity, like one more little spoonful of person being added to a great vat. It was as if individuality had been banished; people merged into the crowd and lost their identity, without a murmur of objection.

The train came along in a few minutes. This was even worse! Daniel thought his pulse must be racing as he stepped onto the train.

'Packed in like sardines?' he thought. 'If sardines were treated like this the animal rights lobby would be up in arms about it! It's like something out of Dante's Inferno!'

He looked around the carriage. 'What a look on everybody's face!' he thought. They seemed to be exuding suppressed anger, as if to say, 'Watch it, Buster! You tread on MY toes and you're dead!'

Eventually the train arrived at his destination. He got out and his torment eased off. He went up the escalator and emerged, to his great relief, from the world underground.

Daniel taught English as a foreign language at a school in Oxford Street, just a short walk from the station. When he got there, he went straight to the teachers' room, which looked out onto Oxford Street from the second floor of the building. The crowds of shoppers, taxis and buses milled around below.

Daniel greeted his colleagues, took off his jacket, collected his books and cassette tapes and climbed more stairs to the teaching room. There was no thought of Brian on his mind now. His students were waiting for him and there was a kind of buzz as he walked into the room. Everyone was keen to begin the day. Daniel knew it would involve challenges, but he was confident in his own abilities. He was an experienced teacher and he could deal with most of the problems most of the time.

The day proceeded as usual. The morning class went without any major hitches. There was a break for lunch, which Daniel took on his own, as normal. Then he returned for the afternoon lesson, which was arranged with an interval half-way through, when the students went into the coffee bar.

The break in the afternoon lesson was a time when the teachers got away from their students and congregated in the teachers' room for a few minutes of reflecting, raging, exploding, resting, pouring out their hearts, gossiping or just recharging the batteries.

One of the teachers, Sarah, kicked off: 'I had to explain "Fuck knows" today,' she said gaily.

'How did that come up?'

'You know that Saudi girl in my Level 3 class? Apparently someone said it to her in a shoe shop. She was asking where a pair of suede slip-ons were made.'

'How did you explain it to her?'

'That was even worse. I said it was like "God knows", only with "fuck" instead of "God". So of course she thought "fuck" was a pseudonym for God. So I had to explain "fuck" too.'

'What did they all make of that?'

'Nothing really. Just went sort of quiet, as if to say we really are as mad in this country as people back home make out.'

The teachers were generally young people, like Daniel and Sarah, who had taught abroad for a couple of years and then returned to Britain. Teaching was a kind of stop-gap, filling in time between graduating from University and working out what they really wanted to do.

It was time to go back into the classroom. Daniel went back upstairs to his Level 4 group. They were doing a cassette tape that afternoon, so there was not too much effort involved on the teacher's part. At the end of the class, Paolo, a young student from Portugal, came up to the teacher's desk. 'Daniel,' he said, 'may I ask you something?'

'Of course!' Daniel replied with a grin.

Paolo produced a well-worn travel guide and showed it to Daniel.

'My parents gave me this book before I came here. I cannot understand one thing in it.'

He pointed out a paragraph describing the lovely English countryside, with its gently rolling hills. The villages, the book declared, were pretty and could be visited on foot or by bicycle, along winding country lanes. Care should be taken though when using maps, as the distances along those winding country lanes were often considerably longer than they appeared. 'It is sometimes a long journey along a circuitous route to reach a place that is near as the crow flies.'

Daniel knew what the problem was before Paolo even asked.

'As the crow flies?'

'Yes, what does it mean, please, Daniel?'

'It means a straight line between two places. You know the shortest distance between two places is always a straight line. A crow is a kind of bird. It always flies in a straight line. It's a black bird.'

Paolo smiled enthusiastically. 'Oh, yes,' he said helpfully, 'I know a blackbird.'

Paolo was in his early twenties, a few years younger than Daniel. He was always terribly polite.

'Oh, no,' Daniel said. 'A crow is a black bird, but a crow is not a blackbird.'

Daniel realised his mistake instantly and, rather apologetically, illustrated the idea on the whiteboard, with lines and dots. He added that it was rather an old-fashioned expression: 'We don't use it much any more.'

Daniel wasn't sure how well Paolo understood, but he was tired and wanted to go home anyway. He collected his bag and coat and battled his way home on the tube. He had a room in a shared house in the East End. He opened the door and went straight to his room on the ground floor, thinking this wasn't going to be his home for much longer. Because in a few days, The Move would happen.

Daniel had something to eat and was watching TV when the doorbell rang. He guessed it was his boyfriend, Brian, and let him in. He always felt a rush of energy when Brian entered the room. They went to Daniel's room and kissed and cuddled and chatted. The imminent Move was the topic of conversation.

'So aren't you nervous about moving in with me?' Brian asked. 'Especially as you've lived with someone before and it didn't work out.'

'Of course I'm nervous. I wouldn't be human if I didn't feel a bit of nerves. But it's worth it.'

'I've still never met Roger. What was he like?'

Daniel laughed. 'What do you want to know for? Want to find out what the competition was like?'

'Just curiosity. What killed the cat.'

'Well, he was tall and slim, muscular. Very charming. Beautifully dressed.'

'And you left that Adonis? AND took up with me?'

'Well, I suppose I was stupid enough to think looks were everything. I eventually wised up and saw his bad side.'

Brian laughed. 'What happens when you wise up and see MY bad side?'

'You're not just the next step along the way. You're where I've got to get to.' He kissed Brian on the lips. 'My goal is now in sight.'

The next morning they left together to get the bus to work, as usual. Daniel said his goodbye to Brian again and got off at the tube station for the rest of his journey into school. Brian stayed on the bus to the mainline station.

The school where Daniel taught had a liberal atmosphere. Daniel had no real problems coming out as gay to the other teachers. The students were another matter. Some of them came from countries where homosexuality carried the death sentence, and could take a dim view of this European decadence. Besides, as most of them didn't stay long enough to form real friendships with the teachers, Daniel saw no point in discussing his private life with them.

Daniel went into the teachers' room. He started talking to Sarah.

'So this weekend is IT!' she said. 'The great Move! Move with a capital M! Are you ready for it?'

'Ready as I'll ever be!' he said.

'Will it be a terrible journey for you?'

'Not really, I can come in on the Victoria line from Brixton.'

'Well, that's all right!'

Daniel thought about it for a second. 'In fact,' he added, 'it should even be quicker to come in from there than where I am now. The transport's better, although of course it's further as the crow flies.'

Daniel had to pack for The Move. Strangely, planning The Move and thinking about it beforehand were more stressful than actually doing it. He methodically packed everything into the appropriate type of box or bag, delicate items surrounded by a lot of padding.

He was at home that night, surrounded by packing cases and his belongings, when the doorbell rang. He answered it and, much to his surprise, Roger's tall, muscular frame was outlined in the doorway. There was a moment of silence as Daniel's eyes narrowed. He no longer felt grief at their parting – just a kind of cold, cynical bitterness whenever the two of them were together.

'Well?'

'It's my books. Can I come in for a minute?'

'You said I could have the books when I left.'

'You said you didn't want them. I heard you were moving this weekend, so I thought I'd come round and claim them before it was too late. Can I come in just for a minute?'

They went inside. 'I haven't slept, you know!' Roger said, trying to raise a little sympathy. 'I was kept up all night by some birds tweeting in the garden!'

'What sort of birds?' Daniel asked the question and immediately realised how futile it was.

Roger looked surprised. 'Fuck knows!' he said.

They went into Daniel's room. Daniel sensed there was some ulterior motive in Roger's visit and had a pretty shrewd idea what it was.

'Of course, you couldn't possibly afford some new books. Not on what you earn in the City. Anyway, they're over there on the shelf. Now I haven't got much time 'cause I'm packing for The Move.'

'So you're all ready to move in with His Nibs.'

'That's not a very nice way to refer to him.'

Roger's face contorted into a look of mock horror. 'Oh, what should I call him? Fat, ugly git?'

By this time Daniel had had enough of Roger's bile. 'Here, Roger,' he said quietly, 'have a little token of my esteem!' and punched him on the jaw.

Roger had not been expecting that and he was speechless for a moment. Daniel continued in a quiet voice 'Now just get out and don't come back. Get out of my room and get out of my life.'

Daniel and Brian's new home was a furnished flat with a pleasant, but not particularly large, garden, reached through a door from the kitchen. It had an apple tree and a lawn. The day they moved in, Daniel took a chair out into the garden and sat peacefully admiring the view while Brian went out to do a bit of shopping.

The garden was starting to bloom with crocuses and bluebells. Daniel sat on the veranda, his gaze darting around the garden as he looked at one thing, then another. His attention was fully occupied: he was completely absorbed in his perception. It suddenly dawned on him that this was a scene of special, magical beauty. This was the magical space he was going to share with the man he loved. At that moment, two magpies flew into the garden and perched on the apple tree branches.

‘Oh,’ he thought, ‘our first visitors! We’re sharing the space already!’

He heard Brian come into the flat and called him to come out on the veranda. ‘We’re entertaining two visitors in our garden!’ he said. ‘Magpies,’ he added, pointing.

Brian smiled. ‘So you can identify different types of birds now,’ he said.

‘That’s right,’ Daniel said, ‘I’ve learnt discernment through you. I can sort the good from the bad now. Before it was just a mass – undifferentiated. Although it has taken me a long time to reach this place. I’ve gone all round the houses. I’ve taken a circuitous route. But I’ve ended up in the right place, with you.’

Brian laughed. ‘Yes, that’s right, darling, you did. You ended up in a place that was nearer your starting point. As the crow flies.’

A GIRL STORY

Simon Dessloch

With my Air Wear trainers I can follow her silently like a cat. This jewel-encrusted geriatric with the shiny black handbag. I pretend I'm her shadow. That way no one else sees me either, when I follow her into the little girls' room. She lets go of the swing door and I catch it. Release it gently so it makes no sound.

On her high heels she hobbles into the second cubicle. I go into the first. Peek through the holes. See her standing that shiny black handbag – patent leather like SM fetish wear – against the partition wall to her right, the one that separates her from me.

Because there's another woman in the Ladies, a fat one in a red tunic, fixing herself in the mirror, I wait.

I watch the old lady peeling herself out of layer after layer of stretchy fabric. She's fucking wearing suspenders, do you believe that? She pulls down her flesh-coloured drawers. I can smell her cunt. I can hear the clack clack of the tunic-woman's heels. The soft thud of the swing door closing.

It's just the fetish lady and me left in the toilet now. I know she won't chase after me with her knickers down, so I pull the little black handbag through the gap under the partition wall to my side. Nowhere safe to stand it. At the far side there would have been. Nowhere to hang it. Nowhere higher up that's level.

I know this loo. I know all the Ladies rooms. My hunting grounds. Stealing is clean. I mean I don't do armed robbery. I don't carry a gun. I don't have to.

She makes a little yelp. They always do. The posh ones. The tunic-woman would have screamed the place down.

But this one just mewls like a puppydog. A subdued soprano, like hitting the right pitch will stop me dead in my tracks.

I'm out the door before she's left the cubicle trilling 'Thief! Thief!'

Outside Trixie is waiting with the boys. We walk fast but we don't run. The handbag is hidden in my rucksack. We leave through the nearest exit and into the square and we squat down behind a thick hedge. I show them what I've got. Inside there's five twenties, credit cards, ID, two stitched cloth hankies, do you believe that? Everyone takes twenty. Trixie finds a thrice-folded slip of lined paper with a list of four-digit numbers. Some crossed out. We end up with six hundred quid before the cards are cancelled. Plus two pairs of kinky boots for Trix and me. I mean I can pretend to be Penelope Ferris but Luke and Pedro and Stu can't.

I can't help thinking that I could have the six hundred all to myself, instead of sharing this stolen money with my friends. Trixie doesn't have the nerve. She can't even shoplift. Dumps her load the moment someone calls thief. She panics even seeing me do it so I can't take her with me inside anywhere. She went red like a tomato when I handed the shop assistant the card to pay for our boots. I was wearing mine already in case I had to do a runner.

Bless her. She's a cute thing. She with the long curly hair. I'm winding and twirling it round my fingers and this is as far as she lets me go. I twist it and pull it and she goes 'ou' and I like that and I want to do it more. Hurt her more.

Instead she does the hurting. Going on about Jesus Eyes and his pale blue eyes and his hairy fucking chest and how she would go all the way with him if he asked her to. So far he hasn't said a single word to her, of course, so she does hand-jobs on fat boy Otto for a tenner. Ten fucking quid. Do you believe that?

This one looks so sad. Because she's dressed all in red, you know, like, cherry-red? Like Little Red Riding Hood. Where the fuck did she get this outfit? Looks like it's hung in a wardrobe for longer than I've been alive. Maybe twice that. I go after her down the corridor that leads to the inevitable destination. No reason to head there except to answer the call of nature.

The woman in red is spindly thin and lame. And so sad. White hair. Red nails. Red shoes. Red bag. She walks like an invalid. I'm beginning to feel sorry for her and I really hate myself for that. And I hate the way that feels. I imagine *her* asking *me* for money. I imagine her sad face. I haven't really seen her front yet.

Her legs are as thin as my arms. Her stockings are several shades paler than her skin. Desiccated Malibu sunburnt.

I feel self-conscious because I'm walking so slowly just because she does.

It's taking twice as long to get to the loo.

I keep a distance. It's only when I get close to her that I notice how bad she smells. Like that vagrant smell. But it's too late now to back out. Because I've opened the door. Broken into her cubicle. Used force.

Most of those cubicles can be opened easily from the outside. There's a mechanism with a groove and you stick a coin in there, any coin, and you turn it and the door opens.

That's how they get to people who've OD'd. That's how the attendants lock the cubicles from the outside so no one can use them and they don't have to clean them.

And that's how I get to the ladies that I can't get to any other way. When I have to break and enter.

She doesn't look like she's going to do any opera-singing. She doesn't look like she's going to do anything. She doesn't look scared.

She looks – sad.

She won't fight.

'Give me that,' I say so softly. She doesn't move. Looks frozen stiff. I close my fist round the strap and pull. Thinking that all I have to do is gently slip it from that gnarled brown witch's claw.

Little Red Riding Hood and the wolf.

But she doesn't let go.

She pulls back hard.

Footsteps. The door thuds.

She smiles.

The witch is fucking smiling at me.

I grab the bag with both hands, get my knee up against her, but it's not enough. Not until I pin her with my kinky boot on her chest and pull as hard as I can. Pull till it gives.

I've got the bag. She's still holding the strap.

The woman that's just come in has locked herself in at the opposite end.

I run out of the toilet. Try to slow down. Walk. Hide the prize in my own shoulder bag. I go clack, clack, clack and my own footsteps freak me out. The witch's bag feels nice and full.

In the square I throw it to Trixie. Like it's a dead rabbit I've slain to feed to my best friend, to provide for my love.

'There's nothing in it.'

'What?'

Trixie rips out entrails of shredded paper. Together we tear the fucking thing apart. It's got red silk lining, little pockets with nothing in them. Smells of attics and dust like it hasn't been opened in a hundred years.

We stomp up and down on it but it's no good. We throw it on the underground tracks. Why the fuck did she even fight for it? I remember her grinning at me. I should have kicked her harder.

For a while I don't do the Ladies.

I feel I'm losing my nerve. When I close my eyes I see Little Red Riding Hood grinning. Laughing at me. What the fuck is her story? Where does she get off?

Instead of stealing I smoke, I drink, I drop Es. I get high only to come down again and each time I fall it's from a greater height. Trixie and me are holding together but I can feel her slipping away.

In the street outside the mall I see Jesus Eyes. He winks at me. Bastard. Absolute creep. Those watery eyes. Dead fish.

'What's your name, little one?' I ignore him. 'It's just that I've seen you around. You're Trixie's friend. You got a reputation for robbing old ladies.'

'And you got one for stealing little girls.'

'But I always give them back after, don't I?' He walks side by side with me now. Too close. Big broad belt round his narrow hips. I think his torso is longer than his legs. I'm waiting for him to tilt over. 'Don't I? You can have her back now. I mean, it's over now. It's done. Trixie and me. I mean, we understand each other, don't we?'

I'm not doing it for Trixie now. I'm not even doing it for the money any longer. I'm walking the corridors. I'm going inside when I don't have to go at all. Passing time. Looking for that special lady.

I've done a few easy ones – pushing down on old-style door jambs on the outside to dislodge the handbag hanging on the inside, ready to drag it out when it drops. Without ever having to see or touch the ladies.

I spot someone I've never seen before. A lady's lady and I want her. Dressed like she's going to the races – a pompous hat and gloves as thin as silk stockings.

Don't quite know what to do about Trix. Now that she's different. She's so overbearing. Wants to cuddle. Wants to hug. I don't think I want her now. Now that Jesus Eyes has had her. I think I'm going to hurt Trixie or Jesus Eyes but first I'm going to pick a fight with this lady.

That coiffured hair makes her look like a Barbie doll. Like I've just taken the wrapper off and she's brand new and untouched. I want to make her naked and with her hair down to her bum. She walks like a model and I imagine she's performing just for me. There's a distance between us still but I'm zooming in on her. She smells of dark dry lavender.

I want to defile my Barbie doll.

I break into her cubicle. Grab that silly hat that she's got, that makes her look taller than she is. It's some kind of Ascot monstrosity. Looks like a dismembered trilby put back together with parts missing. The silly hat's been fastened with a pin, I think. I think I've seen that in movies. Her hair is all messed now, out of kilter and strands of strawberry blonde are obscuring her face, and this is how I want her, with her hair down. A wild thing.

Are those false lashes? I shall try to rip them off her eyelids.

I reach for her face. She pushes me away hard.

'Are you crazy?'

This time I go for the grey suede bag and I get that easy because Barbie's busy rescuing her hat from the bleach suds in the toilet bowl.

I turn to go but she comes after me. She's got heels but so do I. She jumps me from behind. I'm really not expecting that. That she might give as good as she is getting. I hold on securely to the bag. Stuff it in my coat. It's only a tiny little bag with a very slim, very long shoulder strap, almost a wallet on a leash.

She starts hitting me and kicking too. Throws her weight on me and we fall. She's fucking throwing me to the floor is Barbie doll, do you believe that?

She gets me on my back. Really wild now. Tries to get the bag out from inside my coat. I reach for her hair. Grab handfuls and tear. She kicks me and, *ou ou ou*, that really hurts.

She gets the bag. I try to grab it back. I sit up but pain is crippling me. I let go of her hair. I let go of everything. I let her go. She kicks me in the face and then again.

I think I'm bleeding in more than one place. I've managed to hold on to some of her blonde tresses. They're almost a metre long. Almost as long as my leg.

I try to get up. Can't. I hear her go clack clack clack. I hear the soft thud of the door.

SAME AGAIN, PLEASE

John Dixon

'Why is it,' said Jerome, 'that the parents of gay people always live such a bloody long time?'

All his friends had elderly parents, so did several neighbours and most of his undeclared work colleagues. 'Is it a universal truth – or just my reading of a situation I'm familiar with?'

He threw up his hands in exasperation. 'And you needn't think you're going to outlive me! You'd love that, wouldn't you? Then you could make out I was a saint and never married because I was... so, so happy to devote my life to looking after you. Well, I haven't had a life – you stole it – and now I'm about to retire. To what? I work hard and forfeit everything just to... to... God, the years I've spent clearing up your phlegm and diarrhoea – and spooning out your bland, knifeless diet into your toothless gums. And you're even too deaf to hear what I'm saying. Why don't you just die?'

He finished tucking up his father in bed, then gently put a glass of fresh water on the bedside table. 'And now, perhaps...'

Jerome's only escape was at night. He tip-toed out of the house and headed straight for the local park. He walked round and round and when it was obvious there was no new talent worth following he spoke to the regulars, many of whom had elderly relatives.

'By the way, I forgot to ask – how's your old father?'

'Mother, actually.'

'Sorry.'

'Don't be. There's not much difference at that age. How's your... your one?'

Jerome shrugged. 'Life goes on.' He walked round the circuit again and continued the conversation when they passed later.

'Where's old Harry these days? Haven't seen him for weeks.'

'His father died.'

'Oh dear.'

'And Harry doesn't come over here any more.' There was a long pause. 'He goes over the Flats. He says there's a lot of new talent there.'

'Really? It's so difficult to get back from in time.'

'Surely it doesn't matter now you're retired?'

No, thought Jerome, I don't suppose it does. He found comfort from these nightly quests. He returned home better disposed to his father.

'The poor old man; he must be confused, in pain. No wonder he's so irritable. It won't be for much longer.'

When Daddy approached the age of a hundred Jerome spent hours looking for an appropriate card. There were cards for retirement, bereavement, sixty, seventy and eighty. Any age beyond that was obviously not commercially viable. Jerome was forced into a scissors-and-paste effort – 'Daddy will never notice the joins.'

He handed the card to his father early on the birthday morning. His father seemed grateful. Several other cards had arrived; Jerome's one was given pride of place, in the centre of the mantelpiece. Later that day an official-looking envelope – embossed and crested – was delivered by special mail. It was the traditional congratulations telegram from the Queen.

Daddy was well pleased. 'Put it in the middle of the mantelpiece. Move yours; this one's from the real Queen.'

Jerome said nothing and went ahead with the birthday schedule. 'We're going out for a spin,' and he settled his father into the wheelchair. 'Let's go to the park.' His father said nothing. Jerome felt in control pushing the chair; he could not see his father's face, just his hands plucking and gathering at the blanket round his knees; equally Daddy could not see him and Jerome was able to wave to his friends. He pointed to things and shouted. 'Look at the bandstand; they've just finished repainting it.' His father said nothing. Jerome pointed beyond the grass to the far hedge. 'And look at those lovely rhododendrons over there.'

'Yes,' said Daddy, pointing somewhat nearer, 'and look at that couple of pansies on the grass. Is this where you come when you go out after midnight?'

Jerome let go of the handles of the wheelchair.

When Daddy died, and all the funeral and inheritance arrangements were over and all the documentation safely filed away, Jerome decided to move.

He found a small town house, purpose built, but in an old style, and equidistant between the park and the Flats. He had a house-warming get-together for the regulars from the park and announced 'My life is going to change. Bye-bye to Clandestine by Night. I'll go out whenever I want, and invite round whomever I wish! Most of all, I am free to settle down to form a proper relationship.'

Jerome visited the park by day and sat on the bench watching the passers-by. He had missed out on the fun and games of childhood and half wanted to join in the sports that were being played; or at least to teach the players the rules of games he had never played himself.

A regular noticed him and said 'Can see what you're up to. Some young people like older men – especially if they've never had a father figure.'

'Well,' Jerome replied sharply, 'that wouldn't be me then, would it? And I wouldn't want to perpetuate what I suffered from.'

In fact, the footballers did not interest him; he did not care who won and found it an anti-climax when the victors and the defeated shook hands and went off for a drink. He liked their muddy legs, the sweaty shirts and shorts and the dishevelled hair, but he much preferred a broken nose, a black eye, missing teeth, bruises, tattoos and scars – someone to take back and offer sanctuary from the police or rival gangs.

One youth who fitted the description stayed overnight, came back a second time and moved in. He only had a few belongings. 'I travel light,' Vince said, 'and if I get anything I sell it quick.'

Soon all Jerome's time and space were taken over. Vince invited his friends round, some rougher than even Jerome would have dared to smile at. And then, just as quickly, they all disappeared, Vince included.

Two days later a policeman knocked at the front door. He apologised and said, 'Look, I think there's been some mistake but I've got to check it out. Your address has been given as the residence of a gentleman who claims that the owner will know him by the name of Vince.'

'That's no mistake. But he's not here at the moment. Where is he? He's got nowhere else to go but here.'

'I see. You do know him, then. He's quite safe, sir. He's with us in the police cells at the moment. Not for the first time either.'

'Really?' said Jerome.

'There's nothing you can do, sir, if you were thinking about trying. Probably best you keep out of it. He was caught in the act. Nothing missing here?'

'Anything that is mine is his to take.'

'Whatever you say, sir. But not everyone thinks the same as you.'

'I don't suppose they do.'

Jerome's first visit to Vince in prison was a revelation. He felt the need to share the experience. 'It was like a guided tour round a castle,' he confided one midnight to a couple of trollers from the park. 'I was escorted everywhere. I felt like royalty. Such an ordered life, monastic almost. And they were just sitting there – just not doing anything – like a *tableau vivant*. But I bet things go on at night – sharing a cell with another young pretty. You could have a whale of a time. Even one of the officers gave me a long, hard look.'

Jerome never missed the monthly prison visit. And he never failed to rush off and transmit the news to the regulars in the park: all the intimate details – the visit where he bumped into Vince's girlfriend, the later visit when he was introduced to a baby; how he had noticed Vince had a tattoo on his neck and nicotine stains on his fingers, and how his language had deteriorated and his political opinions become unsavoury.

It was not long before Vince was transferred to another prison, way up north and far more difficult to get to. By chance Jerome met someone in the park who had been born in that particular area and who had been only too glad to get away from it. Jerome smiled and took no notice. He convinced himself he had always wanted to go to that part of the country. 'It's no problem. It's only twenty miles from the nearest station. I can get a taxi. I could almost stay overnight. It would be like visiting relatives.'

Vince's first words to him were 'My girlfriend can't afford to visit all the way up here.'

Jerome was tempted to say 'Well, find another one who can.' In the event he handed Vince a note of a fairly low denomination. 'I'd rather you gave it to her.'

'Yes, I think that's best, too,' said Vince, pocketing it.

Jerome never heard about the girlfriend again and when he asked politely the conversation was quickly changed. 'I'm getting out of here soon,' said Vince.

'That's marvellous. I'll have everything ready for you. It's still all as it was.'

Jerome invited round several trollers from the park and asked if they thought the bedroom needed redecorating. Most said yes, but no-one could decide on a colour. And nothing was done.

Several weeks passed and a Prison Welfare Officer visited Jerome's house. She looked round and seemed impressed.

'I'm comfortably off,' said Jerome. 'Daddy left a bit and there's my pension.'

'Yes, but it's a set-up open to abuse. We'll need to monitor his progress.'

'What about mine?'

'It's up to you to look after yourself. Now, as to the neighbours. How might they react if they find Vince has just come out of jail?'

'However they bloody like. They don't come into the equation. He needs me; and I'm all he's got.'

'That's as may be – or not. His morale is low and he cannot cope with hassle. He needs Support in the Home Environment in the widest possible sense, in order to Train for the World of Work.'

When Jerome had a firm date for Vince's return he was galvanized into action. He had a fitted bedroom installed, with a king-size double bed; the old single bed was transferred to the spare bedroom. He filled the fridge with Vince's favourite junk food and the cocktail cabinet with cans. On the day of the release Jerome gave Vince a set of keys on a key ring with his favourite cartoon animal.

Things began to go wrong at once. 'Can I have a Coming-Out Party?'

'Coming-Out?' said Jerome. 'Oh, you mean a release party? I suppose so.'

For the next few hours Vince was on the phone, talking at length to friends, glowering when Jerome listened in. At the end of every call Vince gave Jerome's telephone number and address. 'Yeah. Come round. Any time. And phone. Reverse the charges. No problem.'

Within hours the house was full.

'I phoned for takeaways to be delivered,' said Vince helpfully, as he emptied the last bottle in the cocktail cabinet. 'I know you didn't have time to do any shopping.'

Jerome said nothing. He could have done with a drink himself.

'Well,' said Vince, 'now we're all nicely tanked up, I'll show you round. Come and look at the bedroom. Nice, isn't it? Wanna try it for size?' Two youths jumped on the bed with Vince. One of them turned to Jerome and said 'You can go. And shut the door behind you.'

Next day, Jerome and Vince had a tremendous row and Vince flounced out. Several of Jerome's credit cards were missing. He phoned to stop all transactions. 'And he's taken Daddy's medals – perhaps he thinks they're Nazi heirlooms. Oh God,' he despaired, 'it's obvious he won't be looking after me in my extreme old age. But then I don't suppose I'll live as long as poor Daddy. He'll have the last laugh – from beyond the grave. I should have murdered him – but it's more likely someone'll murder me.'

A few days later Vince sloped back and Jerome, with infinite reluctance, let him in. 'I was going to have the lock changed.'

'Do you want your keys back?'

Jerome reproached him. 'Why have you done this to me? What did you hope to gain? Can't you see – I was the goose? I was the goose who would have laid the golden egg. You didn't have to pluck an illicit feather.'

'It wasn't me,' said Vince. 'It was one of my friends. Former friends. I don't see them anymore.'

For a time things went well; no friends came round, the phone was disconnected. Then small items went missing. Nothing important or useful. Cuff links. And a tie-pin. Jerome desisted for a time from making an issue, thinking 'Perhaps he likes these old fashioned things. Perhaps he's never had anything like them in his own life and he's getting to know their value at long last – or perhaps he even associates them in some way with me.' Then he could hold back no longer; he raised the matter very tactfully.

'Perhaps you've lost them,' said Vince.

'No, I haven't lost them. I live here. I know where I keep things. I haven't moved them. I haven't used them. They've been in the same place for years. I am very particular.'

'Have you had anyone else here?'

Jerome faltered. 'You ask me that?'

'What, never during the time I was in prison? Did you go to their place every time? Or do it under the trees?'

Jerome was lost for words. 'I've been loyal to you. I would never do anything behind your back. You know that. And...' He paused and remembered what the Prison Welfare Officer had said about Vince having low morale and self-esteem. Jerome swallowed hard and said 'Why do you do yourself down in this way? Don't you think anyone could be loyal to you – through whatever circumstances?'

'Yes,' said Vince, getting up. 'But not you.'

Jerome wondered if there was much point contesting this. He felt like saying 'Yes, things were better when you were inside.'

He went upstairs and locked himself in the spare bedroom. There was a lot of noise below. He heard the front door slam. He gave Vince fifteen minutes to go – or rethink – and went downstairs to a deserted house.

'He's taken all his things, has he? What's he taken of mine?'

Everything seemed to be in its place.

Several weeks later Jerome was checking through his desk. 'Good Lord! He's taken Daddy's death certificate. What on earth for?

He continued to check. 'Oh God! He's taken my birth certificate. It's almost...' Jerome felt a stab in the guts. 'Almost... as if... he's...'

THE BLOND AMERICAN

David Reade

I am not affected by triskaidekaphobia, but I shall never forget the date; it was Friday the thirteenth, the month being February and the year 1931. My husband, Linton, Second Earl of Ewelme, had been away for a few days in London staying at his club, Brooks's. To no surprise or pleasure on my part he returned with a young man in tow, informing me that his name was Wayne Ritmueller, that he came from America and that he was to act as his secretary and help him collate and identify the letters of Lord Beckley whose biography Linton was writing. He introduced me to this person, who was then aged about twenty-three and very handsome.

Wayne, who came from North Carolina, was tall, well-built and blond, with a baby face and a fresh complexion he hardly needed to shave. He looked and sounded the all-American boy and had a personality to match: easy-going, ready to laugh heartily at jokes, kindly, helpful and co-operative. His very presence seemed to brighten the gloomy rooms at Stodworth, and after a while his infectious laugh seemed life-enhancing. I was not a young woman then, being over forty, but I had preserved my looks as much as possible and considered myself comely and attractive. I dressed well, as befitted the chatelaine of a large country house who entertained often.

To put matters bluntly, I did not go unnoticed by Wayne, the young American. I guessed his sexual tastes to be somewhat unusual like my husband's, but I knew I had made an impression on him. Gradually, but it seemed fast to me at the time, a rapport, a special understanding developed between us, covert smiles were exchanged and I felt a minor *frisson* every time our paths crossed in the house.

This had not been the case, I hasten to add, with Linton's other young 'helpers', whom I found of no interest; frequently they had been callow youths of no personality, grace or breeding. But Wayne, in spite of his American brashness, seemed to nurse a sensitivity in his soul.

He always addressed me as Lady Ewelme until one morning, as we passed each other on the stairs, he called out in his regular but polite manner 'Good morning, Lady Laura.'

I was shocked at this incorrect use of my title, but secretly pleased, and it must have shown on my face, because after that I was always Lady Laura and I began calling him by his Christian name, Wayne, instead of addressing him formally as Mr Ritmueller. After this, I started to find life exciting, awaking each day wondering what it would bring, thinking of how I could conspire to be near to Wayne, could arrange to be walking in the grounds when he was also there, knowing the places where he would likely be and, carefully and secretly, managing to be not far away. As the weeks passed I began to think this was what being in love was like. Looking back on it, I realise it was not love but infatuation, bringing me little pleasure and eventually much distress.

One thing I could not accept was the unpalatable fact that my husband could be enjoying illicit sexual relations with Wayne, this being something I wished not to think about. What they did – what could they do together? – I wondered, but promised myself to throw the thought away.

I told myself it was ridiculous, that I was a woman of over forty and he was a young man of twenty-three; twenty years lay between us. He was merely a boy – but God, what an attractive one! Linton and I had no children. Linton did not want any; in any case ours was virtually a *mariage blanc*. Perhaps Wayne felt like a son to me, but I soon dismissed that premise because my attraction to him was more than maternal.

Days and weeks passed like this. Linton and Wayne seemed to get on together and were apparently quite close. I had seen this happen before, but knew that after a while Linton would tire of the young man and turn his attentions to a new one. What would happen then if Wayne was obliged to leave Stodworth? I should doubtless never see him again, and this thought haunted me at night, when I would awake with a start and a stab of horror at the idea.

Summer turned into autumn. Wayne could be spied on by me helping to clear the leaves from the lawns, as well as sitting in the library gazing at old letters. One morning in late October, during a most clement period of weather, I passed the french windows of the library while taking a walk around the formal gardens in the vague hope of seeing Wayne's tall and bustling figure. The french windows were open and Wayne called me in. 'Lady Laura, could you spare a minute?'

Trying to stop my heart from beating madly, I entered the library, hoping to look as matter-of-fact as possible. 'Yes, Wayne?' I said brightly.

'It's most kind of you to spare the time,' he replied. 'I understand from Lord Ewelme that you knew Lord Beckley, whose biography we're working on.'

'That's right,' I said, 'but really hardly at all. He used to stay weekends with us from time to time when he wasn't busy with government affairs.'

'That would have been, Lady Laura, about the year 1921?'

'It could have been,' I answered, knowing that this helped him to guess my age. I worried that he would know I was over forty, that my husband had perhaps told him and that he preferred younger women, assuming he preferred women at all. But surely a good-looking man like that could attract most young women if he wanted to? Then I realised my thoughts were running on in the same endless trajectory, leading me nowhere.

'Many people found Lord Beckley a difficult man. Would you say that, Lady Laura?'

'No, I wouldn't. He was always very nice to me.'

'He would be nice to you,' said Wayne, looking straight into my eyes. 'Who couldn't be?'

I hesitated before saying, 'My husband isn't always nice to me. Is he nice to you, Wayne?'

To my surprise and delight, at that moment Wayne took me in his arms and gave me a long embrace. He smelt of eau de cologne and hair oil. The experience was for me ecstatic and extraordinarily sensual. I was shocked at his behaviour, yet at the same time absolutely elated. I was also embarrassed in case someone should see us through the open doors. 'Where is he?' I breathed.

'He's out, gone to the estate office. He took the shooting-brake. There's nothing to worry about.' He released me from his embrace slowly and I walked away from him and out of the library in a daze. So Wayne did desire me as I wanted him. It was frightening, yet terribly exciting, to be on the verge of a secret *affaire de coeur* with a delectable young man who was supposed to be assisting my husband to write a book, but in reality was taken on because of my husband's unusual tastes. I had never seen them together except in the study, and Wayne slept on the other side of the house on a different floor. My husband and I had separate bedrooms, and I supposed it possible for Wayne to enter Linton's bedroom without my knowledge, but if he did so, it was conducted with the utmost discretion and secrecy.

And so there I was in 1931, a titled lady living at Stodworth Hall in Gloucestershire, about to embark on a tumultuous liaison with a man twenty years my junior. It was like being a character in a novel by Colette. Life at Stodworth had been so dull for me really, but now it was exciting beyond words. Romance and danger mixed together were to be the spice of my new life. As for Wayne, I loved him and I hoped he loved me. Maybe we could run away together? Never mind about finances, we could live anywhere: a bed-sitting-room in Bloomsbury, a small cottage in a country village – anywhere, so long as we were together.

That night I could hardly sleep, for I was half expecting that Wayne would come to my room at night to consummate our love, but he did not. Once or twice I heard a noise at the window, which I had carefully left open, but it was nothing. He came not.

The next day I saw him in the hall of Stodworth as I descended the great staircase. He looked up at me and flashed an intimate smile of such promise that I had to clutch at the banister rails to stop me from falling down the stairs in a stupor. I remembered the number of times I had walked down that staircase in splendour, coming down slowly with all eyes upon me, the Lady of Stodworth in my beautiful gowns. Now, clad in a plain but expensive dress, I was hardly able to walk down without the danger of falling because of my husband's 'secretary' and my infatuation with him.

Most of the morning I spent thinking of him, wondering where he was. Twice I walked past the french windows, but they were closed. That evening we were giving a dinner party for twelve and Wayne was to attend. Taking charge of the seating arrangements, I daringly put him next to me.

In the late afternoon of that day, Linton came to my boudoir to see me. 'About the seating arrangements tonight,' he remarked casually. 'Wayne won't be attending. He is leaving us.'

I tried to remain calm and to give nothing away. 'Wayne leaving us?' I queried. 'But why?'

'Well, he's finished the work in hand and wants to move on to something else.'

'But so suddenly! Does he have to leave today?'

'I'm sorry to spoil your seating arrangements, Laura,' he replied, 'but Wayne is leaving today. He's catching the evening train to London.'

With that, he left the room and left me stunned. Wayne was going. I knew Linton would get tired of this one and wish to find another, but so soon! I felt as though my world were imploding. I knew not what to do. My worst nightmare was coming true and there was nothing I could do to stop it. Would he come and say goodbye? It was a stark, hysterical, emotional abyss.

Wayne said goodbye in a manner which was necessary in the circumstances, a formal 'Goodbye, Lady Ewelme. It has been a pleasure to know you.' I sat there trying to behave like the Lady of Stodworth politely bidding farewell to a governess, while underneath my heart was a vortex. How could God be so unkind to me? Wayne gave, I wished to believe, the trace of an intimate smile before he was driven by the chauffeur to Gloucester station for his train to Paddington.

How I managed the dinner party, God only knows. I was living in a dream, forcing myself to smile and make small talk to the guests, supervising the table settings and trying to be the woman I always was. It was hell. That night I took a sleeping draught prescribed for me by a London doctor, which gave me oblivion for the night until the full horror of what had happened dawned again on me in the morning. Surely Wayne would contact me somehow? Where was he now? Would he go back to his family in America? I knew nothing of this man, nothing except that I loved him.

A week passed, but I felt no better. Then after another week, I received a telephone call direct to my boudoir just after breakfast. It was he, still addressing me in his charming way as Lady Laura. I could hardly speak. 'So you wish to see me?' I asked in a low voice. 'How and where shall we meet?'

'Can you come to London, Laura?' he asked, using my plain Christian name for the first time and sending me into paroxysms of joy.

'I'll come anywhere you want me,' I whispered.

It was arranged that we should meet at the Great Western Hotel, the nearest one to Paddington Station, for luncheon at the end of the next week on another Friday the thirteenth, November of that year 1931.

I told Linton I had to go to Mayfair for a fitting. I think I have written enough for anyone reading this to be in no doubt about the intensity of my feelings for Wayne Ritmueller, so that it is not necessary to describe how I felt when he met me off the Gloucester train at Paddington. He was wearing a tweed suit of good quality, but his neck-tie looked homespun; he wore a watch and chain in his waistcoat pocket. He took my arm to lead me to the hotel dining-room where we ordered luncheon and started to talk.

There were many questions I wished to ask, but I was lost in his company, listening to every word he said, the intonations of his American, yet slightly feminine, voice, the oddly literary phraseology he used and the way he looked into my eyes. Although to me not more than a boy, he was very masculine and I felt comfortable and protected in his presence. As the meal progressed he began to tell me about himself, his family in North Carolina and his humble beginnings, his passion for English literature and his attempt to find himself a niche in the world of books.

When it was time for coffee, he asked what I wanted to do after luncheon. I could give only one reply. 'I just want to be with you, Wayne, I just want us to be together.'

He took my hand there and then; I wondered if the other customers would think us mother and son, but I didn't care, I was with him, with my Wayne, and it was heaven on earth.

'Would you like to spend the afternoon in my room here at the Great Western?' he asked suddenly.

I knew it was wrong, I knew it was adulterous, I knew I should say no, but emotionally there was no choice. I agreed.

It was a small room with a double bed and a bathroom attached, overlooking the railway line which would shortly take me back to Stodworth. It was ordinary and everyday, not luxurious or romantic, except for his presence. As soon as we shut the door, Wayne took me in his arms. Matters progressed until we both knew what would happen. Wayne drew the curtains. It was a typical dark mid-November day. I undressed shyly and slipped into the double bed, shivering against the cold white sheets. Wayne dallied in the bathroom. I heard the cistern water running, then he came out wearing a dressing gown, took it off and quickly got in beside me, holding me close for a long time.

I ran my hand down Wayne's soft, warm body towards his symbol of manhood.

But it wasn't. He had, to my horror – and I so hate writing this – a vagina, a woman's vagina! I know, I felt it with my own hand before drawing away in disgust. I shrieked, but Wayne's arms were strong like a man's, and he (or she) would not let me go.

'Don't be upset, darling,' he whispered. 'Yes, you have discovered my secret. I am not a woman, but a man in a woman's body. But tell me you still love me, don't you? I fell for you the moment I saw you, the Lady of Stodworth.'

'But how?' I blundered. Then Wayne began to talk of what he termed Sapphism, telling me I could learn to love a woman as I had once loved a man. All the time I lay there, petrified, unable to escape Wayne's grasp. Finally he released me and I jumped out of bed and began to dress hurriedly, while Wayne watched with reproachful eyes, still asseverating, saying that no one in North Carolina understood him, still trying to persuade me to stay. He got out of bed and stood there naked before me. He (in spite of my discovery I still thought of him as 'he') turned on the bedside light and showed himself so that I could see his small, perfectly formed woman's breasts easily concealed under a jacket and waistcoat, and that aforementioned female pudendum.

'Don't go, Laura,' he implored me, taking hold of my arm. I pushed him away. He began to talk of a book called *The Well of Loneliness*, the subject of a scandal only three years before, then he mentioned the word Lesbianism. 'You ought to try, Laura, many women do. We are much gentler than men, much nicer in every way. Linton is not for you, darling.'

'But Linton,' I began, 'Linton was your – well – '

'Yes,' said Wayne, 'Linton thought he loved me, but I kept my secret away from him as long as I could so as to keep the job and to be near you. But he found out.'

'He found out,' I repeated, gazing at him. 'I presume it was on the day of the dinner party.'

Wayne nodded. 'When he found out, he said I had to leave at once. He is a cruel man. You need someone to love you, Laura.'

'I'm sorry,' I said, 'but I'm going now. I thought you were a man, you see. I have been cruelly deceived. I don't pretend to understand what my husband does with other men, but I have no intention of copying it with other women.'

On my return to Stodworth, a good-looking, rather effeminate young man was introduced to me by Linton. 'This is Nicholas,' he announced. 'He is my new secretary.'

THE SAGA OF ŐGMUND ŐGMUNDSSON

Henrik Harrysson

Őgmund Őgmundsson hated the slush as it soaked through his thick sheepskin boots and into his shins in a way that the snow would never have done. Őgmund Őgmundsson loved the slush because it signalled the great thaw, the thaw that meant that the Parliament, or Alþing, could finally be called. He knew that all across Iceland other groups of men, along with a few women, would be trudging through similar mounds of slush, headed for the great meeting place by the lake.

From his home in the north, the journey took fully six days, as they skirted around the still frozen ice-cap crowning the island's heart, fording streams turned briefly to torrents by the melting waters. At night they huddled around fires, telling stories of their forefathers, and mothers, of feats going back to the days of the old gods. Father Snurisson, who was part of the group, might sneer disapproving, but he knew that the spirits of the pagans, whilst surely no match for the Son of Man, would make short work of the old priest himself. Later they would retire to their sheepskin tents, tents said to be so snug that men had been known to be buried under a ton of snow before they noticed the cold.

And then the next day, more miles, over lava fields or through forests of stunted pines. There were no towns to speak of then, so they would pause at the occasional turf-roofed cottage for some goat's milk and some smoked fish, and exchange news with the local farmer and his wife. This year's Alþing was set to be the biggest gathering for many moons.

Őgmund had attended several times before, in support of his father Őgmund Hákonarson. But now the older Őgmund was ailing. The legs which would once have walked the length of Iceland in a week would now scarcely carry him down to the shore, yards from his home. Luckily young Őgmund had strength more than enough for several men. Taller than three sheep, his shoulders could, they said, support a pregnant cow while he could just as easily wave a two-handed axe over his head with one hand. Were this not enough to instil fear, his long, thick, almost black hair and bushy beard, his black eyebrows arched over grey eyes set deep in his skull, all might have frightened warriors and daemons alike.

As the oldest of five sons and three daughters his claim to lead was one that none but the bravest could contest. And yet he was also known as a gentle man, almost a soft man. The same arms that could carry a cow would bring in a lamb which had been found wandering on the lava fields, far from its mother or any source of food, back to the byre where he would feed it himself. His father hoped that, by the time he was ready to lead, young Őgmund would have filled out to be the father figure, firm but wise, that he saw himself to be. He also saw that his son, now in his majority, wanted above all for a wife, and that this could be the making of him. Since he had shown scant interest in the girls in the village the father hoped that the Alþing would offer opportunities, perhaps for a better alliance. For chiefs often brought their daughters as well as their sons; and many fine marriages, along with much business, were contracted into over the fortnight or so.

Such thoughts were far from young Őgmund's mind as he reached the crest of the last hill and finally saw the waters of the lake spread out in the valley below: Alþingvallvatn, beside whose waters they would spend the next two weeks, was a place of mystery. It was said, like the valley, to grow wider each year. It was further said that, whilst so shallow that one could see the bottom through the clear icy waters at any point, those same waters, fed by a hundred glaciers, would freeze any man foolish enough to swim across it, and turn his blood blue.

Down among the gathering on the flat, boggy, valley floor, Őgmund and his men pitched their tent as soon as they found a convenient dry space. It seemed that most of the clans were already assembled, for few had faced as hard and long a journey as he had. That night they ate and drank hard, catching sight of familiar faces. Őgmund studied the faces carefully, looking for signs from those he remembered, and speculating on those who were strangers. This time, the speculation was heightened, this being the first Alþing since the house of Őgmund had sworn reconciliation with that of Arnórson, ending a feud of seven generations. Őgmund's own mother had sworn bitterly that she would sooner not have lived to see a day when her own son should hold counsel with such men.

In the morning, his head throbbing, he decided to take some fresh air down by the lake. 'Cold air and cold water for a thick head!' as his father always said. He even thought for a moment of swimming, for he was a fair enough swimmer. He dipped a foot into the water, enough to make him almost cry out with pain. Any thoughts of immersing himself further left his head. Then, to his astonishment he realised that the object he had spotted well out in the lake was not a bird, but the head of a man. Soon it was making its way towards him, sending out ripples across the stillness of the lake.

Őgmund stood his ground. Finally the head began to rise from the waters, and smiled at him. It was blond, the skin pale, the eyes sky-blue. Őgmund averted his eyes from what followed. He would rather die than be seen naked himself, even though, for obvious reasons, most people swam unencumbered by clothes. The face smiled, and said 'Góđan dag.' Őgmund need not have worried unduly, for soon enough the man was safely clothed. A decent enough height and pretty well built, though not, Őgmund was sure, someone who could take him on and live to tell the tale.

'They say only a madman would swim in this water. And a dead one at that.'

'Well, as you can see, I'm neither.'

His clothing was plainer than Őgmund's, suggesting that he was part of a supporting party, rather than a leader.

'Who are you with?' asked Őgmund.

'I am Skúli, son of Gissur,' replied the man, almost deliberately not answering the question; then, after a long pause, 'but I am with Smidur Arnórson.'

Őgmund winced involuntarily at the name. So this was the face of the enemy. Still, he admired the young man's cheek. He would like a servant like him; certainly more so than the dutiful but oh-so-dull Ari, who had served his father since before he himself was born, and was now attending him in turn at his first Alþing as leader of his people.

The Parliament didn't take long to get into its stride. There were the usual arguments about land, a chieftain demanding a divorce from his wife of seven years whom he claimed to be both barren and bewitched. But there were also the chieftains of the church, seeking to extend the writ of the Lord, and banish the last remnants of the old gods.

Őgmund was rather on the fence on this one. He smiled at the gods of his ancestors, as though they were rascally uncles, but he did not much like what he heard of the church and he certainly did not much care for Father Snurisson. He was sure that the Father was there to keep a weather eye on him.

In the evenings there were entertainments. Shows of strength were naturally to the fore, and Őgmund was keen to show his mettle. The first two men to take him on were soon dispatched, to the jeers of the crowd. But then he was surprised to see the gauntlet thrown down by a man whose hair and eyes he recognised as those of Skúli.

'You can't swim away this time, young man!' warned Őgmund.

'Neither can you, old man.'

As he expected, it took little for Őgmund to pin him to the ground. But then, in his very submission, Skúli simply stuck his tongue out.

The next round brought Őgmund down to earth with a terrible thud. Used to brute force, he had not expected Skúli's deft footwork. As he felt his shoulder crack on the ground, he dreaded, for a moment, the thought of a broken bone, something that could turn the proudest of men into a bent and helpless cripple, old before his time. He noticed the look of concern on Skúli's face. 'Shall we stop now, Őgmund Őgmundsson?'

'Not on your life. I'd as soon surrender to a goat!'

The third, decisive round was more closely matched. The two men rolled around, egged on by the crowd. Őgmund knew that to lose to a smaller or for that matter a lower-born man would not go down well at home. Finally he had Skúli firmly pinned down, his weight immobilising his adversary. All the same he felt strangely comfortable there, and hesitated to get up. And when he looked at Skúli's face, inches from his own, he saw that he was smiling, broadly; hardly the action of a beaten man.

Őgmund finally, almost reluctantly, pulled himself up above his prone opponent and raised his arm in victory, to the roar of the crowd. Honour and order were upheld. As a gesture of magnanimity, Őgmund invited Skúli to join him and his men over a roasting carcass of a sheep. By the time that Skúli staggered away to rejoin his camp, Őgmund felt very important, very drunk, but above all very happy. In the morning his head was surprisingly clear; fortunately, for he now had an important errand to perform. Before the Alþing assembled for its final meeting, Őgmund made his way over to Smidur Arnórson's encampment. He was both disappointed and relieved not to see Skúli.

Having sought out Smidur Arnórson he got quickly to the point.

'I am Őgmund, son of Őgmund. Last night I was impressed by the bravery of one of your men, who dared to take me on in unarmed combat. You would have thought him hardly in my league, but he gave me some exercise. I could use someone like that, as I will soon assume control of my father's lands. I should like to take him on. I shall, of course, offer you full compensation, and more.'

Arnórson was clearly intrigued, for he had heard much of Őgmund Hákonarson, and was impressed by his son.

'Well, I am honoured, Őgmundsson, though I cannot think who you can be talking about.'

'You are lucky enough to have in your ranks one Skúli Gissurson.'

Arnórson almost laughed. 'Why, that young wastrel! He came back last night roaring drunk and is still in his tent when he should be roasting my mutton and heating my goatsmilk. As far as I am concerned you can have him!' He was going to add 'for nothing!' but then hesitated. 'On one condition: that you also take my daughter Kristín's hand in marriage.' To Arnórson it seemed like an eminently sensible match. 'Unlucky' as he might be in having five daughters to one son, Kristín was the second eldest, the tallest, most practical, and by most men's reckoning, the prettiest of the five.

Őgmund for his part felt a blind panic, which could scarcely have been greater had he faced five men each armed with axes, and with only a cow's leg to defend himself. His panic lessened when Kristín herself appeared and greeted him with a frank, open smile.

'Why Őgmund Őgmundsson,' she said, 'I've seen you fight, and I feel that you are one of the few men who could take me on and hope to win the day.'

Her father's scowl turned to a smile when he saw the smile on Őgmund's face. He little knew that the smile was of relief, of a man sentenced to death, but then told that he would only be banished.

Őgmund supposed that he would have to marry one day. It went with the territory, all hundred and fifty square miles of it. He found it hard to say why he had always resisted the idea. It just seemed to him like a distraction; a duty that men and women forced upon themselves to keep things going. Still, Kristín was a young woman who seemed to know her own mind, and whom he was sure his father and uncles would like, and she was certainly one whom he could call beautiful, whose slender dark figure would look well beside his tall stocky one, and whose eyes suggested an intelligence that had never been much apparent in any of the village girls (or boys for that matter).

He hesitated. 'I am sure we can come to an arrangement; if the young lady herself is willing.'

'How could I dare disobey my own dear father's wishes?' she said, before winking at Őgmund.

With a kiss on the hand it was sealed.

The other part of the business was soon enough accomplished. Skúli was dragged from his tent and pulled by the hand, like a child, between the tents, exciting barely a glance. Őgmund noticed how much warmer, more substantial was the hand he held, roughly, than the one that he, but minutes before, had kissed. It had not the same beauty, the same refinement, but it had a wholeness about it. Only then did Őgmund find the thought odd. And promptly switched his mind to the orders of the day.

It pleased Őgmund to see Skúli helplessly holding his head, as he staggered from side to side.

'So where's your fearlessness this morning, young man, eh?'

Skúli himself, though physically in pain, seemed unsurprised, as though being narrowly beaten in combat by a chieftain's son who then gets you drunk and buys you off your master in return for his daughter's hand in marriage were something that happened to him every day.

Two days later they set off back on the long trek to the north, Őgmund's party the larger by one man and four head of cattle, acquired by slightly more conventional barter.

He spent much time quizzing his new servant. Skúli's impudence hardly seemed diminished by his new status. He was happy to offer up opinions on everything and everyone.

'I wouldn't take that track at this time of year if I were you,' said by someone who had never even seen the region before to someone who had passed that way many times before. Or 'If you don't mind my saying, those cattle are of decidedly poor stock. They won't last three winters in the North.' In fact they only lasted two.

Master and servant (naturally) shared a tent together. If anyone thought that they might be sharing more, then the others in their party either did not care, or thought better than to mention it. Only Father Snurisson asked Őgmund, 'with the greatest respect, Sir,' whether he might be storing up problems for the future by allowing a servant 'and a young one at that' to treat him so familiarly. 'The world needs order; under God, of course.'

Őgmund had slapped Snurisson on the back so heartily that the cleric had almost fallen into the ditch. 'My dear Father Snurisson! Our Lord was but a humble carpenter. Besides, you are strictly my servant, and I allow you to take the most terrible liberties.' Snurrisson had merely frowned.

When they finally reached the village, the older Ögmund noticed at once how much more grown up, how much happier, how altogether full of himself the young Ögmund now seemed. At first he assumed that this was the Alþing talking. He had long sensed that his son needed to show responsibility. But then he learned of the offer of marriage. While he hardly relished an alliance with Smidur Arnórson, he could see how happy all this appeared to have made his son.

His own marriage had been founded on love, and he liked to think that, provided certain conditions were met, each of his sons could enjoy the same freedom. He was less impressed by the new servant who seemed somehow to have become part of the bargain, but could see that he was perhaps more of the nature of a friend. Young Ögmund had always been rather solitary. That he should find companionship with a server might seem odd, but the old man had always treated his own servants well. He also saw that, by coming to this harsh but beautiful land, his ancestors had accepted that everyone had to muck in and abandon their airs and graces.

And so there was peace in the land, and Ögmund and everyone in the village lived happily, for several seasons. There was talk periodically of the marriage, but Ögmund always put it off, keeping to himself and Skúli.

The whole village was in a state of excitement that few, even the elders, could remember. For weeks now, no-one had talked of much else. The men had prepared three oxen and twelve sheep for slaughter. And even the two prized shark carcasses had been dug up from the beach where they had spent the winter 'maturing', the acid produced by their decomposition breaking down the meat to the point where it was truly succulent. Old Varick Björnsson had declared it to be the best hákarl that he had tasted in forty years, though he had drunk a flagon of brennivin to wash it down.

Meanwhile the women had woven new leggings and cloaks for their husbands, and repaired their dresses, or prepared new ones for themselves. Old Őgmund Hákonarson's long-house had been cleared, and then decked out. And now, the men, women and children waited impatiently for what the following days would bring; all, that is, except for young Őgmund and his servant Skúli Gissurson.

Their only solace was that this was not the wedding itself. That would entail a week's journey into the depths of the South East, to the lands of Kristín's father Smidur Arnórson, when the festivities would if anything be longer and more spectacular. No, this was to be an initial, formal meeting of the two families and their immediate clans, when old Arnórson could confirm the honour that was being done to his line by this alliance with that of old Őgmund Hákonarson. They had been invited for the feast of the Summer Solstice, which the church had taken to calling that of St John. However, given the state of the roads, even in high summer, they could be expected a day or two on either side.

Őgmund Őgmundsson saw no way, in honour or practicality, of avoiding the wedding. He needed to wed. His position, his future depended on it. All, from his father down, expected it. He owed it to Kristín Smidursdottir, whose letters to him, written in a fine hand, had shown a kind concern that could all so easily develop into love. (Had she detected a civil coolness in his own replies, he wondered.) Above all, he had given his word, something as close to the sacred for him as anything could be.

And then, as if to put an end to his wandering worryings, they had arrived, two days early as it transpired. Őgmund strode out to greet Smidur Arnórson, who seemed noticeably thinner and paler, but assured the younger man that they had made excellent progress, over dried roads now largely cleared of melt-water floods. Kristín, who followed close behind, smiled nervously. A younger man, little more than a boy, acknowledged him gruffly. He resembled Kristín in his face if little else; her brother, Őgmund assumed.

The opening banquet and revelries seemed to go well, but young Őgmund, seated at the high table next to Smidur Arnórson, experienced it as more of a last supper. By the time the guests had retired to their houses and tents it was past two in the morning, and the sun had already risen in the northern sky. He saw but one faint hope, and resolved to take it. When he sought out Kristín she was, as the day before, friendly but a little on edge, as though she half anticipated what he was about to say. 'Kristín Smidursdottir, you are truly the most beautiful woman in Iceland.'

'Improbable. And besides that, not very original, Őgmund Őgmundsson!'

He went on to try to explain, in awkward words, why he believed he could not, in all conscience, marry her.

'You are a woman as wonderful, and deserving of love, as any that I have met. I admire you more than any other, and I had thought that nothing would make me happier than to be your husband.'

'Őgmund, if you no longer wish to marry me, please sir, do me the courtesy of telling me why in words that a sensible woman can grasp.'

'You deserve wholehearted love. I can honour you, even love you, to a point, but' (he paused and tried to look her in the eye, but could not) 'I have given my heart to another.'

'Is it a woman in the village?'

'No!' He almost spat it out.

She saw his eyes dart away to a distant blond-haired figure that she also recognised from her past.

'Is it' – and this time she paused long, before uttering the name – 'Is it Skúli?'

He felt as though shot through with a spear, but also a sense of a terrible wound being lanced and opened. He simply nodded.

She remained silent for a while. She had of course known Skúli for some years, but had been taken aback to see how, even at the banquet, Ögmund had seemed to have eyes only for him.

At last, shakily and coldly, she replied.

'In one sense, I cannot reproach you. I swear I thought I was myself in love with him once. But now this?'

'I release you from any obligations, of course,' he stuttered.

'You release me! It was you who promised! If I am now rejected, what will become of me? Our wedding was to have been the proudest day of my father's life. And now I am to be cast aside, like a cow with an unexpected limp. What man will look at me now?'

'You could tell your father that you do not love me. I will tell him that I release you both.'

She laughed.

'I hardly see how that will help me. And as for you? How will your father take it, that his great son has wasted his time, and made a complete fool of him, and all for the sake of a servant boy?'

'Skúli is hardly a boy!' he said, defensively but irrelevantly.

There was only one other possible way out that he could see, and it promptly appeared, in the form of Ögmund's younger brother, Sigurður.

Whilst sharing his elder brother's thick black hair and grey eyes, Sigurður seemed to differ from him in every other respect. Slight rather than sturdy, charming and gregarious rather than solitary, famed far and wide for his beautiful singing voice, he was as skilled at dancing as he was hopeless in a fight. He had won the heart of many a local girl, and broken just as many. Their father had often thanked fate that he had at least in Őgmund a real man for a son, and wished that Sigurður might learn to follow his example. His one comfort had been that the younger son would never inherit.

And yet, Őgmund had also followed Kristín's wayward eyes at the banquet. He had seen her watch Sigurður's dancing with rapt gaze, and her all-too-ready acceptance of her betrothed's suggestion that she take to the floor with her future brother-in-law. He had noticed their graceful ease. And as to Sigurður, his elder brother knew that, whilst Kristín might be wasted on him, he would only too eagerly jump at the chance to take her.

And thus was a further bargain arranged, so much more unusual than the first: Sigurður and Kristín would declare their love one for another, and Őgmund would generously waive his right. And yet, there would have to be more. No first-born son could tamely surrender his wife to his brother and hope to remain in line for the helm. The loss of face, both to him, and more importantly to the clan, would be too great. He would have, in effect, to surrender his inheritance, and with it, much of his claim to be a man.

The moment that held him most in dread was that of approaching his father.

'You say that you cannot give her your love, but that your brother can. You will bring ridicule on yourself. And all for what? All this smells of bad fish. Is there another? Perhaps someone too low?'

'Father, there is no woman in all Iceland whom I love or honour more. I just cannot. I need time, time to withdraw from the world.'

It was finally agreed that young Őgmund would indeed withdraw down to the old boat-house by the shore, and gather fish for the village.

'All I ask is that I be allowed to retain a servant, to help me.'

His father's answer was as a deliberate provocation.

'Very well, I shall give you Ari.'

His son's face turned almost red.

'I shall either have Skúli as my server here, or I shall take him to serve me elsewhere.'

'There is something not right here. But try as I might, I cannot cast you out. You shall have your wish. But I thank the gods that your mother is not here to see this sorry tale.'

And thus it was that, the following summer, the old Őgmund made the last long journey of his life down to the south east, to see Sigurður and Kristín joined in marriage. There was much talk in the village, but few guessed the truth that lay behind it.

Őgmund and Skúli settled down in the old boat house, and soon were half-forgotten. Skúli's family had formerly been sea folk, before his father had been shipwrecked and killed, and he was quick and eager to show Őgmund the ropes. They would often be at sea for days, but seldom needed to venture far, so rich were the seas around Iceland in those days. And it was said that the finest fish to be had in all of the North were those from the nets of Őgmund Őgmundsson and Skúli Gissurson.

THE JEWISH BAG LADY AND THE MUSLIM SECURITY GUARD

Rochelle Baker

He'd seen her for months now, a scarf on her head, gold hoops through her pierced ears, about seventy years old he figured, small and thin, floppy Birkenstocks on her tiny feet. Once, maybe twice, a week just before closing time she'd sidle in, kind of waft like a ghost, shopping bag in hand, up and down the aisles – an organic tomato, an organic red onion – into the bag.

Small time – he let it pass; he was tired and bored out of his mind. Another half-hour and he could change into civvies, get a pint and an Indian takeaway, go back to his cosy flat and the TV. He didn't want any trouble but tonight she went up-market – smoked salmon, five pounds forty-nine for one hundred and fifty grammes; the red onion and tomato of course; Welsh goat cheese one pound ninety-nine for a tiny circle of it and wholemeal rye, organic, no yeast, three twenty-nine. She started out of the door.

'Shit,' he thought, 'didn't anyone see what she was doing?' Guess they all left it to him, they were all too busy talking and laughing and flirting and taking the money in. He followed her to the door. Just as she stepped outside he put his hand on her bony shoulder. She jumped sky-high and spun around.

'Excuse me,' he said. 'Have you taken anything you haven't paid for?'

'Why?' she said.

'Can I look in your bag?'

'No,' she said.

'No?' he replied, wondering what to do next. She looked so fragile. 'Look, I've watched you for months. A tomato here, an onion, once in a while a cucumber. But tonight, I mean, organic smoked salmon? Come on!'

'It's for my birthday,' she said.

'What?'

'Tomorrow I'm eighty.'

'Eighty,' he said, surprised. She looked good. Well, for someone who was eighty. Must be all this organic food.

'Yeah,' she said. 'I'm inviting the landlady for brunch.'

He didn't know the word but figured it must be some sort of special meal.

'But look,' he tried again more gently. 'You can't go around just taking things, stealing.' He didn't like to say the word – it seemed somehow inappropriate and he didn't want to hurt her feelings. She leaped on it.

'Stealing?' She raised her arm.

He saw the numbers. All the digits clearly defined. He looked away.

'Who's stealing, me or them?' and she waved towards the shop. 'You know how much these bastards make? Who owns these organic shops? Big American corporations. How much they mark this stuff up – and how little the farmers make?'

'OK, OK,' he stopped her tirade. Surprised, he hadn't expected an ancient shoplifting crone to be so articulate.

'OK, I'll let you go this time, but don't do it again!'

This sounded silly even to him. She didn't even say 'Why not?' but he could see it in her eyes.

Suddenly he said 'Do you drink wine?'

She looked suspicious.

'I mean on your birthday, for the brunch with the landlady and the smoked salmon.'

'Yeah,' she said, 'but only organic and white. The women in the vineyards in Chile are giving birth to deformed children from all the pesticides...'

'OK, OK.' He went back into the shop.

'Make sure it's dry!' she called after him. He looked around: no-one was watching. He grabbed a bottle of French Chablis. Ten pounds ninety-nine, what the hell! He took it outside and put it into her shopping bag. She didn't thank him – turned and walked away.

'Happy birthday,' he called to her – no response.

He didn't see her for two weeks. Did she have other places she acquired things at? He couldn't call it shopping. Then one night she came in – ten minutes before closing time – yes, the tomato, red onion, oh, and organic hummus, two pounds forty-nine, and falafel. Then as a sort of afterthought she came back from the door – organic wholemeal pitta bread and olives, black, organic, a small tub – all of it into the shopping bag, which said, he hadn't noticed before, 'The Organic Trade Show Olympia' on it; nice touch. Did she actually go to that? OK, he let it slide. Middle Eastern night. What's the occasion this time? Maybe the landlady's birthday. He followed her to the door.

'Hello,' he smiled.

She grimaced, annoyed by this obstacle – by having to stop.

'Listen,' he said. 'Can we meet for coffee? Tomorrow maybe? I get an hour for lunch, one to two.'

'I should come in then,' she thought, but what she said was 'Why?'

'I don't know, I want to know you better, find out who you are.' He glanced at her arm. She pulled her sleeve down, covering the numbers.

'What's to know? I survived. My mother and father murdered – my brothers worked and starved to death – everyone gone. Me, they used; every day maybe twenty men, sometimes a woman, everything they wanted – my cunt, my ass, my mouth – lick the shit from their filthy asses. What do you want to know? Does it turn you on thinking about what they did to me?'

'No,' he said. 'No, please.'

'OK.' She relented. He looked so young.

'You can buy me a coffee, but only organic and Fair Trade. No Starbucks. Decaffeinated,' she added. 'I have enough trouble trying to sleep – but only by the natural water method, no chemicals.'

'Great,' he said. 'Tomorrow, one o'clock, across the street, Caffe Nero.'

She nodded and turned away. He watched her disappear into the dusk and went back into the shop.

The next day he found himself looking forward to their meeting. He was early. He waited and waited – she didn't show. He'd brought a jar of organic Italian sun-dried tomatoes in virgin olive oil, a treat. He'd thought she couldn't have had them very often. At least he'd never seen her take any! Eventually he got a coffee and a toasted cheese panini and ate and drank absent-mindedly. Then he went back to the store, disappointed. He put the jar back on the shelf.

Two weeks later she came in, ten minutes before closing. She didn't take anything. She came up to him and reached into her bag and took out a book.

'Where are you from?' she asked.

'Iran,' he said.

'You got a mother?'

'Yeah,' he said, 'and a grandmother.' You remind me of her, he almost said, but decided not to. 'They're in Iran,' he said, sadly.

'Here, this is for you. It's by Cynthia Ozick.' *Rosa*, it was called. It looked as if it had been read many times. 'Maybe you could read it?'

He took it and started to thank her, but she waved her arm. He told her he was leaving – he'd given them notice. He couldn't take it any more – the long, empty hours, watching the yuppies consume all day, the ridiculous uniform, not to mention his aching feet. He was going back to school to study journalism. He wanted to write.

'Good!' she said. 'What's your name?'

'Ahmed,' he said.

'I'm Roseanna.' She started down the vegetable display. She put a tomato and a red onion into her bag. Then, just as she was cradling an avocado in her hand, she turned to him and smiled shyly, like a little girl, as she dropped it into her bag.

He smiled back and watched her stroll, graceful and with great dignity, out of the door.

PATRON PROTÉGÉ

Jeffrey Doorn

Alan sat at his desk unable to concentrate on his work. Normally, preparing a brief on the effects of the latest piece of EU legislation was not that difficult a task. Today, though, the words before him merged and reformed into words he had said, or not said, to Brian and responses made, or not made, by Brian. Brian, Brian on the brain; how did Alan get into such a state?

He hadn't been so besotted with anyone since he was a teenager. A blurred vision of Hal began to form; Alan hadn't thought of him in years. They had met in King's Cross Station one crisp autumn day.

'Wotcha, mate?' the tall blond had greeted him. 'Just off the train, are ya?'

'Not exactly.'

'No? Well, you don't want to go hanging round railway stations, mate. Pretty piece like you. Asking for trouble, that is. Course, trouble may be what you're after.' Alan shook his head. 'Run away from home, have ya? I know. You probably think: come 'ere, stand 'round looking innocent, nice gentleman gives you a meal, bed for the night, maybe a bit of cash in the morning if you let him have his way, then off again.'

In fact, that had been, more or less, what had happened to Alan his first night in London, and once more since then. But money runs out, and sleeping rough is uncomfortable, so he'd come back.

'See that old geezer over there? He's got his eye on you. But don't go wiv 'im, he's a pimp. Get in his clutches, you'll be bought and sold ten times a night. He gets the dosh, and a freebie wiv you now and then as a bonus.'

Alan shuddered. 'What are you doing here, then?' he ventured to ask.

'Whadja think? I'm rent, me. Been at it three years, since I was eighteen. How old are you?'

'Sixteen.'

'Crikey!' Hal had taken Alan under his wing, the first and youngest of the wings under whose protection Alan had grown. For four months Alan lived with Hal, sleeping on a settee, sometimes lying awake listening to the sounds Hal and his clients made on the other side of a thin wall. Some clients offered more money if the lad would join them for a threesome. These offers were always refused, unless Alan signalled he wouldn't mind. Very often, though, the tiny flat was silent, as Hal entertained men in hotels or elsewhere.

That period, tied as it was with Alan's exploration and discovery of London's attractions, was a time of intense emotional and sexual longing. He was head over heels in love with Hal, as only a sixteen-year-old can be; but despite his efforts, he couldn't persuade Hal to sleep with him.

'I don't shag mates.'

Once he'd started working, Alan moved to a bedsit; and as he made friends, he and Hal drifted apart. His good looks won him admirers; and he had some casual affairs with other young men. But it was the older men who took a fancy to him who helped change his life. One even arranged for him to take classes to qualify for a diploma course, for which the patron paid. Sadly, his benefactor died soon after, leaving Alan bereft.

The diploma was a factor in his securing a job in a large and expanding firm of consultants. He did well, and after a year or so was promoted to a junior administrative post at head office. While researching in the firm's library one afternoon, he met a man thirty years his senior, who introduced himself as Douglas Courtney. He seemed affable and unassuming. When Alan later checked in the staff handbook, he found Mr Courtney was Director, Technical Services, so fairly senior in the hierarchy.

The next morning, an internal envelope arrived containing a note.

Very much enjoyed our little chat. You struck me as someone I'd like to get to know. Perhaps you'd care to meet for dinner one evening. There's a good French restaurant I sometimes visit. I'm sure you'd like it, and I'd be glad of the company. Ring my extension when you have a moment. Douglas.

They met at five o'clock in Courtney's office; and after a long, friendly talk, in which it was established that they were both gay and unattached, they set out. The pink-decorated restaurant was quiet, the service pleasant, the food and wine excellent.

'I do like having younger friends,' Douglas said at one point; 'they help me stay fresh and keep me feeling young. But what makes a chap like you go out with a man of 54?'

'I've never chosen my friends based on age or anything like that. If I like someone, those surface things don't matter. It's character and personality that count. Besides, you always learn something from people of different ages and experience.'

'True, but a lot of young people don't see it like that.'

'Well, it's their loss.'

Soon, Alan and Douglas were meeting regularly for coffee, a stroll during lunch breaks, a concert or film in the evening or a weekend drive for lunch at a country inn and a visit to a stately home or other attraction. The only awkward moment came during their first overnight stay together. After a day's sightseeing and al fresco dinner on a starry, moonlight evening, Douglas confessed he was in love with Alan. It was clear how he hoped the evening would end.

'I don't know what to say,' Alan stammered. 'I'm flattered; and I'll cherish your love. But while I'm very fond of you, I just think sex might spoil our friendship.' The discussion continued into the bedroom and long into the night. In the end, they slept cuddled together; and for the next eighteen years they remained affectionate friends and confidants, but never lovers.

Over those years, Alan shared with Douglas the ups and downs of his relationships, initially exciting but ultimately less than satisfying affairs with men of around his age. Douglas, for his part, acquired a handful of young companions, at least half of whom took advantage of his generosity, milking him for treats and presents without giving anything back. One in particular, a persistent liar with a volatile temper, continually tapped Douglas for money, using one sob story after another as pretexts. Despite Alan's admonitions and warnings not to believe the lies or to give in to the bullying which invariably followed a refusal, it took a long time for Douglas to see through it all.

Quite often Alan felt helpless as Douglas, who had by now retired, lived way out in the suburbs, where it wasn't easy to keep a watchful eye on him or protect him from spongers. Then too, with Douglas either devoting his time to these scamps, or licking his wounds when they'd cleaned him out, he had less time to see Alan. Their former pattern of outings was reduced to lunch every six weeks or so. Perhaps it would be selfish to want more; perhaps it was petty to resent the attentions shifted to younger men when he himself was approaching middle age; but he did feel the bonds of friendship and loyalty should count for something. Besides, he was fonder than ever of Douglas and now felt that, should he be invited for a weekend or longer break, he would be quite happy to sleep with him.

In an attempt to ease his mid-life crisis, if that was what

it was, and stave off stultification, Alan enrolled in evening classes to rekindle his creative side. He had always been interested in photography and film, and found he enjoyed developing his skills with camera, video and DVD recorder. After a couple of years, he became proficient and took a lead in organising film projects.

As a new spring term began, two things happened which threw his settled life into turmoil. First, among the newcomers arriving to get involved in making a DVD was a gorgeous young man named Brian. Then, when Alan phoned Douglas, intending to tell him how things were going and to describe the new arrival who had set his heart aflutter, a strange voice answered. Douglas was, the voice informed him, in hospital and he (the voice) was a relative looking after the house for the time being.

That weekend, Alan went to visit Douglas. Seeing his friend lying in a hospital bed looking pale and gaunt, it seemed to Alan that age had finally caught up with him. Remembering their conversation on their first evening, a notion occurred to Alan that he had somehow failed Douglas. It had been his job to keep his friend young and fresh; but he'd blinked and Douglas had grown old.

'Oh, Alan, it's good to see you. How did you get here?'

'Train and taxi. Not a bad journey. It's nice out here in the country.'

'Yes, I have a good view from that window. How are you?'

'Oh, you know. How are *you*, that's the question?'

'I think I'm alive. At least, I didn't see my obituary in *The Times* this morning.'

'When are they letting you out? I want to make a date to take you dancing.'

'As long as it's not one of those discos of yours.'

'Don't worry. Actually, between you and me, I don't go to clubs any more, or very rarely.'

'No, I suppose not. How old are you now, anyway?'

'Come on Douglas, it's easy to remember. You're 72, so I'm 42.'

'Of course. You know, I still can't believe I'm 72. Suppose I'll be passing the torch before long. I had hoped to live another dozen years. Then you'll be the age I was when we met.'

'Oh, you'll make it, don't worry.'

'I'm not so sure. But we'll see, we'll see.'

The financial year end and pre-Easter rush at the office, plus work on the film project, provided some distraction for Alan, which was intensified by his growing infatuation with Brian. Whether the young man was aware of his feelings wasn't clear; in fact, Alan didn't know whether Brian was gay or straight, until one coffee break chat about what they'd done over the weekend, when Brian mentioned the name of a club.

'Oh, I used to go there.'

'Why did you stop?'

'Just got out of the habit. And it seemed to be taken over by twinks.'

Brian laughed. 'I'm no twink, I'm 22. What are you, about 38?'

'Something like that.'

'Alan, I've been thinking. With the break coming up we're going to lose ground, and I'm worried I won't be able to catch up. Would you mind if we met over the holiday weekend? I could really use your help.'

'Certainly. Glad to. Where?'

'Could I come to your place?'

Alan awaited Brian's arrival as nervously as an adolescent on a first date. Several scenarios ran through his head, all involving increasing intimacy leading to bed. He had to keep reminding himself the young man was visiting only for technical advice and guidance. Then he imagined another scenario, where he became Brian's mentor and patron, as Alan's diploma course sponsor, and later Douglas, had been.

Brian breezed into Alan's flat like a rush of fresh air. His keenness and energy fired Alan's mind, while his physical proximity fired lust. It was all Alan could do to keep his hands to himself. Over tea, Brian spoke of his plans, hopes and dreams.

'I want to get into television, work on a few documentaries until I get a chance to produce my own. I have lots of ideas, not only for television, but feature films as well. I think it's important to build up my skills, as a cameraman, lighting, sound, editing – really, every aspect so I can ultimately be a director.'

'That sounds very sensible, Brian. You not only have ambition, but practical notions of how to achieve it. I'm sure you'll succeed: you've got talent, youth, charm and determination.'

'Oh, I'm determined all right.'

Brian's departure was like the shutting of a window, leaving Alan gasping in the stifling atmosphere of frustrated longing. Over the following few weeks the film project developed; but not till its conclusion did Alan catch another moment alone with Brian. They returned the equipment and props to the storage cupboard, and Brian wiped his dusty hands on his jeans.

'Well, that's the last of it. It's been good working with you, Alan; thanks for everything.'

Alan felt they'd reached a now or never moment.

'Would you kiss me good-bye?'

'Sure.' They embraced. The kiss was swift, but Alan held on; and when at length they broke apart, he spilled out his feelings.

'I didn't want to say anything earlier, but now it's over I have to confess I've grown rather fond of you, in fact maybe too fond...'

'Whoa, don't start getting intense.'

‘No, but, well, if we could see each other from time to time...’

‘I don’t think so. Don’t get me wrong, I value your friendship and I’m grateful for the way you helped me on this course; but it can’t be any more than that.’

‘Why not? I can still help you, in other ways perhaps, and we can at least socialise.’

‘But I don’t want any more help. I have to be independent, make my own way. And as for socialising, I already have a circle of friends, friends my own age.’

‘Oh, I didn’t know that would matter so much. I’ve always had friends of all ages. One is thirty years older, and he says going around with younger guys keeps him young. I think we still have a lot to offer each other, Brian.’

‘No, Alan, it wouldn’t work. Can we go now?’

With the coming of summer, Alan tried to distract himself from his constant replaying of his last conversation with Brian and a dozen imaginary variants on it. He made three or four visits to Douglas, now recuperating at home, but still not fully recovered. Alan dreaded losing his dear friend and regretted not having had sex with him in the past. He wondered whether he could have done more to give Douglas pleasure and show how much their relationship meant to him.

Work was intensifying at the office, with seminars, conferences and international committee meetings to attend or service. Elaine, Alan’s assistant, was generally helpful, though somewhat distracted at times, absorbed as she was with her marriage and four-year-old child. For a week the office had been unusually quiet, as their young colleague, Fran, was in Strasbourg interpreting for the British team. Not that Fran was noisy, quite the contrary; but Elaine tended to use her as a sounding board, and Alan felt she was just waiting for Fran to return to offload her pent-up gossip. She also loved dealing out motherly advice; though at 22, Fran was only three years her junior.

Alan put his unfinished report to one side. 'I'm off to lunch, Elaine; do you mind holding the fort?'

' 'S all right, I'll wait for Frannie; she's due in soon.'

All through lunch break, Alan toyed with the idea of contacting Brian. If he could just explain his vision of playing Douglas to Brian's Alan, taking up the torch his older friend was about to pass on, and becoming even an occasional adviser, confidant and potential sponsor. He had to stop brooding, but felt he could not while there was so much left unsaid.

That afternoon, Fran and Elaine were in full flow. 'I don't know what to do. I love this job, and it's great to have the chance to travel and everything; but I just can't face another meeting with that horrible Grogan.'

'What did he do, Frannie?'

'At first it was just staring; every time I looked up I'd notice him leering at me. It made me really self-conscious. Then he made a point of sitting next to me at lunch, and again at dinner. I don't know, he kept dropping little remarks and innuendoes. And sometimes he'd press his leg against mine. I moved away, but there wasn't much room.'

'I'd have kicked him.'

'I felt like it, but I didn't want to make a scene or cause embarrassment. Anyway, I can't prove he did it on purpose. Just like, when his hand grazed mine, or his arm brushed against me; I'm sure he'd say it was unintentional.'

'Still, you should complain; it sounds like a clear case of sexual harassment.'

'Oh, I'd hate to make a fuss and run the risk of being branded hysterical. He's a respected senior manager.'

'Sounds like a scumbag to me; he shouldn't get away with it.'

'At least I don't have to see him for another two months, until the next meeting. I can look for another job, though

I'd never find one like this at my age.'

'You shouldn't have to change jobs because of that sleaze-ball.'

'But I haven't told you the last of it. He insisted we share a taxi to the airport this morning, though he was flying direct to Birmingham nearly two hours after my London flight. All the way, he kept pressing close to me, saying how lovely I was and how I had so much potential and that he was "quite taken" with me.'

'Puke! How old is this geezer?'

'At least twice my age. I told him not to talk like that, and you know what he said? He could help me in my career. And, get this, he wants to be my mentor and patron!'

'Ooh, it makes my skin creep.'

Alan heard all this with increasing disquiet. Was that how Brian saw him? Suddenly his vision of himself as patron seemed hollow. Unless he changed course, he was, he feared, in danger of repeating the worst of Douglas's follies with callous, grasping young men, while appearing to others as another Mr Grogan. That must not happen. He extracted Brian's number from his address book and quietly tore it up. With a sigh of relief, he set about completing his brief.

MOTHER'S WARNING

Michael Harth

Looking at me now you may find it difficult to believe, but I was a shy retiring boy, unsure of myself and picking my way delicately through the difficulties and hazards of growing up. My father was well into his forties, and Mother just entering hers, by the time I, their only child, was born, so that the age-gap between their friends' children and me prevented more than casual contact, and I had a fairly solitary childhood.

In any case I didn't make friends easily. Regularly, when my term reports arrived, I would be harangued: 'The Head says you don't show any team spirit,' to which I would reply that was because I didn't have any, a notion they seemed to find as difficult to comprehend as the Head himself. He and my Housemaster both remonstrated with me over that and my 'not being a good mixer', but by then I had already learnt to hide my true opinions, so I would just explain 'I prefer my own company.'

I filled my time mostly with reading, but when I was twelve I was given a computer, and this proved something of a life-saver: in fact I spent so much time on it that my parents began to regret they had bought it for me, though this feeling was mitigated by the thought that my proficiency in such an up-and-coming area should stand me in good stead in an increasingly electronic world.

When I moved to senior school I became aware that some of the other boys exerted a strange fascination. Scholastically I was so far ahead of the rest of my age-group that I was moved to a form higher than my age warranted, where I was mixing with boys a year or so older than me. They never took any particular notice of me at first and I was far too shy to do anything more than harbour longings, which I didn't understand and kept to myself. It felt as if there was a much bigger gap in our respective ages than was actually the case, but I was soon at the top of this new class in most subjects, which seemed to elicit a certain reluctant admiration from at least some of the others.

One in particular, named Jimmy Purfitt, was no great shakes academically, which didn't stop him drawing me like a magnet. He wasn't even particularly good-looking, but to me he seemed pretty irresistible, though looking back I suspect it was his air of physical vitality and self-assurance that made up most of his appeal. We sat at adjoining desks, and one day he asked me to help him with his homework. As I willingly obliged, and even took him through the simultaneous equations he was having trouble with, he soon made a habit of turning to me whenever he had work problems, while I for my part gradually relaxed my façade of disinterest.

Jimmy was the nearest I had to a friend, and he gradually became quite protective, almost proprietorial, towards me, standing up for me on several occasions, while he basked in the admiration I didn't try to hide. As we progressed through the school, he must have decided I was to be trusted, for one day, when I commented on a new and obviously expensive pair of trainers he was sporting, he told me that he had bought them himself, having acquired the money to pay for them by allowing some guy to take a few liberties.

I was both shocked and awed, though at the same time gratified that he should confide in me.

'You mean he...?' I asked, gesturing with my hand, though I paused there, unable to complete my question.

Jimmy, however, was not so shy. He just laughed and said carelessly 'A bit more than that. I had to let him give me a blow-job.'

To my intense annoyance, this made me blush, but I didn't let it deter me, enquiring timidly 'You didn't mind?'

'It didn't bother me,' he boasted. 'Of course I'd rather it had been a girl doing it, but I just shut my eyes and imagined it was my girlfriend on the job, and there are a lot harder ways of earning a few quid.'

I thought to myself that I wouldn't mind following in his footsteps. I didn't think it would be any great hardship to let some guy do that to me, and when I said something along those lines, Jimmy suggested I should give it a try. But though I found no difficulty in imagining him in that sort of situation, I couldn't see my timid retiring self exerting a similar fascination.

Mother gave the impression that she rather disapproved of sex, and I suspect that it was a side of life she would have preferred to sweep under the carpet, for the subject was never discussed *en famille*. But when I was fifteen she was offered a promotion which meant that she would no longer be able to drive me to and from school. She had compensated for not being as devoted to me as most mothers of her acquaintance were with their offspring by being over-protective, and now she felt she had to warn me of possible dangers. So the weekend before starting her new timetable, she took me on one side, looking both solemn and uncomfortable.

'I want you to be very careful when you're out on your own: on no account must you talk to strange men, and if they try to speak to you, you must get away as quickly as possible.'

When contrasted with her frequent admonitions to be more sociable, this was somewhat surprising, and I reminded her in the pedantic style I favoured at that age 'It has never been a habit of mine to strike up a conversation with anybody, let alone total strangers.'

That didn't satisfy her. 'You must be particularly wary of being offered sweets or money,' she emphasised.

'Why on earth should anybody do that?' I asked, playing the innocent, but this just got her more flustered.

'They might want something from you,' she said darkly, fortunately quite unconscious that she was having the opposite effect from what was intended.

'Whatever have I got that they could possibly want?' I asked, but at that point her courage failed her, and she lapsed into vague warnings. Of course I was well aware of what she was going on about, but even while I was assuring her I would keep my wits about me, I was privately wondering, since she seemed so sure I would attract what she considered undesirable attentions, whether I might not after all be able to follow Jimmy's example.

If I took the short cut through Meyrick Park, I reflected, I could be home almost as quickly as by bus, and there was the possibility – the likelihood, if Mother was correct – of my being accosted by someone prepared to pay cash for a degree of intimate acquaintance. Jimmy had told me he frequented Dean Park, nearest to where he lived, and if he was to be believed there was no shortage of interested men – punters, he called them – so I supposed and hoped that Meyrick Park would be the same.

It was something of an anti-climax when I saw no sign of the crowd of eager men I had optimistically anticipated, and I supposed that no doubt my original assessment of my pulling power had been accurate and Mother had got it wrong. But when the next day I collared Jimmy to tell him of my lack of success, he laughed.

'You should have told me you were going on the game,' he said, grinning, 'and I would have given you a few hints.'

'Would you?' I asked eagerly.

'Sure,' he said casually, and took me home with him. There he demonstrated that our school uniform was not designed to display the youthful male body to best advantage, and showed me how to make it sufficiently obvious to those who might be interested in renting my services that I was available. I also learnt, among other things, what particular area of the parks functioned as a hunting-ground. Some of his instruction was more intimate than I would have dared hope, and afterwards I felt a lot more confident of success in my endeavours, and was looking forward to putting what I had learnt into practice.

The next day he asked me 'Want to try something else?' so I went back with him again and sure enough he did take things further. Then at the weekend I was able to try out what I had learnt. I had a pair of jeans I had never worn, because they gave me the sort of look which I had wanted to avoid but was now aiming for. I had filled out since they were bought, and now they were a bit tight, but that should only add to the effect, I thought, quite pleased with what I saw in the mirror. Then I replaced my shirt and tie with a T-shirt, and the effect was even better.

But when I got to the park, no-one actually approached me, and I realised I would have to take the initiative. This involved a degree of blatancy that was foreign to my nature, but I was fairly desperate, and at least it worked OK, so that one of the men plucked up the courage to speak to me.

'Do you have the time?' was the best he could come up with.

I made sure to smile at him when I replied, but even so he stuck there, so I did my best to encourage him. 'I usually come here about this time, to give myself a break from sitting at my computer.'

He brightened immediately, obviously happy to have found some common ground, and soon we were comparing the specs of our machines. His was a good deal more powerful than mine, and when I expressed interest, he seized on the opportunity, asking 'Would you like to take a look at it?'

I didn't have to fake my interest this time, and soon I was in his little semi watching him put his machine through its paces. It was actually quite interesting, but it wasn't what I'd gone back with him for, and I couldn't think of a way to get down to the nitty-gritty. So when he offered me a drink I went into the kitchen with him, but nothing ensued. It was up to me again, but I couldn't quite see myself explaining that my services were for hire.

However, on going back into his sitting-room I saw that his screensaver was a nude man only too obviously ready for action. My new acquaintance blushed, obviously flustered, and began to stammer out an apology, but I couldn't miss such a golden opportunity to cut out a lot of beating around the bush, so I interrupted him with 'Do you have any more pictures like that?'

Soon I was sufficiently aroused that I would almost have let him into my pants for free, but Jimmy had dinned into me 'Always remember it's a job: you're there to make a few quid, not to enjoy yourself.'

So when he tried to touch me up I moved away, saying 'I don't think I should let you do that.'

Of course I let myself be talked around, and when I left I was very pleased with myself. I had almost enjoyed his not particularly expert ministrations, while I was quite a bit richer than when I'd arrived. Then, once the dam, so to speak, had been breached the news spread surprisingly rapidly and I had little trouble in securing further work. The problem was now how to account for the purchases I was keen to make with my new wealth, since anything too blatant would have roused the darkest suspicions in my mother's mind.

I asked Jimmy 'Don't your parents ever ask you where you get all your money from?'

But he merely shrugged his shoulders and said 'They know I can look after myself.'

In fact, having all these men willing to pay money to enjoy my favours, and even more the fact that they mostly returned for another helping, was doing wonders for my self-assurance. I began to carry myself more confidently, and even walk with a bit of a swagger. My parents noticed the difference in me, but assumed that it just meant I was maturing. I would have loved to set them right, but I had already learned that parents are best left in ignorance.

Jimmy, of course, knew which of our fellow-pupils were supplementing their pocket-money in this particular way, and we came to form a little clique. I was both shocked and horrified by the way they talked about their clients, when it seemed that their aim was to extract as much as possible from them while giving them the minimum in return. This not only offended my moral sense but struck me as bad business practice, since, I reasoned, a customer who didn't get value for money would surely look elsewhere.

I remember one of them, Tommy Forrest, who was a good two stone heavier than me, mostly in the wrong places, boasting 'I took it out and asked him "You want this, don't you?" When he said yes, I made him say "please" and then I got him to crawl across the room on his knees before I let him have it.'

'That's it,' Walt Norman agreed. 'Make the dirty cocksuckers grovel.'

I kept quiet, comfortably aware that I earned a lot more than they did by being more obliging, and also offering a wider range of services. But then I also kept quiet about the fact that Jimmy and I regularly got together, and on these occasions he nearly always ended up being the passive partner, a fact he was extremely anxious to keep hidden from the others.

I once asked him curiously 'Do you let any of your punters do that?'

'Of course not,' he replied indignantly. 'I only let you cos you're my mate.'

In fact I was quite sure he enjoyed our times together at least as much as I did, but if he felt he had to hide the fact that he enjoyed being screwed, I wasn't going to ram it down his throat. Besides, as most of the punters wanted the same, it all helped to improve my technique.

I had already discovered that sex, while certainly creating a degree of short-lived excitement, was not actually very interesting, and the obsessive fascination it held for so many of my punters, not to mention my schoolmates, was a constant source of amazement – and scorn, I might add. To me it was on a level with eating, and no doubt this is why I was so easily able to fall in with my punters' requirements, and my more extensive repertoire meant that I could charge rather more than the competition. It also meant that I tended to attract the more affluent clients, most of whom came to me because they had been recommended by another punter.

You may wonder how I was able to get away with all this while still living with my parents, but it wasn't really a problem. I remember reading somewhere that male offspring inherit their temperament from their fathers and their intellectual qualities from their mothers, and this certainly seems to be true of me. There was something vague about my dad: you never felt you had the whole of his attention, and similarly I don't think he was more than mildly interested in anything. He sort of strolled through life without letting it touch him deeply, while he certainly didn't have any intellectual interests. So we weren't particularly close, and he largely left me to my own devices, not taking any great interest in how I spent my time, though he did make sure I knew he was there if I needed him.

Mother, on the other hand, was much more emotional, not to say volatile, and she had lots of intellectual interests: in fact, she had a reasonably high level of intelligence, but it was vitiated by a whole collection of irrational prejudices. One of these, incidentally, ensured I would be safe from inspection if I chose to live in London, since I knew she would never visit me there – not, as one might imagine, because she considered it a sink of corruption, but because she harboured the conviction that life there was too hectic.

By then they had both decided they didn't understand me, and I didn't tell them I had gradually been losing any interest in the career path that had been laid out for me. I kept up my studies, and my exam results were more than sufficient to get me a place at university. I chose London, largely because I would be able to live more or less where I wished instead of on campus, though of course I didn't explain that to them.

I did say to Jimmy 'Why don't you come to London? Then we could take a flat together.'

'I've already fixed to go to Cheltenham,' he explained uncomfortably.

'Cheltenham?'

'There are reasons,' he said vaguely, so I left it, reflecting that at least I wouldn't find the flat invaded by the females that had come to form the larger part of his sexual diet. I had already observed that straight men, while they may have a certain charm when they are young, speedily mature – save the word – into dull boring adults, and I supposed sadly that Jimmy would follow the pattern.

As it happened, a few days later I was chatting to one of my most frequent clients, a guy named Gordon Watson. Unlike the large majority of my punters, with whom I had to be constantly on my guard for signs of their becoming too emotionally attached, Gordon wanted sex, not romance. The frequent sessions created some sort of bond between us, so that in spite of the disparity in our ages – he was forty-six at the time – I was able to talk much more freely to him, keeping him abreast of my doings, and on this occasion, after I'd serviced him, he asked me 'What arrangements have you made for living in town?'

'I'm going up next week to look for a flat,' I told him.

'I might be able to help,' he said. 'I have a small pied-à-terre, conveniently central, for when I come up, and I guess you could stay there except that you'd have to put up with me every so often.' He laughed apologetically, though why he felt he had to apologise for doing me a favour I couldn't imagine.

'You could tell your parents you were looking after the place for someone who was away most of the time but didn't like the idea of it being left empty,' he went on, and they accepted this much more easily than I had expected, aided, no doubt, by the fact that they wouldn't be called on to pay for my London accommodation.

Dad did ask curiously 'How did you get to hear of this?'

I answered vaguely 'Through the friend of a friend,' and he didn't question me any further.

I had guessed that Gordon's visits to London would become rather more frequent if I took up his offer, and that did indeed prove to be the case, but it was no problem. Before long I was looking forward to them: I had never felt able to reveal my true thoughts and feelings to Jimmy, but with Gordon I had finally found someone I could confide in.

As the end of my time at college approached, I asked him what he thought I should do.

'What do you really want to do?' he asked me in return.

'My parents are expecting me to get my degree and then go into a steady job,' I answered, the idea depressing me even as I enunciated it.

'It comes down to how much you feel you owe them,' he pointed out, going to the nub with the perspicacity I had come to expect from him.

'I've not really been the sort of son they would have liked,' I mused.

'Having children is something of a lottery: you have to take what you get. If you can show them that you are on a course that will enable you to live comfortably, that should be sufficient.'

We left it there for the moment, but he'd obviously been thinking my situation over, for on his next visit he made me an offer.

'This little place is worth silly money because it's so central: with what I could get for it I could buy something quite a bit larger but further out. I'd need a small mortgage, and if you were willing to pay that, you would have somewhere a bit more spacious than this, and then, if you wanted, there'd be more scope for you to expand your professional activities.'

Once I was settled in London and had finished my studies I maintained only desultory contact with my parents: I would visit them three or four times a year and made sure to send Mother a card and some flowers on her birthday. Then Father died of a heart attack. He had always been a heavy smoker, and though he regularly gave it up, he could never stay on the wagon and was soon puffing away again, so I wasn't entirely surprised. Mother, however, was devastated, much more than I would have expected since she had always 'worn the trousers' in their relationship (a fact I resented) and I had naturally assumed she would be able to cope with independence. But instead she gradually fell to pieces: he had always been the centre of her life, much more so than her son, and without him she seemed to lose interest in life.

There was no way I could have her to live with me, of course, even if she'd wanted to, and I rather chafed at having to assume responsibility for her. But I reminded myself that it was, even if indirectly, due to her that I was in my present extremely comfortable situation, while happily once again one of my contacts was able to help. He was the main shareholder in an old people's home, and told me 'If you buy a few shares in it, you'll be able to place her there at a greatly reduced rate.'

Even so, I balked at first, but when he told me just how profitable an investment it would be, I agreed, besides which I reflected that if it hadn't been for her, I might be slaving away at some more or less tedious job, impatiently waiting to reach retirement age, so that I owed her this much.

'I've found you a very nice place to stay, where they'll look after you properly,' was how I broke the news to her, taking her down there to see it before she could think up sufficient reasons for not going.

'I don't think I'd like it there,' Mother complained on the way back, but we both knew it was decided.

Fortunately Matron who ran the place had plenty of experience, and with her help, Mother settled in much more quickly than I had expected. I visited her conscientiously till her deteriorating faculties meant there was no point.

At the funeral I had the wreath inscribed 'With grateful thanks for setting me on the right road,' which was felt by the other mourners, not in any case a large crowd, to show true filial feeling.

STILL FIT

V. G. Lee

I don't really understand Pat's popularity, particularly with younger women. Pat's fifty two – younger than me but to be honest you wouldn't think it.

For instance – last Thursday. We'd been invited (along with about a hundred and fifty other women of our ilk) to the launch of a famous lesbian chanteuse's autobiography.

Fancy dress was optional but, of course, we both dressed up. The two of us (we're not a couple, never were, never will be) are known for our fondness for costume which our other friend Joan (who's been in and out of therapy for years) says can often signify a dislike of 'self'.

I thought I looked pretty spiffing in a Burton suit, double breasted, wide lapelled, purchased from my local charity shop, shirt and tie also from the same establishment. I'd borrowed my brother's natty brown trilby. I'm still fairly slim and above average height so I can carry off a bit of cross-dressing rather successfully. I'd travelled up to London on the train and sensed that the glances I got from my few fellow passengers were curious but not uncomplimentary.

At Charing Cross I met Pat pacing up and down outside Next, expression dour.

'I'm bloody frozen,' were her first words. 'I've had two Big Macs and a mega-sized hot chocolate to warm me up and now I feel bloated and unhealthy.'

'Hello, Pat. What's happened to your face? Gone three rounds with the girlfriend?'

Pat's hand shot up to what looked like a nasty cut on her cheek. 'It's a pimple,' she said. 'Does it show?'

'I'll say it does...'

'Look, I need to go into Next. I want to check this woolly hat in their mirror.'

Into Next we went. Their sale was still on – last few days. To say the least, the staff, just ready to shut up shop for the night, looked at us askance. Under Pat's trench coat she wore military gear: camouflage combats, tee shirt, and khaki leg warmers rolled to look like puttees over her leather walking boots, still muddy from her disastrous walking holiday in the Peak District, which I won't go into now. In front of a mirror she tried out various alluring or otherwise ways to wear a brown knitted hat while I feigned interest in a fuchsia-coloured cardigan with ruffled front, to appease the restless sales personnel.

'How do I look?' she asked.

'Fabulous,' which wasn't true but, as Joan says, Pat can't take negative feedback.

The venue near Trafalgar Square was packed. Ratio of drink to food about seventy-thirty, ratio of costumed to uncostumed guests, fifty-fifty. I've noticed during my decades of dressing up that those who don't, tend to take themselves rather more seriously than those who do, with the exception of those who dress up for a living such as, say, Imelda Staunton (not at this gathering but one of my own personal show-biz favourites).

At the far end of the room was a small stage. Three women dressed as Wrens (they may have been Wrens) were singing the 1965 Keely Smith hit *You're Breaking My Heart*, which was also the title of the famous lesbian chanteuse's autobiography.

'That brings back memories.' I turned to Pat but she'd already commandeered a glass of red wine and with it held above her head, dour expression changed to one of supreme satisfaction, was heading for the tiny dance floor. You see, Pat was in her element.

In quick succession I drank two glasses of white wine with a still water chaser to maintain my equilibrium, then went in search of Joan. Me and Joan, we get on rather well. We put this down to both being Virgoans which Pat says equals 'one pair of fusspots'.

Spot Joan. I have a piece of information regarding myself to impart. The previous week when I'd been at a celebration for the Chinese New Year, a reliable source had told me that, as an Ox, I was a possible leader of men, or in my case women. I'd asked after Joan and she was a Rabbit, pleasant enough but not a leader of anybody. Pat was a Snake. No surprises there.

'I see Pat's enjoying herself,' observed Joan before I could begin. Joan wasn't in fancy dress although she'd had the hairdresser carve a pound sign into her cropped hair just above her forehead, which I chose not to comment on.

'Is she? I'm so relieved. Book launches aren't really her thing.'

'Don't worry about it. She's dancing.'

'I wasn't worrying...' Yes, Pat was dancing. With an attractive dark-haired woman in a black velvet trouser suit. 'Isn't that the famous chanteuse's agent?'

'Yes. What's Pat done to her face?'

'She says it's a pimple.'

'Looks more like she's been in a fight,' Joan sniffed. 'Some women go for that "damaged" look.'

'Do they? I was going to offer my beige concealer but you know how prickly Pat can be.'

Joan said 'To change the subject a tad, a woman patted my bottom just now with more than sisterly pressure.'

'What did you do?'

'Nothing. I'm waiting to see what her game is.' Joan gulped from her glass of fresh orange juice. She won't touch alcohol; says she has a nervous reaction to it. Won't even eat wine gums or put a dribble of sherry in her boeuf bourguignon.

'So?' I prompted.

'So nothing. She took her hand away after a few seconds. Still, from little acorns etcetera.'

In silence we watched Pat dancing enthusiastically to the Wrens' rendition of *Chattanooga Choo Choo.*

'Why don't you bring me on home?' Pat sang out, her voice loud and slightly drunk-sounding, above the polite murmur of revellers. I winced. Turned back to Joan to share my news about Ox and Rabbit.

'I'm off to mingle,' she said.

'Me too,' I said.

What a wonderful evening! Had another glass of wine, several unspecifiable vol-au-vents and at least a dozen mini-sausage rolls. Bought a copy of *You're Breaking My Heart* and got the famous chanteuse to sign it. Was rather disappointed that she didn't once look into my eyes – they are my best feature and ageless. Like Joan, I mingled a good deal, exchanging pleasantries, tipping my trilby at personable people. Joan reported back with news of further pats on her bottom, which made me wonder if her admirer wasn't in fact a clumsy pick-pocket. However, no pick-pocketing to report in my own buttock area. Back to famous lesbian chanteuse to apologise for Pat destroying the card table bearing the display of her autobiography.

'Pat is so-o very clumsy.'

'Don't worry about it,' she said laughingly.

'Oh, I wasn't worrying *per se*,' I said, also laughingly.

Went in search of Pat. Found her still sticking like glue to agent. Both looked cheerful, sipping from the same beaker of red wine. Made another circuit of the room and finally cornered the agent on her own.

'You don't know me...' I began.

'No, I don't.'

'I'm a friend of Pat. You danced with her earlier.'

'I did indeed and hope to do so again.'

'I just want to apologise on her behalf. She can be impossible.'

'Can she?' Agent raised her beautifully pencilled eyebrows. 'I look forward to that. She's very fit, isn't she? I'd better get hold of her before the music packs up.'

For some minutes I stood alone, feeling I don't know quite what. Like a prize... fusspot? Joined Joan who was slumped, ragdoll fashion, against the wall. 'All right, Joan?'

'I've overdosed on fresh orange. You can do that, you know.'

'So I've heard. Look here, Pat's new agent friend reckons Pat's "very fit". Now what do you think she means? "Fit" as in attractive or "fit" as in athletically able?'

'We all know what "fit" means,' Joan responded with unnecessary irritation. 'I expect she meant both of those although I can't for the life of me imagine why.'

We watched Pat and the agent fox-trotting and had to admit that they danced well together: same height, same build, same rather over-excitable expressions on their faces. Quite an age disparity, Pat being a good fifteen years older.

Joan said gloomily 'They're getting on like a house on fire,' and I neighed back 'I'm surprised. I'd have thought that a pimple the size of a sixpence would be a complete turn-off.'

'What's a sixpence?'

'Oh really, Joan, don't be obtuse. I'm getting my coat.'

We were all getting our coats. The main lights switched on and the singing Wrens marched briskly off their makeshift stage. Pat finally emerged from the scrum, heading for the cloakroom, grinning – that horrible expression – from ear to ear.

'Great evening,' she said breathlessly.

'I've had my bottom touched at least five times,' Joan said. 'In fact I wouldn't be surprised to find some discoloration of the skin by morning.'

'How about you?' Pat turned to me. 'Anyone been touching your bum?'

'I've experienced the enveloping warmth of loving friendship all night.'

'That's a "no", then?'

Pat's popularity continued into the queue for our coats. Several times she was kissed by complete strangers. I definitely saw admiring glances lingering on what was in truth a pimple. Pat's agent friend held on to her hand for ages.

'Such an amazing grip,' she enthused. 'I really like you. Has anyone ever told you, you have a fabulous face?'

Joan and I exchanged bewildered glances and refrained from snorting. I whispered 'She's young enough to be Pat's daughter.'

'Granddaughter.'

Pat's 'fabulous face' was wreathed in smiles – a rare sight since she'd reached fifty.

'Why not come along to the pub with me?' the agent enticed.

Pat hesitated.

'Don't mind us,' Joan said with a stiff little laugh. I buttoned up my overcoat and straightened my trilby, cramming it further down on my head lest a gust of wind whip it away once we got outside.

'Thanks but no,' Pat said, 'I'm with my friends.'

Joan and I waited while she retrieved her trench coat, kissed a few more women, squeezed a few more hands. Finally the three of us set off into the freezing night.

'Only ten o'clock,' I said. 'There's time for a pizza before I catch my train.'

'My buttocks are smarting,' Joan said, but good-naturedly. 'I hope they've got comfy banquettes.'

Pat said nothing. She lit a cigarette and strolled along peaceably between us.

'You really shouldn't smoke,' I said.

'You're not wrong,' Pat replied and blew a perfect circle into the cold night air.

THE CARD SENDER

John Dixon

'What's up?' asked Patrick.

He was hovering behind me, pretending not to be interested in the contents of the letter I was reading. He often did this when he recognised the handwriting of a former lover.

'Oh, nothing. Well, there is actually. It's from Barnabas.'

'Oh, is it now?'

'You know it is. Read from here down.'

It is a source of regret that I am unable to invite you to my wedding.

'His wedding?'

'So it says. First I heard of it.'

I'm sure you will want to wish us well; and will be thinking of us at 3 p.m. on Saturday 14th September. Should you wish to send us a present the forwarding address is:

'What a bloody cheek!' Patrick went off alarmingly – as he so often did. He had replaced Barnabas as my lover and was ever-eager to run him down. '*"Should you wish to send..."* No home address. Just a forwarding address – for the present!'

It was odd, hurtful and frankly out of character for Barnabas to be so secretive. He was usually so open, inquisitive and full of himself, rather like Patrick. He looked a bit like him, too.

I wondered what the woman was like. Martha. No, beg her pardon, Mary. Not that it mattered. Barnabas tended not to call people by their names, but by endearments. Dear, Darling, My Other Half; sometimes perhaps even My Better Half. How long before he'd call her The Wife? I'd always hated that expression – when the word 'The' is made more possessive than 'My', and more institutionalised; the only possible one, the one taken for granted.

Patrick was about to embark again but I stopped him.

'Now that he's married he's no danger to you. Why keep on?'

'Aren't you even offended?'

'Intrigued.'

'He should have told you. It's quite soon after splitting up. Think it's on the rebound? Well, do you?' he repeated. 'Or even a shotgun wedding?'

'I can't honestly believe that.'

'Why not?'

'Because in the three years we were together he showed no more inclination to take the so-called dominant role than you have.'

This ended the conversation and no further mention was made of the subject until Christmas.

The card was a very religious one. It was signed by Barnabas and Mary.

Looking forward to meeting you. Have heard so much about you.

The handwriting was not Barnabas's, not even his signature, as Patrick was not slow to point out.

'She obviously does all the organising in the household.'

'We can't know that.'

'Shall I put it on the tree with the other cards? In pride of place? Or chuck it?'

I was about to hand it to him when I noticed a message on the other side – again in her handwriting.

Thou shalt not spill thy seed.

'What's up?' asked Patrick.

'Nothing important. I'll chuck it.'

'Aren't you going to send them a card?'

'I've only got a forwarding address.'

Thou shalt not spill thy seed. I wondered how much Barnabas had told her. And how much she had guessed or surmised. And why – after being married for three months – should she still be interested?

My birthday comes just after New Year. I wish it didn't. It is one celebration after another. I received a card from Barnabas and Mary. Inside was a piece of writing paper and in her hand the message

I hope the conjunction of Christmas, the New Year and your birthday will give you the strength to turn over a new leaf.

'Well,' I laughed. 'It never has done before!' I turned the card over to see if there was a further message. This time she had written their home address, presumably a hint for my not having sent a Christmas card. Damn, I thought, now I suppose I'll have to send Barnabas a birthday card. I checked the date. It was in May.

There was, however, an intervening communication. I always go on holiday in March – not from choice, but because it fits in with my job. I have been going in March for several years. Barnabas came with me on three occasions. This year was the first time with Patrick. When we returned there was a card waiting for us. It read

We'll be in your area next week. Will drop in.

'Oh, God, what's the date?'

'Over two weeks ago,' said Patrick.

'Thank God for that.'

'Isn't it typical, inviting themselves round here but not inviting you to their wedding.'

'Married couples can be like that. They assume single people need them so much that they can drop in as they please.'

'But why isn't there a note saying they called and found us out?'

'That's a point. She wouldn't have missed an opportunity to send a card.'

'Do you think they actually came?'

It was rather strange. Barnabas would have known we'd be away this time of year. Perhaps he'd told her, and she was writing without his knowledge.

In May I duly sent Barnabas a birthday card. Four days later I received a thank-you card from her.

'A thank-you card for a birthday card?' shrieked Patrick. 'For a present, yes. But not for a card. It wasn't even HER birthday, either.'

We were most grateful for the card you sent Barnabas. I thought the picture on the card and the poem inside were quite delightful. I always read the poem. Some people don't.

I'm sure I hadn't when I bought the card. Even if I had it couldn't have been worse than the quotation she added to the back of her card

Thou shalt not lie with another man.

There was no doubting the implication of that. I felt now I had to show Patrick and tell him about the other cryptic messages.

'I should've told you before. But I didn't know how long it was going to go on for.'

'I understand. I only wish I could understand this woman. She's determined to let you know she knows, isn't she?'

'Knows what?'

'Exactly.' He paused. 'And what's more, she's dividing the year up neatly.'

'That's true. You think she'll keep up the pressure?'

We both shrugged. We were tempted to ignore the whole thing but instead we agreed to confide in Randolph, a close friend of mine. Patrick, who sees everyone as a threat, isn't very keen on him. It's true that years ago Randolph was a bit of a loose cannon. But he can be very helpful; he's now deeply into psycho-babble and keeps threatening to do a part-time counselling course. We showed him the cards and after the initial hilarity and disbelief we settled down to a serious discussion.

'There are lots of women,' began Randolph, 'who like our sort – simply because they don't feel threatened.'

'Yes,' yawned Patrick. 'They're called fag-hags. Tell us something we don't know.'

'Hold on. There are also some women who want to get married and – for one reason or another – haven't done so. Perhaps the opportunity has not arisen – '

'– or they are just plain ugly,' cut in Patrick.

'Barnabas would never have made that remark,' I rebuked him.

' – and,' continued Randolph, 'when the opportunity does arise, even with a person they suspect is gay, they would rather take the risk – and it is a risk – than stay on the shelf.'

'It's a risk for the man, too, Randolph,' interrupted Patrick, 'as you must know yourself.' He gave me a look as much as to say *Would Barnabas have said that?* 'Oops! Sorry. Do go on.'

'I was just going to observe,' Randolph continued, 'that as late converts they will be extra eager to make the set-up work, to stress family life, religion, morality and, of course, cut the links with former friends.'

'But surely this is the point,' said Patrick. 'She's not cutting the links. She's writing to us on every pretext.'

Randolph shrugged. 'Perhaps she wants to convert you.'

'Which is quite uncalled-for as I pose no threat to her.'

'Granted,' said Randolph, 'but she has managed, by whatever means, not only to find a husband but to change his sexuality. This must give her an enormous boost. A mission accomplished. Now she's proved one person can be "won over" she must believe others can as well.'

'Which makes it a form of seduction? Or flirting?'

'That is actually,' mulled Randolph, 'a very perceptive remark.'

'Bet you wish you'd made it,' smiled Patrick and added, 'Let's change the subject. I really can't feel sympathy for her.'

'No,' said Randolph, 'but it's good trying to understand an opposite viewpoint. Specially as you'll almost certainly be hearing from her again.'

And he was right. The next communication was a change of address card. Underneath was written

We needed a larger place. We want to start a family. Why don't YOU settle down? It CAN be done.

The quotation on the back was inevitably

Be fruitful and multiply.

'Well,' said Patrick. 'She's certainly using her success with Barnabas to encourage you.'

'She needn't bother.' I threw the card and address away. I wasn't going to make contact and only hoped she wouldn't either.

A month later another card arrived. It read

Is everything all right? This is to confirm our new address. We thought you might have lost it as we did not get a card wishing us a happy move. It was also our first wedding anniversary last week. If there is anything we can do to help please let us know.

We showed the card to Randolph.

'Don't you think it's a cheek?' I said. 'Why should I send an anniversary card to them when I wasn't even invited to the wedding!'

'Well, she couldn't invite you before she'd got her man in the bag; now she has, she's making amends – albeit on her own terms.'

'Why? I'm not after Barnabas. I would have written to him if I was. It was me who turned him out.'

'Perhaps she's trying to tell you she's found qualities in Barnabas you never discovered.'

'Pooh!' said Patrick. 'And do you suppose there'll be any more cards?'

'Bound to be. Could go on for ages.'

Despite Randolph's prediction – and I was getting rather fed up with his knowingness – there were no cards for a long time.

'She must have got the message,' said Patrick.

'I'll believe it if we get through Christmas and my birthday unscathed.'

We did. It was amazing. We sent no cards and received none. We rejoiced too soon. There was a card when we returned from our March holiday. It read

We're not having any success trying for a family. It is a great tragedy. We have both been for hospital checks. There should really be no problem. It is some time since we started trying and since we heard from you. Things seemed to go much better when you wrote.

'I can't recall I ever did. Anyhow, Randolph, what's your verdict on that one?'

'She thinks you've put a jinx on her. That you still have some power over Barnabas.'

'He might well wish he was back here. But that's none of my doing.'

'Tell me,' said Randolph. 'Can Barnabas – do it?'

'He always left that side of things to me. But there is no reason to suppose he can't – or that he is any less fertile than... '

'No, indeed.'

'Will I be receiving... ?'

'Why ask? She'll write again.'

And he was right, of course. Damn him! But this time it was a letter, firmly sealed.

You have always been Barnabas's friend though you have not met for some time. Lately we have both been very sad. I know you would wish to correct the situation. After long discussion we have both agreed that you should give me a baby.

'Just like that,' laughed Patrick. 'And to be named after you as well? Insist on that.'

'Be serious, Patrick.'

'Why should I be? She's now suggesting adultery with a man she's condemned for being gay.'

'There's actually some logic in her position,' said Randolph.

'Is there?' said Patrick, not bothering to enquire further. He turned to me. 'What quotation are you going to use in your reply? "Thou shalt not commit adultery"?'

'No,' I said. 'I was thinking of something for myself. "Thou shalt not fuck another man's wife, especially if you've already fucked the husband".'

'I like it,' Patrick smiled. 'Why not go one better? Tell Barnabas to leave the house. She's never met you and we could send someone else round there instead? It could even be me. She's never seen me. They don't even know I exist.'

'Don't they?' asked Randolph, surprised. 'I assumed that... That puts things...'

'Don't,' I begged.

I wrote back at once. It took me about ten minutes to think up a couple of lines.

'Let's see,' said Patrick.

I handed it to him. 'You'll have to sign it as well.'

I'm sorry to learn about your sadness. But stable relationships can be maintained without children, as Patrick and I have discovered.

'Yes,' nodded Randolph. 'That should stop her writing any more cards.'

And he was right. We never heard from her again. And we didn't see so much of Randolph either.

UNDER THE BED

David Reade

When I left school, I dreamed of being an airline pilot. But I was not well qualified, indeed not at all qualified, having left school with only one O Level pass under my belt.

Hence I took a job as a clerk in the County Architect's Department at the County Hall in my County Town; a dull, repetitive occupation of no interest or glamour whatsoever, with salary to match. I carried on living in this small town with my ageing parents in their semi-detached house for far too long. I never thought of marriage, realising during my teenage years that I was homosexual and my desires led me only to males, preferably younger than myself. However, that was in my mind and of many fantasies only; the County Town produced not the slightest possibility of the hoped-for realisation of dreams.

This was fairly understandable, as I spent all my evenings sitting with my parents watching television, which was very new then and had only one service from the BBC; or sitting in my small bedroom which overlooked the back garden reading and dreaming. The latter was possible in the summer only and at Christmas, since the rest of the time the temperature of the bedroom precluded any use of the room other than for sleeping under heavy blankets. At Christmas time I was allowed to light a fire in my bedroom fireplace so that we could feign Christmas joy in a modicum of comfort. The same applied to our front sitting room, which during most of the year was out of bounds because of its chill.

I was an only child – sent to school at five years old, then to Grammar School after passing what was called the Scholarship Examination. At the Grammar School, sex became a reality for a time. It was a kind of Arcadia in that every boy was young enough to excite and most boys were attractive in some way or other, except for the ugliest ones. I never gave any thought to what I should do about sex after school, assuming that it would continue or that I might change and find a woman to marry and, as the Bible says, put away childish things. But this did not happen and the life I led became completely celibate – the carnal solitude of a County Town.

The male staff at County Hall were not attractive and they and the female staff used to make fun of me, talking about girl friends and sniggering if I didn't reply. Only the office boy excited me, but I was too shy even to speak to him except on matters relating to work, which was mainly filing of papers. I thought of myself as a clerical labourer, indeed sometimes I would stand on ladders in dingy basements lit by strip-lights, grasping dust-covered files and taking them down to unwrap the red tape, putting them back and starting again. It was a miserable job, like my life. My parents were getting older and showing it. Father had never liked me and he made that obvious. Mother was kindly towards me, but had become very remote and forgetful. I knew that after they died I would inherit the house, and supposed I would carry on living there, hoping I might find some boy to live with me; though I knew not how this could be achieved in this County Town.

My parents kept hardly any alcoholic drinks in the house, except at Christmas – and little enough of that – and I managed quite well without it, until one night in the dead of winter, the ground covered with snow, I tired of the flickering television screen and announced that I was going out for a walk.

'A walk, Peter, on a night like this?' my father queried. 'It's probably still snowing.'

'It's not actually snowing now, Dad,' I replied. 'I've checked. I'm going out for a short while. Don't wait up for me, I've got my key.' And out I went into the icy air bundled up in coat and scarf.

A short, slippery walk brought me to the door of the White Horse pub, where lights were still shining and the sound of voices could be heard. I plucked up courage and walked through the swing door.

The bar was uninviting to say the least; down at heel, in need of a coat of paint, dimly lit and under-patronised. In spite of this I stayed, ordering a pint of best bitter and sitting alone at a table near the door drinking it. Then I ordered another one. No-one took any notice of me whatsoever. After finishing the second pint, I asked for another.

'It's nearly closing time, mate,' said the barman. 'Are you sure you want another whole pint?'

'Yes,' I replied defiantly. 'I want another whole pint, please.'

The parents were in bed when I got home and did not see my condition, that I could hardly walk straight, almost sliding along the slush-covered pavements, that I left my spectacles in the bathroom sink and crept into bed intoxicated, but retrieved them when getting up to pee at two o'clock.

The next morning my father entered the bedroom to announce that it was time to get up.

'Pooh, it smells of alcohol in here!' he complained. 'Wherever did you go last night?'

'I just had half of bitter at the White Horse, Dad.'

'Seems like you had more than that, son. Mother says breakfast is ready.'

That morning I could hardly eat my eggs and bacon. 'He's a bit worse for wear,' my father said to my mother. 'He went to the White Horse last night.'

'Oh, you didn't, Peter,' said Mother. 'You didn't go into that horrible place. That's where Mr Perry goes, you know, the one who hoots his horn every morning at seven o'clock when he passes the house of his fancy woman, Mrs Raines. He always wakes me up with his hooting. Did you see him?'

'I didn't see anyone, Mum. No-one I knew, at any rate.'

'Did you drink too much, Peter?' my father asked.

'Course not, Dad, I just had a half of bitter, or maybe two.'

'Or maybe three or four,' said Dad.

'Have some more tomato sauce on your egg, dear,' Mother offered.

'No thank you, Mum, I must go and finish getting ready now.'

Father gave me a lift in his car to the County Hall. 'I'm going to Wrightlings to see about the mower. It's never too early to deal with these things. Course, you wouldn't want to mow a lawn now in the snow, but I want the mower working properly by the time spring arrives.'

Spring – now that was a thought. When, I wondered to myself, was spring going to arrive in my life? I read about other people's lives in the Daily Express, people like Errol Flynn and film stars of his ilk, who seemed to have wonderful exciting, interesting lives. And I would bet those lives were full of sex, too. Mine certainly wasn't.

It was a funny thing, though; last night's drinking experiment seemed to give me Dutch courage, as they call it, and I greeted the lovely office boy cheerily. 'Hullo Martin, how are you this morning? I like your new hairstyle – suits you.'

Martin smiled back. 'It's for me new girl friend,' he advised. 'She said I need a DA haircut.'

Oh well, I tried. 'What's her name, Martin?' I tried again.

'Anne,' he said. 'And she's a smasher. I'll show you a snap if you like.'

'Love to see it,' I said. At least I was being friendly with this boy for a change, even though it wouldn't get me the attention he was giving to Anne. Better to talk to an attractive boy even if there was no hope, rather than just sitting at home with the old people, watching Sylvia Peters and MacDonald Hobley.

The girls giggled as I walked through the typing pool. Were they giggling at me? I would never know; was I paranoid? At about noon, I rang my mother to tell her I wouldn't be home for lunch that day.

'Where will you have your dinner, dear?'

'Don't worry, I'll be all right. See you this evening.'

At lunchtime I made my way down the street to the Cottage Restaurant, ordering shepherd's pie, one of their specialities. 'I'll have a half of bitter with it, please,' I said to the waitress.

'You mean beer? We don't serve alcohol here, sir.' She looked shocked. 'We haven't got a licence for it. But you can have a soft drink – we've got several varieties of lemonade and there's...'

'OK,' I replied, 'just give me a lemonade with it. And a pot of tea afterwards.'

The fact was that I couldn't really afford to lunch out like this at the Cottage, at least not every day, but this was a special occasion, the time of my life which was going to lead to a release, a new life, a new enjoyment, instead of just an existence. The bill came to four shillings and sixpence – 'pot of tea 6d.' I wouldn't tell my parents about it, otherwise Dad would say, 'Oh Peter, you'll always be poor!'

In the afternoon, Martin showed me three snapshots of his girl friend, Anne. I couldn't understand what he saw in her, she looked so ordinary compared to him. He deserved someone much more glamorous, more like him. What a beautiful face he had – sensuous lips, blue eyes and blond hair; sinuous, muscular body. How I should have liked to kidnap him and take him back to my parents' house when they had gone away or died, and keep him a prisoner, attending to my every sexual need. Stop it, Peter, you're going too far. But how would it feel if life were different? I could only contemplate.

The afternoon passed slowly, and it seemed that I had very little to do. Mrs Bond called me into her office for a chat. She was one of the few staff members I really liked, and was quite important, and being secretary to the County Architect inhabited a large office of her own with huge filing cabinets. It raised my status being specially friendly with her.

'Any more news on the girl friend front?' Mrs Bond asked me, though I wished she wouldn't.

'None at all,' I replied. 'I don't think any girls like me.'

'Oh nonsense, Mr Edwards,' she parried. 'There's always someone for everyone. In any case you're not a bad-looking young man, you should have no trouble in finding a girl for you.'

'I wonder when we'll have a thaw?' I said, trying to change the subject.

'Soon, I hope, Mr Edwards. I can't bear it, it ruins my shoes,' she held out an elegantly shod foot, 'and it makes me feel so cold all the time. Runs right through me, it does.'

'I must say your shoes don't look ruined, Mrs Bond. They always look brand new to me.'

Mrs Bond smiled.

When I left that evening, I made a special point of saying good night to Martin, the office boy. 'Going out with Anne tonight, Martin?'

'Yeah, meeting her under the clock tower at the bus station at six.'

Instead of going straight home on the bus, I hid behind a barrier and looked out for Martin. Sure enough there he was waiting for this ugly female to arrive, which she did just after six. I saw her, looking even more dowdy and plain than in the photograph, sidle up to Martin and surprise him. Surely he couldn't really like this girl? But apparently he did, as they walked off arm in arm.

I caught the bus home sick at heart, soon turning my key in the front door of 29 Bramble Road. 'Dad's out,' said Mother, 'at a Photographic Society meeting. He's had his tea, but yours is on the table. Come on, dear, hurry up, it's waiting, you don't want the tea to get cold. Come on, a good cup of tea will warm you up. It doesn't get any better, does it, the weather?'

I sat down as bidden to consume my sardines on toast, bread, jam, buns and tea. 'I hope you won't be going out to that White Horse place tonight, dear,' Mother said.

'I might, Mum, I just might. After all, I'm twenty-six now, old enough to make up my own mind about things.'

'Yes, but you live under our roof,' said Mother, accusingly.

That decided me. I was going out whether they liked it or not, although snow still covered the footpaths and it was necessary to walk very carefully. Mum and Dad looked on disapprovingly when I announced my intention to go out.

'It's not a nice night to go out, Peter,' Mum said. 'Why don't you stay in with us and watch the telly? Or listen to the wireless? You haven't heard The Archers lately, and it's Life with the Lyons tonight.'

'No, Mum, I'm going out. Dad went out, didn't he? To the Photographic Society meeting.'

'Yes, but he's back now, dear, sitting in his chair. You ought to wait until the weather's better.'

'Sorry, Mum. I'm going out now.'

'Well, don't drink too much, will you, dear?'

'Good evening,' I said to the barman, who grunted 'Pint of best is it?'

I sat down at a table again for a long time, then I couldn't believe the coincidence when I saw Martin and his girl friend Anne enter the bar, going straight up and ordering Babycham, brown ale and crisps. Of course, I remembered that Martin had told me Anne lived not far from Bramble Road and I supposed that was why he was in the area. So far they hadn't seen me and went to sit down a few tables away, close together and holding hands. I opened a packet of cigarettes which I had bought that evening, though I was not generally a smoker, and lit one, puffing on it voraciously. It did my nerves in seeing that boy with that girl who wasn't worthy of him. Why did it upset me so? 'You must pull yourself together,' I told myself. 'That boy doesn't share your preferences, and in any case why should he fancy a bespectacled man of twenty-six when he could have all the boys in the world? – that is, those that like that sort of thing.'

I ordered a second pint. 'Live round here, do you?' asked the barman in a casual way as he pulled the pint. He was a short, fat, middle-aged, rather grubby, balding bloke, sporting a toothbrush moustache.

'Maybe,' was my reply.

'I thought I could have seen you somewhere,' he continued. 'Your face looks familiar.'

'Maybe,' I answered mysteriously, returning to my table with the pint and lighting another cigarette.

I drank only two pints that night, but still I could have done with more, and so I took a bottled pale ale away with me and hid it under my bed. During the night I woke up remembering, and wandered down to the kitchen to find a bottle opener. It was about two o'clock in the morning. I had a thick dressing-gown on, but was still cold, my feet frozen in the slippers.

'This is not ideal for you, Peter,' I said to myself. 'On a cold night like this, and let's face it, most nights are bloody cold, you need some spirits to buck you up. Maybe whisky or brandy.' I didn't usually swear, but there was no one to hear me. I opened the beer bottle and stood there drinking, looking from the kitchen window onto the snow-covered back yard, wondering what Martin was doing. Probably he was asleep and dreaming of Anne – to be sure he wasn't dreaming of me. What a bloody life! Tomorrow I would buy some spirits and hide them under the bed.

The next morning my face flannel contained a block of ice and I had to rinse it under the bathroom tap. It seemed more than ever sensible to buy liquor and I had decided on Johnnie Walker Black Label from an off-licence rather than from the White Horse, and so I bought it from a place near the County Hall and covered it up well in a bag. The girls in the typing pool were their usual idiot selves. 'Ooh Peter, what have you got in that bag then?'

I wanted to tell them to eff off, but I was polite, ignoring their badinage. But I showed it to Martin, I don't know why, perhaps hoping he would want to drink it with me. 'That's a rather good whisky, Peter,' he remarked.

Back I went to my desk and the afternoon's work and my teatime chat with Mrs Bond. When the evening came, I said goodnight to Martin, asking if he was going to meet Anne, but he said it was the night she washed her hair and she wouldn't be available. Then I went back home to tea.

'Not going out again tonight, Peter, I hope,' said my mother. 'There's a play on the telly tonight. And the weather's just as bad as ever.'

'Well, Mum, I might, or I might not. But I think I probably won't tonight.' As I said this, I thought of the full bottle of Johnnie Walker concealed beneath my bed. There was no need to go to that boring White Horse. On the other hand, if I stayed in I would have no chance of meeting a boy like Martin, or even any boy.

But what was I talking about? What chance had I in this County Town of ever meeting any boy by just sitting at a table in the bloody White Horse or any other pub? About as much chance as sitting in my own bedroom or in the snowed-up garden of our semi. What a life! Maybe I should go and live in London, but the problem was, among other things, money. I would have no job – although I supposed I could find one – but I would have nowhere to live and knew that London was expensive, everyone told me. In any case, it was important to admit that I was frightened of leaving the cosy prison of 29 Bramble Road where I was born and nurtured.

All evening I kept leaving the warm back sitting room for the ice cold of my bedroom and taking sips of whisky. I kept away from the parents so that they would not smell the spirit on me, but then I remembered what someone had told me: vodka left no smell on the breath. Of course, that was the answer. Why ever did I buy whisky? Tomorrow it would be vodka – after I had finished the whisky, of course. But maybe tomorrow anyway, just in case I found myself without anything.

In bed that night I felt better, thinking as usual about Martin and other boys of my imagination. At least this was my private domain, my fantasy private life in which no-one could interfere, no-one could snigger. At three o'clock that morning I got up to take another swig of Johnnie Walker.

I was surprised the next morning at how little whisky was left in the bottle. It was definitely necessary to buy some vodka on that day without fail.

'Another parcel?' asked Tricia in the typing pool. 'I'll bet it's a present for some girl, isn't it? You are a dark horse, Peter.'

When I didn't answer, another girl remarked, 'The strong, silent type,' and they all giggled.

'Do you like vodka, Martin?' I asked the boy when I had the chance.

'Never tried it,' was his reply. 'Anne likes Babycham and I like a bottle of brown.'

'You can come and drink vodka with me,' I said, suddenly emboldened by the thought.

Martin grinned, but said nothing.

After my chat with Mrs Bond I had to walk through the typing pool again. 'Ooh, vodka!' I heard one of the boring women say. 'Would you like to drink vodka with me?'

So Martin had told on me. Never mind; I was wasting my time there in any case. He liked girls, and that was it. I hadn't much chance of getting a boy, but I had got the vodka. It didn't taste too bad either. It came very chilled too, hidden under my bed. And best of all, it didn't smell on the breath and the parents never knew I was drinking it.

So what? All this happened quite a few years ago. Both Mum and Dad are dead now; it was a hard time watching them go, but the drink got me through that and the funerals. Martin married Anne and they live in the town. He doesn't work at County Hall anymore; in any case I don't fancy him, he's too old: looking quite middle-aged, I should say, and getting plump.

I still work at County Hall myself. I take vodka in a plastic cup with my tea, hiding the bottle in my briefcase. I had a bit of trouble about my drinking, but NALGO got me through it. Mrs Bond has retired, and I really have no friends at work now and I need a drink to get me through the days there.

I still live at 29 Bramble Road. It's more than a little lonely, but I can imbibe as much as I like and there's no one to say anything. The weekends are the worst, just sitting there looking at the four walls, especially since the telly went wrong. Nothing has been done to the house since they died. I keep meaning to have it repainted, but it's rather too expensive. I have to admit that a lot of my money is spent on drink. I suppose I am what you would call a heavy drinker, and I must admit to being absolutely blotto at weekends. I wish I could find a boy to live with me, but that's not very likely now because of my age. Although there are some boys in this County Town who look so fantastic that I nearly fall off my stool in the Rose &

Crown off the High Street, especially in the Public Bar, there is never one who so much as glances at me.

And so I have another drink. But there is just one glimmer of hope and I must cling to it. A new office boy has started in my department. His name is Trevor, he's sixteen and he's absolutely gorgeous. I offered to buy him a drink when he is eighteen and he said he would like it. At least there's a hope in two years' time. And I have plenty of drink in the house until then – vodka, whisky, gin, brandy, rum, port, Bailey's – you name it.

STONES IN HER POCKETS

David Downing

As her song drew to a close she stretched out the final note until indifferent applause overlapped it and hid its dying. It was on nights like this she became aware of how lazy and nasal her voice had grown. She sang from the chest. Missed notes jarred but went unnoticed, so she let them go. Afterwards she slipped out into the night. The sea called to her but she turned towards the village and took the quiet backstreets uphill, home.

The light from the window told her Christos was back. He would often not return until sunrise, especially while the island was busy with tourists. The tirelessness of youth: it made her a little uneasy. An already opened bottle of wine stood on the table and she poured herself a glass before wandering down the cool-tiled corridor and listening patiently at her son's bedroom door. There was only the warm silence of an unempty room. Sneaking a peek inside she was brushed, as always, by the tenderness motherhood instilled in her. Until she noticed he was not alone.

She pulled back, surprised and uncertain. She supposed she had always known this moment would come, but had remained maternally unprepared for the reality of it.

Collecting herself, she peered round again, quietly curious. A splash of fair hair was all she could make out. The island boys were always distracted by the blond foreign girls, fascinated by the contrast. Then recognition hit. She emitted only a silent gasp before quickly pulling the door to, shutting what she had seen in. Or out. The head that rested on her son's chest was not a girl's. Dazed, she crept back to the kitchen.

She sat at the table long into the night, adding another bottle to the one that had been waiting for her. Motherhood suddenly seemed more distant than it had.

In the early morning light Christos and Henrick pushed the moped downhill before turning on the engine, then sped along empty back roads, bounced over cobbles, skirted the waking harbour. They pulled up outside one of the new hotel blocks and stole a kiss before Henrick strode inside. Christos revved the engine and was gone.

The previous evening Christos had been chatting to friends by the harbour when he had spotted someone sitting in a café, watching him. When everyone headed off to a beach, Christos dismissed the idea, saying he might follow later. Suddenly self-conscious he got off his moped, straddled the seawall and felt the familiar island-breeze touch his face. Minutes later he sensed someone behind him, and he tensed nervously. The stranger sat down next to him.

Silently they watched a boat float through the night, blaring music and flashing lights, a myriad dancing shapes reflected back in rippled abstract form.

'They put so much effort into lighting their shops and bars and still we all continue to stare into the dark.' Henrick nodded up at the empty sky. 'You lose the stars.'

Christos grunted in a half-hearted agreement, briefly catching the stranger's eyes as he did so. Then silence again.

'Didn't you want to go with your friends?'

'No. Not really.' Christos feigned indifference.

The words formed in Henrick's face before he found the nerve to release them.

'So, do you know anywhere quieter? To show a tourist?' He nodded towards the moped.

Christos looked back out over the waves, into the darkness, his heart pumping. He let time pass.

'Yes,' he said. 'I know somewhere.'

They raced through the crowded streets, tooting tourists out of their path, Henrick's hands holding onto Christos's waist. The faint electric glow of the village slowly disappeared behind them. The wind whistling past blew all that away. Christos turned onto a dirt track he knew almost instinctively, billowing dust that covered their tracks, before pulling up by a tree, its old wind-bowed branches reaching forever out to sea.

This was his own private place, somewhere he had never shared with anyone before. He wondered, briefly, why he did so now, but knew the answer already.

They scrambled down over rocks and perched themselves on a ledge. Henrick busied himself with a joint, lit it, inhaled deeply, then offered it to Christos, who filled his lungs with the sweet smoke, and together they exhaled grey-blue clouds. The awkward formality of before disappeared on the breeze and they chatted, looking out to sea, at the near-far sky and the refound stars.

'Let's swim,' Christos said.

Henrick stared down dopily at his clothes so Christos simply shed his, ran forward and dived. He turned to the shore and watched Henrick clumsily pull off his own shorts and shirt. Light from the moon caught his body as Christos watched.

Henrick dived in and surfaced. Behind, the landscape had become insubstantial, spectral and distant. Christos trod water. Without breaking eye contact, Henrick took one easy stroke towards him. Christos tensed as foreign hands rested on his shoulders, bringing his skin alive, then slid again to his waist. Then his own hands reached out for this other foreign body. He felt the brush of their legs as they kicked to stay afloat, and, as Henrick leant towards him, the touch of their lips as they pressed on each other salt-wet kisses.

Now, Christos parked his moped back under the tree, clambered over the rocks, shed his clothes and launched himself into the sea. The morning sun was rising, the heat just beginning. He swam out, invincible, until he reached the weatherworn hull of a small fishing boat tugging vainly at its anchor. He pulled himself aboard, staining its wooden planks dark with water. He lay across them and let himself be rocked by the ever-undulating motion of the sea.

He knew he would not see Henrick again. Tourists came and went. He understood. But he wondered why this one had been the one, the right one, at the right time, for him. It did not matter.

His happiness slipped him into sleep as the sun rose in the sky.

Suddenly the boat tipped violently to one side, startling him awake.

'I thought you might be here,' said Henrick, smiling. 'I saw you from the rocks.'

Standing over Christos he shook out his wet blond hair like a dog drying its fur. Then he kissed him, a single sure kiss on the lips.

'I didn't think I'd be seeing you again.'

'You almost didn't. I had to pay the cab driver a small fortune to convince him to go off-road in his car. Bloody stupid tourists, eh!' And he leant over and kissed him again.

The tourists had begun to arrive when she was still a girl, and island life had changed, forever. The islanders were wary of foreigners, keeping their distance, happy to take their money but that was all. This cosmopolitan influx was threatening age-old ways that began to be clung to ever more tightly. Yet, for the young, unburdened by tradition, the island had become alive with possibilities.

As she had grown older, the summer Saturday nights had become something of a ritual for her. She waited until her parents were asleep before applying makeup and tying up her hair, creaking open the shutters, climbing onto the roof below and jumping down into the lane that ran behind the house. She wandered back into town, safe from the prying eyes of her mother's friends who stayed away from the bright lights of the expensive tourist area. She breathed in the foreign perfumes, eyed the unfamiliar fashions, listened to the babble of languages and accents. All this difference intrigued her as much as it frightened her. That her parents forbade her it only added to the excitement.

One of these nights, as she weaved her way through the alleys and lanes, she stopped to stare in a shop window. As she did so, she felt someone standing beside her, looking too, then sensed eyes upon her. She took time to turn. She was looking at a tall handsome youth with a thick mat of prematurely silver-grey hair. He smiled at her and his ice-blue eyes sparkled. She had never seen eyes like that before. Quickly she walked on.

She looked through other shop windows, smelt the aromas wafting from restaurants, heard foreign music spilling out of bars. She happily lost herself amongst the crowds until, slipping off into a back street, she saw, once again, the blue-eyed boy she had stood next to earlier. She watched him. He was about her age, maybe a year or two older. He had something about him that seemed to register inside her, something she had not felt before. He seemed lost, but then he noticed her, and when he saw the recognition in her face, he smiled again and moved towards her. He spoke, the foreign tongue making him seem more awkward than she had expected.

'I am going to the beach,' he said, waving a bottle of wine as if in evidence. 'Escaping. You know where?'

She was silent.

'You can come too?' he asked, as if to encourage directions from her.

Something in her overwhelmed the instinct to refuse, politely. Her mother had always warned her about the tourists, especially the boys, and she wondered now just what her mother saw as so threatening in them. She did not speak before turning and walking away. At the corner she paused and looked back, and he began to follow.

He walked a few paces behind, allowing her to lead the way. As she headed down the steps to the beach she noticed he was no longer with her and there was a brief feeling of loss before he came running, waving two glasses he had pilfered from an empty table of a bar. She giggled, his mischief an offering to her. She pulled off her shoes and swung them in her hand in time to her stride in a way she imagined a young woman might when walking with her lover.

At the shoreline they turned and strolled out of sight of the busy seafront, heading along to a quiet part of the beach, out of view.

The glass shook nervously in her hand as he poured her first drink. She sipped as she thought she might when she was older. The wine tasted bitter but she hid her dislike, feeling the warmth it created in her stomach and the tingling it left in her face. Her silver-haired youth was talking, but she just nodded and smiled.

From the bar at the far end of the village, the one that sat out on its own, she could hear the singer glide her way through another sad song. Although she could not make out the words, she could tell by their tone that the woman sang of some inner hurt, but could not understand why anyone would choose to listen to another's unhappiness. Still, she sat and listened, to the songs and the sea, and sipped at the wine.

By the time the bottle was empty she felt giddy, unsteady. Her stranger stood and nodded his head towards the unlit end of the beach, took a few steps and waited for her. He looked nervous, uncertain, and she felt it had something to do with her. She stumbled as she stood, and giggled, happily silly, feeling grown-up wearing makeup and drinking wine and having power over men.

They wandered along in silence. Night closed in around them, her eyes straining as light drained from the scene. As they walked, past empty sunloungers stacked away for the night, his hand reached out for hers and crept into her palm, subtle yet unstoppable, like the rising tide. As the beach began to run out he stopped and took her other hand and leant down to kiss her. His lips were cold and dry. He kissed her again, more insistent this time. She had never been kissed before, not like that. She thought she should push him away, but there was something, too, that made her feel there was an inevitability to it all.

His hand slid down her back, round her waist. He felt for the buttons on the front of her dress, undid the first, then slowly, one by one, the others seemed to melt too. The night air crept across her skin as the material fell aside. She shivered uneasily. She no longer felt as grown up as she had and part of her wished she was at home in bed.

Bending down, still-cold lips pressed against young breasts. She pulled away but the wine was disorientating, costing her her balance. He caught her, but that only slowed the motion: instead of falling she felt herself being gently laid on the sand.

A hand ran its way up her thigh and, when it stopped, she gasped. He leant over her and she pressed her hands against his chest. She did not understand what she was becoming part of, but something instinctive hinted at clues. He went to kiss her but she turned away, and as she did so, she felt him clumsily push his way into her. She stifled the pain. She started to cry but he shushed her, gently, insistently.

The sand scraped at her back and she wrapped her arm over her eyes, escaping from what was happening. She tried to imagine herself as the sea, fluid and unbreakable. Not to see, not to feel. She concentrated on the rhythm of the waves, made herself distant, put herself elsewhere. It was only when the still deadweight of him pressed down on her that she realised it was over. He pulled away, leaving behind an emptiness that filled with the cool softness of the sea breeze.

Brushing sand from his trousers and hands he reached out to help her up, but she scrambled to her feet on her own, fumbling with the buttons he had undone so dextrously. He was not smiling any more, and the effects of the alcohol had left her. A sharp stab from inside bent her double until it eased. She thought she might vomit. A thin thread of dark blood was moving slowly down her thigh. She smeared it away with her palm.

They walked along the beach in silence until the light from the bar grew closer and the sad songs reached her: they sounded different now, as if they knew, as if they were sung about her.

Back in the maze of streets he went to peck her on the cheek but she moved herself out of reach. The rejection allowed her to regain a little of herself. She watched him walk away before making her way uphill home, numb to the pain that still shot through her.

She had tried to hide the little life that grew inside her, but these things can be hidden only for so long. With venom in her eyes her mother had cursed her, for shaming herself, for shaming the family. Later she heard her parents arguing in the kitchen.

She expected to be parcelled off to a distant relative on another island. An agreement would be struck: a wayward son or a burdensome in-law would be sent in her place, familial difficulties, embarrassments, exchanged.

But it did not happen and that was, perhaps, worse. An unbreachable divide had appeared, orchestrated, she imagined, by her mother. Their exchanges became perfunctory. It was her punishment and she must take it. The island had its ways.

She gave birth to a baby boy and it was only Christos's crying or, later, his first few words, which broke the silence. She got a job at a bar, singing songs to tourists, and it brought in money for their keep. She did her best for him, always, and he grew up happily unaware. She, however, was constantly reminded of her shame: as she walked through the streets groups of women would turn to look, her mother amongst them, and then return to their mutterings. For her mother it had been self-preservation. She had had to take sides, and she had chosen that which was easier.

She was not sure if she could face work tonight. She needed to see her son, but Christos had not come home. She would not be able to sing. Nevertheless, routine casts a powerful spell and, at the usual time, she found herself applying makeup and curling her hair. Her reflection showed the guilt that had accumulated over the years. And now her badness had leached into the thing she loved most, and they would blame her, again. She was too tired for the fight.

Raising her hands, she slid the long black dress over her head as if diving into a shimmering nocturnal sea. The shoes she chose were black too, with impossible heels, sharp as knife blades. She draped a coat over her shoulders, the incongruous luxury of a fur: it had been her mother's. She remembered seeing it in the wardrobe when she was young, loving the texture between her fingers as she ran them through it, stroking an animal that would not have tolerated being petted whilst alive.

Tonight she chose different songs to sing, sad songs, songs that seemed broken in some way. Her breath came from the pit of her stomach, her voice echoing deep inside her, and she forgot her audience as the words carried away a little of the hurt though left no void as they flew off on the wind. Pain such as this seems endless; it feeds on itself and does not burn itself out. She saw the concern of the bar owner but could tell he sensed she sang for other reasons tonight. People filtered out, in search of a livelier scene, but a few recognised where she was coming from; knew, in their own way, why she was singing; knew, for themselves, what the words meant, and what it felt like to have lived them. Each line of someone else's hurt held a mirror up to her own, and she blamed herself as she sang.

At the end of the evening she left the stage in silence. For some of the audience there was a sense of relief, as if something had lifted. She reached for the fur coat, wrapped herself in it, and headed out into the cool night air.

A breeze was coming in off the sea as she made her way to the beach. She cast her shoes aside. Her fears having left her, she traced out the path she had taken many times in her mind though had walked only once before, as a girl, when her life had changed forever because of it. She ventured past the sunloungers, still stacked high each night, and she continued until the lights of the village began to fade. She kept walking, the sand slowing her pace, holding her back, but the wind and the waves called to her, and she grew surer of where she was heading.

She walked until there was no more beach. She had expected the place to carry some legacy of that fateful night, a scar to match her own. But it seemed smaller now, innocent even. A circle of empty opalescent shells, half-dissolved by the sea, sat as a broken memento of a child's game. It would be erased completely before morning.

Bending down she picked up a brown stone, ribbed with purple-red veins, like a petrified heart. She rolled it in her palms, feeling its cool smoothness. She dropped it into her pocket and felt the coat shift slightly from her shoulders. She picked up another, letting it fall into the opposite pocket, the weights almost balancing. Then another, and another, trying to get it exact. She loaded her pockets with stones until the coat cut sharply into her skin. Only then did she take a tentative step forward, letting the waves swirl round her ankles, the stones knock against her legs. She headed slowly out.

The texture underfoot changed. She walked out on a long flat rock, invisible beneath the surface. Further out, but still the depth did not change. Then, suddenly, the water cooled and she knew. She knelt down, feeling it rise above her waist. She twisted her legs from under her and sat, letting the submerged rock support the weight she carried. Feeling for the edge with her feet she sidled herself forwards until she sat on the precipice. Waves splashed her, the spray wiping away tears she did not realise she was shedding, salt water and salt water, dissolving her. She fanned her hands gently beneath the surface, back and forward, feeling the water resist. A tourist boat intruded on the night as it sped towards the harbour. After it vanished she felt the impact of the large waves such a small vessel could radiate out long after it was only a memory. They had force and she tried to grip hold of the rock as they buffeted her.

Then one large one, an accumulation of all the others, caught her, loosening her grip as the weight of the water tipped her backwards. She slid, the stones pulling her out and down. She felt herself launched into the sea.

Silence.

Weightlessness.

The sea enveloped her. Panic and peace weighed themselves in the balance. Surely this was what she had been waiting, hoping, for. The chance to be free. The past could not follow her here. The sea would wash all that away.

The weight she carried was pulling her down, the sea claiming her. She let it take her.

Timelessness.

Escape.

She remembered the silver-haired boy whom she had never seen again. They had been young, neither had known, truly, what they were doing. It had been only the folly of children. A mistake which had trapped her ever since.

Free.

Free.

Then she thought of her son. Guiltless through all of this. Even now? Who was she to judge? Who was she judging for? She suddenly understood, after all this time. That was sufficient. Now she began to struggle, trying to disentangle herself from the burden that she wore. Her lungs burned. Fear pierced through her. No! Briefly, her feet touched soft sand. The load that had carried her down continued to fall. It fell from her shoulders. And she began to rise. She kicked and pushed, reaching for the surface. She cried out, air escaping from her mouth in bubbles that raced ahead of her, as she struggled upwards.

She broke the surface, gasping.

The lights were a long way off and she was a long way out but she started to swim, gently, purposefully, towards the shore. The waves pulled at her dress, still trying to claim her. As she tired she feared that the sea might win after all, despite everything, until her knees finally grazed the bottom and she found her way to her feet. Water dripped from her as she stumbled to the shore, away from the fringe of the waves, up past the hem of seaweed, and fell onto the beach.

The night settled peacefully around her.

Eventually, standing, she loosened the cold folds of the wet dress that still clung to her. She ran her fingers through her salt-matted hair, teasing it free. A rivulet of blood ran from below her knee, tributaried off round her calf.

She made her way back towards the village, past the now-silent bar. She did not turn off but walked barefoot right up the main street. People looked but she did not see them.

Christos's bedside light was on, its glow warm and reassuring as she approached. He was alone. And asleep. Her salty fingers settled the covers gently round him and, on his forehead, she left the imprint of a soft briny kiss.

ABOUT THE AUTHORS

Rochelle Baker was born in Brooklyn, NY and went out west to San Francisco and Seattle. She's been published in poetry journals, notably *Prospero's Cell* in Seattle. She's given poetry workshops in Seattle and London, most recently as part of LGBT History month 2008 at Forest Gate Library in East London. A member of GAW for over a year, she finds it very inspiring.

Rex Batten became a student at RADA in 1951 in the same class with Joe Orton, but eventually took up teaching. He has written plays for radio and produced books on Nunhead Cemetery but his most important work is *Rid England of this Plague*, based on personal experience of the 1950s purge when simply being gay was a crime.

Simon Dessloch (clavel@poetic.com) is presently studying for a Certificate in Creative Writing at Birkbeck, University of London. His writing has appeared in *Nth Position, Faster Than Life, Rouge and Mister X.* Simon writes, reads and lives on the dark side.

John Dixon has written several short stories, one of which won the Bridport Prize, another appearing in *Chroma*. Poems of his have appeared in *Envoi, Iota* and *Chroma*. He has completed three novels and hopes to have one published by Paradise Press in the near future.

David Downing has recently been de-urbanised and now lives a blissful existence in a remote croft house in the Highlands of Scotland where he is working on a novel and several new short stories. He can be contacted at: daviddowning@scotlandmail.com

Jimmy Driver is a bisexual skinhead, living in Surrey. He was born in London and brought up in Ilford, before 'Essex Man' was heard of. He studied English Literature at Sussex University and did a number of jobs before getting ME. His favourite writers include Chaucer, Shakespeare, Dante, Wordsworth, Woolf and Henri Bosco.

Jeffrey Doorn, warned by his mother to 'get out of it' (homosexuality), got out of New Jersey. His work has appeared in *Gawp and Gaze*, *Queer Words, Queer Haunts, Gazebo, Slivers of Silver*, and *Oysters and Pearls*, the last two of which he also co-edited. A community activist, Jeff lives with his civil partner in South London.

Henrik Harrysson was born in Lebanon, but grew up in Surrey and Dorset, before studying at the University of Oxford.

After teaching in Germany and France, he moved into IT, and settled in Berkshire with his partner. His ambition is to write an internationally acclaimed literary masterpiece set in Bracknell.

Michael Harth, a contributor to the GAW anthology *Queer Haunts*, is also the author of three volumes of short stories: *The Picnic, A Little Chat* and *The Physent*, while two more wait in the wings, as does a novel *Guru On Hire*. He is currently putting finishing touches to his monograph *Male Love: the Meaning and Purpose of Homosexuality*, which offers new insights by looking at the subject from a teleological standpoint.

V. G. Lee lives and writes in a cottage on the West Hill, Hastings. Her most recent novel is *Diary of a Provincial Lesbian*. She has published two others, plus numerous short stories and poems while looking after three cats and a wayward toad. www.vglee.co.uk

Zanna C. Mayhew has been hooked on horses for even longer than she has been part of the gay liberation movement – and she won't say how long that is. In between writing fiction, going to the races, and attending meetings, she works freelance and potters slowly round Essex on horseback.

David Reade was born during the Second World War, attended a grammar school whose headmaster, like David's father, was a fierce disciplinarian, and thereafter rebelled against any kind of authority. Now resident in Bangkok after thirty years in London, he has written four novels, some poems and many short stories.

Hilary Stanhope was born in Chesterfield in 1937. She read English Literature at Reading University, where she published *The Sapphic Muse in Tudor England*, which proved a popular success, while attracting general critical opprobrium. In 1979 she defected to Finland, and is currently Professor of Feminist Studies at the University of Turku.

Elsa Wallace lived in Africa for the first thirty years of her life, and has been writing for forty years, mostly short stories. Her favourite authors are Ivy Compton Burnett and Dickens. Interests are human and animal welfare, veganism, ghosts and tapestry. She works with a number of lesbian and gay groups.

Tom Wright is 35 years old and grew up in the Midlands. He studied English at Sheffield Hallam University before moving to London in 1999, where he is currently working in education. Tom has been writing short stories for just a couple of years and this is his first story to be published.

All these writers are members of Gay Authors Workshop. Founded in 1978, GAW is an association of lesbian, gay, bisexual and transgender creative writers – poets, dramatists, fiction writers. Our aim is to support writers by providing opportunities for them to meet, to read, to discuss and develop their work.

We hold monthly meetings at different places, mostly in the London area, for that purpose. Some meetings are accessible to wheelchair users.

We are a national organisation and welcome members from all over the country. We give what help we can in enabling members to set up local branches of GAW. Our quarterly newsletter keeps members in touch.

Membership is open to all lesbian, gay, bisexual and transgender writers, beginners as well as published authors. The yearly subscription is £7/£3 unwaged. Enquiries with SAE to: Kathryn Bell, GAW, BM Box 5700, London WC1N 3XX, or email: eandk2@btinternet.com

GASPS (Gay Authors Self Publishing Society) is an associated group of members providing editorial and practical support.

Some other publications from Paradise Press:

Oysters and Pearls edited by Jeff Doorn and Adrian Risdon. 80 pages, £3.99

In this anthology, 14 poets prise open the oyster of life in search of riches: love, sex, food, days at the beach, journeys through nature, cities and time.

These 30 poems peer into lives of isolation and communion, explore relationships open and closed, tenuous or tenacious.

Homo Jihad by Timothy Graves. 298 pages, £8.99

A powerful first novel. Londoner David Underwood must choose between his new lover, an Israeli Jew, and his ex, Ahmed, who suddenly comes back into his life.

Rid England of this Plague by Rex Batten. 320 pages, £8.99

Two young lovers find both solidarity and oppression as gay Britons in the 1950s.

A Little Chat by Michael Harth. 166 pages, £6.99

An entertaining medley of crafty stories, from an expert writer. Light-hearted and ironic, even chilling, but never dull.

The Physent by Michael Harth. 156 pages, £6.99

Sixteen more supernatural tales from this masterful author, appealing to anyone with a taste for the fantastic.

First and Fiftieth by Martin Foreman. 151 pages, £6.99

Imaginative first-person narratives, set around the globe as women and men from teenagers to grandparents relate their stories in a distinctive voice.

The Picnic by Michael Harth. 147 pages, £6.99

Male au-pairs, sex services for OAPs, alien abduction and a picnic that goes wrong are among the themes in this picaresque collection of stories.

A New Man in Old Steine by Graham Robertson. 204 pages, £7.99

James Weston leaves family and friends for a mid-life plunge into Brighton's gay scene, in this riveting satire on small town life.

The Monkey Mirror by Elsa Wallace. 135 pages, £6.99.

Fourteen ghost stories set in Britain and South and Central Africa deal with regions where animal and human lives touch, for good or ill.